The Harp Q

# The Harp Quartet

## Book One of the Beethoven Trilogy

by

## Tess Alps

*For Indra & Charlie*

*Love,*

*Tess -*

YouCaxton Publications
Oxford & Shrewsbury

For Tim, Tom and Joanna

And in memory of my Mum, Kay

# Contents

Acknowledgements _____ ix

Chapter 1 - April 1916 _____ 1

Chapter 2 – July 1916 _____ 12

Chapter 3 – September 1916 _____ 21

Chapter 4 - October 1916 _____ 30

Chapter 5 – December 1916 _____ 38

Chapter 6 – Christmas 1916 _____ 44

Chapter 7 – January 1917 _____ 53

Chapter 8 – March 24th 1917 _____ 58

Chapter 9 – June 1917 _____ 64

Chapter 10 – July 7th 1917 _____ 70

Chapter 11 – Late July 1917 _____ 79

Chapter 12 – August 1917 _____ 83

Chapter 13 – September 1917 _____ 93

Chapter 14 – Early October 1917 _____ 100

Chapter 15 – Late October 1917 _____ 107

Chapter 16 – November 1917 _____ 113

Chapter 17 – November 1917 _____ 118

Chapter 18 – November 1917 _____ 129

Chapter 19 – December 1917 _____ 133

Chapter 20 - December 16th 1917 _____ 138

Chapter 21 – December 20th 1917 _____ 146

Chapter 22 – January 1918_____ 151

Chapter 23 – Mid-February 1918 _____ 160

Chapter 24 – Late February 1918 _____ 169

Chapter 25 – March 1918 _____ 175

Chapter 26 – Easter 1918_____ 182

Chapter 27 – April 1918 _____ 190

Chapter 28 - May 1918 _____ 196

Chapter 29 – July 1918_____ 203

Chapter 30 – December 1918 _____ 210

Chapter 31 - Christmas 1918_____ 217

Chapter 32 - April 1919_____ 228

Chapter 33 – January 1920_____ 233

Chapter 34 – May 22nd 1920 _____ 239

# Acknowledgements

Imight never have had the courage to publish this book had I not been introduced to Kate and Greg Mosse at a party. No, I didn't tell them I was trying to write a novel but my friend Stevie Spring did, and I am so grateful to her, even though it was jolly embarrassing at the time. Kate and Greg gave me lots of encouragement - on the spot and later - and some great advice, introducing me to the wonderful Felicity Bryan. Felicity was patient and generous with this novice writer and The Harp Quartet is much the better book for all her insight and wisdom. I must also thank the friends and family who read it in its less polished state and shared their thoughts.

I read widely as background to the story but I would like to acknowledge the debt I owe to three books in particular that I came to depend on:

*Modern Ireland 1600-1972*

R.F. Foster

*Founded on Fear*

Peter Tyrell edited by Diarmuid Whelan

*The Collected Poems of WB Yeats*

WB Yeats (Wordsworth Poetry Library)

# Chapter 1 - April 1916

Thin blades of sunshine pierced the side-windows of the chapel. Dust danced in the light as sixty-two schoolgirls of Our Lady's Convent bent their heads in devout contemplation of Christ's passion at Good Friday mass.

The sixty-third was contemplating only the hole in the new priest's left sock, just above his ankle. Hannah wondered how on earth you could get a hole just there. Maybe snagging it while climbing over a gate? Did priests do such things? Hannah's eyes moved up to study his bitten nails. A nervous fella then. His stubbly chin and his greasy black curls stopped him looking as handsome as Hannah thought he probably could be. Maybe priests did not get time to wash properly? Or was it more a rejection of sinful vanity? Whatever it was, Hannah realised she must be mortally bored to be letting such things occupy her mind.

"Jeeezus, how much longer do we have to sit here? My arse is totally numb," Hannah whispered to her neighbour. She caught the frowning eye of a nun so ducked her head and started flicking the pages of her prayer book, until the sister turned her gaze on another row.

Finally, after two hours on the hard pew, Hannah was relieved to stand and join the line of nuns and girls shuffling towards the altar in order to demonstrate their devotion to the cross in a more physical way. The priest was offering up the large oak crucifix with the tortured ivory figure of Christ to each girl, so they could kiss his cold, nailed feet before they took communion.

Such a weird ritual, thought Hannah, as she watched the priest patiently walk along the row of kneeling worshippers, holding out the crucifix with trembling hands, leaving the scrawny altar boy to wipe away each dry kiss with a screwed-up linen cloth. Five years of Good Friday masses

1

at the convent hadn't made Hannah find it any less bizarre an expression of faith.

Hannah's turn came to kneel. She sank down onto the stone step next to her schoolmates, all with hands clasped together in pious submission, eyes lowered modestly. Hannah held her head high, tracking the progress of the priest and altar boy towards her.

Father Stephen stopped in front of Hannah and presented the crucifix. She looked up at him and smiled as she held onto the lower branch of the cross. She placed her lips onto the feet of Jesus, then dragged her tongue along his lifeless limbs, pausing provocatively at his loincloth, on over his bony ribs, and until she rested finally on his face, where she kissed his icy lips passionately. Hannah let go and stood, looking Father Stephen defiantly in the eye before marching back to her pew.

Father Stephen was transfixed. Several witnessing nuns stood up. The intakes and outputs of disapproving breath could be heard by many and even felt by a few. "Good," thought Hannah. "That'll wake them up."

******

Two hours later, Hannah's elder sister, Stasia arrived home, red in the face and out of breath.

"Father! Father, where are you?" Stasia slammed the front door behind her and searched first the study, then the parlour, and finally the kitchen, where she found their father sitting with a cup of tea, warming his besocked feet in front of the range. No holes in those socks, thanks to Stasia's expert darning. Aggie, their housemaid, was idly stirring a pan, whistling tunelessly.

"Father, Hannah is an utter disgrace. She is depraved. You simply have to do something. I cannot bear the shame for a day longer. Can you not control her?"

As head girl of the convent, Stasia was doubly pained at her younger sister's challenging behaviour, but this sort of episode was hardly a novelty. Ever since their mother had died four years earlier, for every inch Stasia had become more responsible, Hannah had become a foot more disruptive.

"What's happened now, my love?" James McDermott liked a peaceful life but rarely got one.

"She made a complete exhibition of herself at mass. I can't even bring myself to describe what she did, but it was ...well... very unladylike. Really lewd behaviour." Aggie, behind Stasia's back, raised an eyebrow and suppressed a smile.

"She defiled the body of Christ. In front of the whole school. I thought Mother Veronica was going to have a heart attack. And the new priest didn't know what to do with himself. Don't ask me to say any more. But it's just not fair. How can I get any respect as head girl when my own sister does such disgusting things." Tears pricked Stasia's eyes.

"Come and sit here, my love." James patted his knee but Stasia chose to perch on the edge of his armchair instead. He put his arm around her waist and held her hand. "I know Hannah can be naughty, but you just have to try and ignore her. She's trying to rile you. She's missing your mother badly..."

"And so am I, but I don't behave like that..."

"I know, but Hannah is different. And you're two years older and you've always been very grown up. You have to understand her and forgive her."

"Huh! It doesn't matter whether I forgive her or not. It's what Mother Veronica does that counts."

"Where is Hannah now? Did she not come home on the bus with you? asked Aggie.

"Yes, but she just ran off down towards the river instead of walking home with me. I'm sure she can't bear to come and face you. Frankly, I don't care if she never comes home." And, before her father could protest, Stasia picked up her school bag and marched upstairs to her bedroom to start her Latin homework.

"Bloody hell, Aggie. What am I going to do with them both?"

Aggie topped up James's teacup. "Don't worry yourself now, Mr McDermott. It'll all come right in the end. I'll have a word with the scallywag tonight."

******

After half an hour sitting, throwing stones into the brown, rushing water of the River Nore, Hannah clambered up the bank and started to head for home, but, as she passed the churchyard, she paused. She wandered in. The path to her mother's grave was well-trodden and familiar; her father always brought his two girls to lay fresh flowers there every Sunday morning before mass. The headstone was clean and moss-free. Hannah traced the engraving with her fingertips:

Evaline McDermott, 1876-1912

Beloved wife of James and treasured mother of Anastasia and Johannah

Rest in Peace with God and his Angels

"Oh, Mammy, I'm in such trouble. I don't know why I let myself do these stupid things. I think I'm so clever, getting my own back at Stasia, but all it does is get me into hot water and then Stasia is even more of a pain in the arse afterwards. Did you see what I did to the crucifix from up there in heaven? Was it awfully rude? I've seen Aggie do it in the barn to one of the delivery men. Will you say sorry to Jesus for me, please. If you were still down here with us, you'd tell me what to do now and you'd stop Stasia being such a bossy old bitch, wouldn't you."

Hannah went over to the hedge around the churchyard and picked the odd primrose and violet bravely blooming in the shade. She laid them on her mother's grave, then kissed her fingers and gently touched the headstone, by her mother's name.

"I am really sorry and everything. And I suppose I should apologise to someone – just not Stasia. I'll confess it to

Father Gregory tomorrow, but I hope you'll forgive me first?"

As Hannah walked back home, she was startled when Father Gregory himself appeared in front of her, turning the corner by McLoughlin's bar, carrying some shopping and leaning heavily on his stick.

"Is that you, young Hannah McDermott?"

"It is, Father." Hannah held her breath in case word of her misdemeanour had already reached the ancient priest, but no mention was made.

"I wasn't sure. My old eyes can't make out much these days and you young girls grow up so fast."

"Here, let me carry your shopping back for you." Hannah took Father's Gregory's basket from him. "Is Mrs Logan not around today?"

"That's very kind of you, Hannah. Mrs L has gone on a little trip to see her sister for Easter and I thought I would manage fine. But it's a long time since I've been without a housekeeper and I've forgotten how to cook. I've been living on cheese on toast for the last two days," he chuckled. "It could be worse. And she'll be back after Easter Monday."

Hannah peered into the basket. Sure enough, all it contained was a loaf, a packet of tea, a lump of cheddar, a packet of shortbread biscuits and some apples.

After delivering Father Gregory and his groceries safely to the rectory, Hannah resumed her journey home; she walked in through the kitchen door just before six thirty.

"About bloody time too. Quite apart from wondering whether you'd thrown yourself into the river, racked with guilt and shame, I need a hand with the supper." Aggie jerked her head towards a tureen on the kitchen table.

"Oh Jeezus. Has Stasia told you then?"

"Yes, and your Daddy. You're in the soup it seems. But if you don't get those filthy hands washed and take this soup into the dining room you'll be in some more."

James and Stasia were seated in their customary places, her father with his napkin already tucked into the neck of his shirt and Stasia with her hands folded on her lap.

"Here she is!" James beckoned to Hannah as she placed the tureen in the middle of the table and then went to kiss him. "We were starting to get worried about you. Weren't we Stasia?"

"The return of the Prodigal Daughter. It seems that whatever terrible things you do, Hannah, you will always be forgiven – at least by father." Stasia stood to serve out the soup as Aggie walked in with a basket of bread.

"It wasn't a terrible thing, Stasia. It was just a bit of fun."

"You defiled the body of Christ."

"It's not a body, Stasia, it's just a bit of old bone and wood. Dada, I didn't mean any harm. I was only after having a laugh after sitting for two fecking hours in that gloomy chapel."

"Now, you little monkey, you really mustn't be doing this sort of thing all the time – whatever it was that you did. It drives your sister mental. And then we all get it in the neck."

James and Hannah laughed together while Aggie bit her lip. Stasia looked at them all and shook her head.

"Well, I think you should be punished properly, Hannah, you know," joked James. "For penance, I order you to play me one of my favourites after supper before I have to go off and close the bar."

When the meal was over, Stasia immediately returned to her bedroom, James to his comfy armchair by the kitchen range and Aggie to the sink, while Hannah cleared the table.

"Aggie, can I have this leftover shepherd's pie?" Hannah held out the dish to show how much was left.

"What in God's name do you want that for?"

"I'm going to take it to Father Gregory tomorrow. He's been living on cheese and apples the last few days without Mrs Logan."

"Fine. There's some nice boiled ham you can take him too. And half a fruit cake."

As Aggie and Hannah discussed what they could parcel up for the next day's gastronomic rescue mission, James called over to the conspiratorial pair.

"Stop your whispering. It's punishment time now," said James in mock seriousness. "What shall I order you to play for me?" In truth, Hannah was only too happy to play her fiddle any time for anyone but particularly for her lovely Dada. That could never be a punishment.

"How about 'The Minstrel Boy' - for young Dennis," suggested Aggie.

Eighteen-year old Dennis had been one of James McDermott's best farmhands. Two years ago, he had volunteered to go off to fight the beastly Germans in France. Yesterday, his mother had come weeping to the pub with a telegram in her shaking hand.

As Hannah's fiddle sang out the sad, sweet melody, James watched the logs flickering. He blew his nose for a long time and silently thanked God for giving him only daughters, even though they could be a whole heap of trouble at times.

\*\*\*\*\*\*

A week later, James McDermott was sitting outside Mother Veronica's office. He was a busy man, with farms and shops and pubs to run in and around Rowanbridge, and he really shouldn't be wasting all this time talking to silly nuns. But yesterday - the girls' first day back at school after Easter - Stasia had brought home the stiffly worded letter for him, and it gave him no option but to make an appearance.

Two novice nuns were on their knees, swaying from side to side, silently polishing the corridor floor with lavender-scented beeswax.

James looked at his watch. He turned his tweed hat round and round in his hands. He'd like to have sneaked a look at the racing pages in the paper secreted in his inside jacket pocket but he guessed that wouldn't look quite right in a convent.

Hannah bounced around the corner and sat herself next to her father. She stared at the retreating backsides of the skivvying novices. Hannah thought they looked like nothing more than a pair of grazing cows, inching forward in the fields, heads down, methodically chomping the grass. Polishing floors would not be her fate.

"So, like we agreed last night, I'll do the big old apology act and you can promise to keep me on a tighter lead. OK?"

James nodded but he didn't feel at all confident.

When the McDermotts were finally shown into the Mother Superior's office, James was offered a seat but no cup of tea. That had never happened before. Mother Veronica was sitting at her desk, behind her on the wall a portrait of Queen Victoria. She looked even grimmer than the dead monarch.

"Mr McDermott, I'm sorry to have to conduct this meeting but it is unavoidable. We have spoken several times over the last few years about Johannah's disrespectful and frankly defiant behaviour. Things are not improving. On the contrary, they are getting much worse. It is one thing to torment her teachers day in and day out, but quite another to disgrace the convent in front of our new priest and to desecrate the sacred body of Christ in his presence."

"I'm really, really sorry, Reverend Mother." Hannah walked up to Mother Veronica's desk, placed her hands on its edge and bowed her head in seeming penitence. "I honestly didn't…"

"Silence. I wish to hear nothing from you, Johannah. We are beyond apologies. I have heard far too many from you over the last two years, I'm sorry to say. Absolutely no respect, that's what's wrong with the country. I really don't know what is happening to the world. While our brave boys are over in France fighting the Germans, others take the opportunity to try and overthrow the government."

The news of the failed Easter Uprising on the previous Monday, fighting for Irish Home Rule, had even reached Rowanbridge.

"A total lack of discipline - anarchy even. I appreciate it is hard for you to manage Johannah without your wife, Mr McDermott, but Anastasia could not be more different. How is that possible? Two such different girls from the same parents. Anastasia is a shining beacon of studiousness and piety within our convent. She tells me she has tried everything to bring Johannah into line but sadly to no avail. I believe her. I'm afraid my conclusion is simply that Johannah is an evil girl and we do not want her in our school."

"Well, that's grand..." Hannah stepped backwards from the desk and jutted out her chin, "... because I hate all of you too and frankly you can all..."

"Reverend Mother, please wait," interrupted James before Hannah could burn the last plank on the bridge. "I give you my solemn word that Hannah will be a changed girl from now on. I haven't been keeping an eye on her like I should, what with all there is to do. But that'll all change from now."

"No Dada. Don't beg. I don't want to stay at this awful place a day longer with all these dried-up frights. I believe in God but I don't think I believe in religion any more, so why would I want to stay here and pretend to? That's a bigger sin, surely, than a little bit of a tease of the priest?"

Hannah opened the door and, without another word, left the office.

"I'm very sorry, Reverend Mother. Sure, she doesn't mean that. She just has a bit of a temper on her."

"Whether she means it or not is no longer my concern, Mr McDermott. Good luck, and may God forgive Johannah and protect you both. Good day."

Hannah was nowhere to be seen when James left Mother Veronica's office, and she didn't come home with Stasia on the bus. But she appeared through the kitchen door just as supper had been served and, after giving Aggie a big hug, walked through to the dining room, sat down and served herself some soup.

"Where did you get to then?" asked James. "I tried to find you afterwards. You're in very big trouble now, you know."

Hannah laughed and shrugged her shoulders. But, in truth, she had been shocked by Mother Veronica's verdict and her expulsion. What would happen now? She sucked down a spoonful of soup noisily.

"Hannah, stop making that disgusting noise." Stasia glared at her father as he slurped his soup too, but she couldn't bring herself to correct his behaviour.

"Why do we have to have soup every day anyway before we have our supper? We never used to when Mammy was alive. It's just you trying to be all posh, Stasia, isn't it? The Byrnes have soup so we have to have soup too." Hannah lifted a spoonful above her dish and let it dribble down. "And it's disgusting. Tastes like the spillings from the pump."

"It's chicken consommé, Hannah, with a little sherry in it. You need to learn to eat more than just eggs and potatoes. If only that was all we needed to change in you."

"I don't want to change."

"Well, you'd better or heaven knows where you'll end up. Isn't that right, Father?" Stasia looked across to her father for support but he just hunched further over his soup.

"What on earth are we going to do with you? The school won't have you back and there's no way Daddy and I can

trust you left at home all day, running around the farmyard
with the men and boys."

"No need to worry about me. All the handsome boys are
over in France. There's just the idiots and cripples left, like
Tricky Byrne."

"Don't you dare talk about Patrick Byrne like that. He's
neither a cripple nor an idiot. He's just a bit slow." Stasia's
cheeks glowed.

"Ha-ha! Everyone knows you have your eyes on Nicholas,
and you don't want to marry someone with an idiot brother."

The Byrnes were widely acknowledged to be the richest
family in this part of Kilkenny county, with many farms and
businesses competing with James McDermott's own. Their
younger son, Nicholas, was an officer in the 8th Hussars
and he was over in France fighting while his older brother
Patrick – Tricky to most of the village - was left at home,
declared unfit for military service on account of his squint.

Tricky was generally known as 'an odd one', being very
withdrawn and unable to look anyone in the eye. But his
nickname acknowledged that he was by no means stupid
and had a certain sly intelligence as well as a real skill as a
farmer.

"Well, maybe that's what we need to do with you. Marry
you off to someone who'll put you in your place for once."
Stasia banged her water glass on the table and the rest of
the meal continued in silence.

# Chapter 2 – July 1916

Hannah watched as beads of sweat trickled down Mrs Magee's wrinkled forehead and upper lip, only to be dabbed away with her lace-edged handkerchief just at the moment they were about to drip onto her massive purple silk bosom. Hannah was supposed to be reading Whyte's Appreciation of Saint Teresa of Avila but she must have read this page at least ten times without taking in a word.

She looked out of the front parlour window where she could hear her father laughing and joking in the sun with the brewery man delivering the barrels of stout and beer. The horses pulling the dray swished away the flies with their luxuriant tails. Hannah wished she could unpin her chestnut mane and give it a good old swish too but Aggie had braided it so tightly that it would take a crowbar to undo.

"Mrs Magee, I need a glass of water, please. Would you like one too?"

Mrs Magee looked up from her knitting. "No thank you, Hannah. But make sure you come straight back."

"I will, Mrs Magee."

Hannah closed the parlour door gently and then danced down the hall to the back kitchen. She gulped some water from the jug in the cool pantry and then opened the back door, letting the sun explode into the kitchen. Aggie was sitting on the steps, podding peas, a cigarette dangling from her lips.

"Oh, jeezus, you frightened the life out of me, Hannah."

"Sorry Aggie, but I just had to escape from the old trout for a few minutes. She's almost as bad as the nuns, but at least there's less of the God bit and she nods off so often I can read my own books instead of her hideous stuff. Then she forgets what she told me to do before her forty winks."

"Well, best make sure Miss Stasia doesn't catch you."

Hannah was putting on a brave face for Aggie but she was actually missing the convent. What was the point of misbehaving if there was no audience to appreciate it? Hannah jumped down the three steps, brushing past Aggie, and caught up the bin of chicken-feed by the back door.

"You don't need to do that, Hannah. I'll feed them when I've finished these."

"Don't worry, Aggie. I love my little chucks. They'll lay me some big fat eggs for my breakfast if I'm kind to them."

Hannah skipped around the yard, singing 'It's a Long Way to Tipperary', broadcasting the seed, followed by a faithful retinue of greedy chickens.

"Right, I'd better be off back to the old girl before she notices I've been gone too long. But I think I'll take her a little present…"

Hannah poured another glass of water and crept up the hall back to the parlour door. As expected, a refined snoring was coming from behind it. Hannah turned the doorknob gently. The knitting had dropped to the floor and Mrs Magee's hand was resting on the shelf of her bosom; into it Hannah delicately balanced the glass of water.

She slid into her seat, picked up her book and coughed loudly. Mrs Magee woke up with a start, sending a flood of water down her shiny dress and the glass rolling across the rug.

"Oh, dear God. What on earth…?" Mrs Magee flapped about, trying to brush off the water before it soaked in, dabbing here and there with her hankie. But she couldn't prevent the shame of a dark purple stain from her chest to her lap forming.

"Never mind, Mrs Magee. You must have dropped off to sleep for a second or so." Hannah picked up the glass and the knitting.

"Well, I must have. I don't even remember having a glass of water."

"Yes, you asked me to bring you one back from the kitchen. Sure, it's only water and it'll dry out just fine. And the glass hasn't even broken. No harm done at all."

"I suppose so, but I can't let your father see me like this. I shall have to go straight home and change, and it'll be too late then to return. So, Hannah, do you promise me you'll read the next three chapters before tomorrow?"

"Of course, Mrs Magee." Hannah smiled sweetly.

"If he asks, tell your father I have a terrible headache. It's just a little white lie."

"I'll be sure to do that, Mrs Magee."

The instant the front door closed, Hannah raced back out to the sunny yard to find Aggie so she could brag about her latest victory over the forces of oppression. But there was no Aggie. Hannah sat on the kitchen steps and unpinned her hair, drinking in the sunshine and watching the hens scratch about. She wandered further through the yard, checking each outbuilding as she went, collecting up the couple of fresh eggs she came across.

As she approached the big hay barn, she could hear Aggie moaning softly, a deeper grunting, and the rhythmic shuffling of the drayman's trousers against the bales of straw.

Fifteen minutes later, Hannah was making a pot of tea when Aggie walked back in.

"Cutting it a bit fine there, eh, Aggie? Stasia will be home any minute."

"Don't you worry about my timings. I have them down to a fine art."

Stasia soon arrived home from school, looking very flushed and animated.

"What's up with you? Has Mother Veronica given you an A+ again for arse-licking in your end of term report?"

"You really are disgusting, aren't you. Where do you pick up such vile language? I hope it's not from you, Agnes." Stasia poured herself a cup of tea and went upstairs. Hannah and Aggie hugged each other and laughed.

Hannah had to wait until suppertime to discover the reason for Stasia's excitement.

"Father, guess who's home: Nicholas Byrne. He came back on the bus with me. He's on sick leave and looks very fine indeed in his uniform, though he has his arm in a sling. We must invite him and his parents over to tea while he's here."

"Ooh, Nicholas, darling Nicholas," mocked Hannah. "And what about Tricky? Why can't he come too?"

"Patrick will, of course, be included."

That evening, Stasia wrote out, in her much-praised copper-plate hand, a formal invitation to all the Byrnes to come to tea a week on Sunday and she left it on the hall table for Aggie to post on her way home.

"They only live the other side of Rowanbridge. What a waste of a bloody stamp – and an extra job for me."

"Yes, but you know Stasia must have everything done by the book. I'll take it to the post for you."

Before popping it in the postbox, Hannah considered whether it might be fun to 'lose' the invitation. But it would be interesting to hear Nicholas's account of the war in truth and she was desperate to have some different company than Mrs Magee and her family. That - and cakes.

******

As soon as lunch was over the following Sunday, Stasia started fretting.

"You must put on a fresh collar and tie, Father. And Aggie needs to scrub her hands properly and put on a clean pinny. I'll get mother's best cups down but, Aggie, you'll need to give them a rinse."

By the time the Byrnes knocked on the front door at four o'clock, Stasia had tweaked and primped the house and its inhabitants into a state she deemed worthy of their visitors.

Mr Byrne was a man clearly in poor health. After dutiful handshakes all round, he dragged his emaciated frame upstairs to the drawing room, helped by his dumpy wife. Nicholas followed them up, resplendent in his Hussars uniform, but with his right arm bound up across his chest and some healing scratches on his tanned and chiselled face. Tricky trailed in at the back and followed the McDermotts up the stairs.

Nicholas was full of tales from the front line: the horror of Bazentin, the bravery of his Irish soldiers and the savagery of the Hun. The two fathers shared their thoughts and concerns about the progress of the war with Nicholas.

Hannah watched her sister watching Nicholas. Stasia hardly took her eyes from his admittedly handsome face, and it was true; he did look very dashing and sounded so brave. Stasia drank in his every word as greedily as James swigged his tea and Tricky scoffed the dainty potted-shrimp sandwiches.

Hannah and Tricky were sitting side by side on chairs at the edge of the room, slightly apart from the main conversation. Hannah was fascinated by the quantities of food Tricky was packing away. As soon as his plate was empty, Hannah offered him another selection, as a sort of experiment, curious to see exactly how much he could consume in one sitting.

"Would you like some Madeira cake now?"

Tricky nodded and took a piece. Hannah held the plate a little closer, willing him to take another piece. Two seconds later, he did so without looking up at her.

"I'll be off back to the Somme in no time, just as soon as this arm mends," sighed Nicholas. "But I must say it's a privilege to be back home for more than a couple of days, to see the harvest started … and …to see such dear friends again."

Nicholas looked around the room. Stasia blushed at his words.

"Mr McDermott, would it be okay to stay behind when we have finished tea? There's a bit of land business I'd like to talk to you about, and I wouldn't want to bore the ladies with talk of drains and ditches."

The church clock struck half past five. Mr Byrne rose and began the slow, agonising descent to the front door, followed by his family. After saying their goodbyes, Mr and Mrs Byrne and Tricky left through the front door, Stasia instantly ran up to her bedroom, Hannah dashed out to the yard and James showed Nicholas into his study.

James looked around the small room, the desk piled with paper and ledgers, all of which demanded his attention. He offered Nicholas the leather wing chair. It was his own favourite chair really but, seeing as how the lad was in uniform and had a broken arm, he thought it was only right. He drew up the side chair with the cane seat for himself, slightly anxious whether it would hold his weight.

"Now Nicholas, you're wanting to talk about the bottom fields are you? I've noticed that both our fields are flooding when the rain is heavy."

"There is a job to be done there, sir. But I don't actually want to talk about that today. I've asked for some time alone with you because I've been thinking hard about my future. This war makes you do that, Mr McDermott. I'm lucky that all I got was a broken arm but I can't tell you how many broken bodies I've seen over the last two years. Broken minds too."

Nicholas bent his head down and put his hand up to shield his eyes from the older man.

"I honestly don't know whether I'll make it through to the end of the war. They're saying it'll be over in a matter of months, but who really knows? So, I've decided that I should make plans and ... they involve your family."

James shifted his weight on the fragile chair wondering what was coming next.

"I would like to ask permission to ask for your daughter's hand in marriage and for your blessing. We have grown up close to each other and I think she likes me. I certainly very much admire her. Patrick will not be able to run our farms alone if I should die, so I would like to marry as soon as possible and start a family. And, given you have no sons, it could maybe solve some of your own issues."

"Well now, you've taken the wind out of my sails there, young Nicholas. Goodness me. And here was me thinking we were going to talk dredging." The two men gave an uneasy laugh.

"Well, I am very fond of you, Nicholas, and any girl would be flattered to be asked to marry you, I'm sure. But, as you might well imagine, my daughter has a very strong mind of her own. There is no way she'd be letting me accept on her behalf. I'll call her in so you can ask her yourself." James stood up gratefully. "But, I think you can be hopeful about the answer because I know for a fact that Stasia has been sweet on you for a couple of years now." James gave Nicholas a wink.

"Wait. I'm sorry." Nicholas jumped up and put his free hand on the door handle to prevent James from opening it. "I should have been clearer, Mr McDermott. It's Hannah I intend to propose to."

The two men looked at each other in silence. Nicholas could see that James was shocked and thinking hard.

"Right then. I don't know what to say about that, to be fair. It's not very usual is it, to ask the younger daughter before the older one is off married herself. I'd say that Stasia is more ready to be married than Hannah. She practically runs this house already and Hannah is…well, she is a little bit lively."

"That's what I love about her, Mr McDermott, her love of life, her spirit and sense of freedom. Stasia is an admirable girl of course, but perhaps a little too … how shall I say… unbending, for us to be happy together."

"Well, I suppose all I can do is let you talk to Hannah yourself. I'll get her for you. She's probably out with the chickens." James took a very deep breath, opened the door to the hall and stepped out.

"I wish you luck."

As he waited for Hannah to appear, Nicholas stood and paced around the small study, patting his left jacket pocket from time to time, mentally rehearsing the words he was about to say. The door opened behind him.

"Did you want me for something, Nicholas?"

Nicholas jumped at Hannah's words and spun around.

"Yes, yes. Come in, Hannah. Have a seat – this seat." Nicholas gestured to the big leather chair and then turned to shut the study door, gathering up some courage before he turned to look at his intended.

"Hannah, I have been talking to your father. I've explained my situation and what I need to do and he was happy for me to talk to you directly."

Hannah was curious and cocked her head to one side. What on earth was Nicholas going on about that had anything to do with her? She had no interest in ditches.

"We've always got on well, haven't we Hannah? You used to come over and ride my pony when you were little, do you remember?"

"Course I remember Champion. He was a darling. Gosh, he loved a carrot. Yes, those were grand times."

Nicholas started fumbling in his jacket pocket and managed to take out a little box with his left hand. Then he went down on one knee.

"Hannah, would you do me the great honour of becoming my wife?" Nicholas tried to open the box with his one good hand, dropping it in the process. A ring fell out, glinting as it rolled away over the rug. Hannah laughed and jumped up to retrieve it, before Nicholas could get back on his feet.

"Here you are." Hannah held the ring out for Nicholas to take. He struggled to his feet but declined to take the ring.

"No, it's for you Hannah. I hope it fits but if not, we can get it changed. I know we aren't in love – yet - but that will come. I think you're lovely - so pretty and clever and fun to be with…"

"God, no. You're joking, aren't you? I can't marry you, Nicholas. I don't want to get married to you – or anybody else for that matter. I'm going to have adventures and travel to far-off countries. I'd die if I had to stay in boring old Rowanbridge for the rest of my life."

Hannah laughed again and shook her head. Where had that come from? Nicholas was a decent enough fella but marry him? Not on your nelly.

"Here, Nicholas. Take the ring. Save it for some nice girl – or even for Stasia." Hannah winked at Nicholas as she popped the ring into his jacket pocket.

"Hannah, I would look after you so well and you would want for nothing."

"I'm sure. And you're a very nice man. But I don't love you, Nicholas, and I never could."

Hannah walked to the door and opened it.

"I'm really sorry, Nicholas. I hope your arm gets better soon and that you stay safe at the front."

Hannah walked out leaving the door ajar and Nicholas could hear her running down the hall to the kitchen. He managed to put the ring back in its box, the box back in his pocket and went to let himself out. He thought he heard laughter coming from the kitchen as he shut the front door behind himself.

# Chapter 3 – September 1916

Stasia and Hannah boarded the morning train to Dublin while their father passed their suitcases up to them from the platform.

"Give your Aunt Lily my love. Tell her I'll be up to the city soon enough on business. And I don't need to tell you two to be helpful and polite while you are staying with her."

"Well, of course, you don't need to tell me, Father." said Stasia. "But I think reminding Hannah how to behave properly is never wasted."

The girls found an empty carriage; Hannah opened the window and leaned as far out of it as she could without toppling onto the platform. She was thrilled to be escaping Rowanbridge to go and stay in Dublin for a week with her Aunt Lily.

"Let me give you a kiss, Dada. I'll be back soon. Oh, and tell Aggie that there's something wrong with the big black hen's foot."

Her hat fell onto the platform as she embraced James. The whistle sounded and the train started to move away but, amid frantic shouts and giggles, James managed to throw the straw and ribbon confection into the carriage just in time.

"Perfect." Stasia was already sitting by the window reading her book. "Now you have a grubby hat. Which is, I suppose, better than no hat at all."

Stasia stared at her book intently. She had said very little to her sister since the day Hannah had rejected Nicholas Byrne's proposal of marriage, though she had cried plenty in the privacy of her bedroom.

A part of Stasia was furious that her sister had spurned a truly honourable man - an injured soldier and a friend no less - in such a high-handed way, making jokes about it to

Aggie and acting out how he had gone down on one knee and dropped the ring. How could she do such a thing?

Another part of her was bitterly resentful and humiliated that Nicholas had passed her over to propose to her spoiled brat of a sister. Stasia had always been the McDermott who had been friendliest to the Byrnes over the years; she and Nicholas had taken their communion and confirmation instructions from Father Gregory at the same time and attended the same dancing classes. Stasia had been most concerned for Nicholas's welfare in the war and always enquired after him whenever she met his mother in Kilkenny or at mass. How could he do such a hurtful thing to her? But the remaining part of her was also relieved that Hannah had refused the proposal, and she was secretly hopeful that Nicholas might yet realise he had had a lucky escape and which of the two sisters was in reality the better catch.

Hannah's rejection of Nicholas had spurred on Stasia to look for another solution to Hannah's schooling before the end of the summer, one well away from Rowanbridge. Mrs Magee had been complaining about Hannah's inattentiveness and her endless pranks and Hannah had certainly grown very weary of the devout matron. Not only that, it would be embarrassing for Hannah to bump into the Byrne family all the time, in town or at mass. And, of course, next time Nicholas was home from the front, there would be no Hannah around to distract him if she had been packed off elsewhere. So, they were off to their glamorous Aunt Lily in Dublin who would think of something.

Lily Murphy, their mother's younger sister, had shocked the family by becoming an actress in her early twenties. But an older, rich admirer had saved her from that life and had also, very considerately, died just two years after their marriage. Mr Murphy had left Lily in possession of a generous income, a handsome town house in Pembroke Street, a full cellar and no children to cramp her style. Still only thirty-eight years old and with a fine face, figure and fortune, Lily was the recipient of many admiring advances from would-be suitors but none had yet persuaded her to give up her freedom. James always called his sister-in-law 'The Merry Widow'; it fitted her like one of her fine kid-leather gloves.

Hannah adored her Aunt Lily, with her flowing scarves and colourful dresses. She was the next best thing to having her own mother alive still; Lily had a full store of memories about her sister Evaline that Hannah never tired of hearing. Stasia was much less enamoured of her exotic aunt.

On the rare occasions the sisters were allowed to stay in Dublin for any length of time, Lily took them on jaunts to museums and concerts and they met lots of their aunt's interesting friends. Lily didn't exactly have a salon but she knew some writers and painters and people from the theatre. She had once been introduced to George Bernard Shaw on one of his visits to the Abbey Theatre, as she never failed to remind them.

Lily was there to meet them off the train, unmissable in a burnt orange velvet coat and a hat with peacock feathers sweeping upwards.

"My darling girls. How I've yearned to see you. Let me see you both now. It's been nearly a year and, goodness me, Hannah, you have blossomed into such a beautiful young lady."

Lily flung her arms around Hannah who responded in like fashion.

"Stasia, you are looking well too." Stasia allowed herself to be kissed on the cheek.

Lily summoned a porter to take the girls' luggage to her waiting driver, slipped her fur-trimmed arms into the girls' and led them off to start their Dublin stay with lunch at the Shelbourne Hotel.

As they ate their Dover sole, the girls gave Lily their news and Lily told the girls what was preoccupying the Dublin intelligentsia.

"Since the Easter Rising and the death of the martyrs, so many of Dublin's artists have been trying to tell their story: Augusta Gregory and John Synge at the Abbey - and George Russell is writing a new poem about it, I hear. People are playing John McCormack's recording of 'The Wearing of the Green' whenever they meet up. If artists cannot take up arms they can at least take up their pens, brushes and bows."

Stasia was appalled to hear her aunt support the rebels but kept her disapproval to herself.

"They even cancelled the Feis Ceoil because of the Rising but it went ahead anyway in July. I do hope that you, Hannah, will enter it next year. Any young talented musician would surely want to take part in the greatest music festival in the world. John McCormack himself won in 1903 and it gives budding performers a great boost."

"Have you thought at all, Aunt Lily, about Hannah's need for a finishing school of some sort?" Stasia decided to steer the conversation to the main purpose of their visit.

"I have indeed. I have the perfect place in mind. It is a school run by my great friend, Mrs Letitia Fitzgerald; a great thinker and human being. A serious connoisseur of art and theatre and a wonderful nurturer of the many ... special souls in her care. There's only a dozen or so students, boys and girls."

Hannah couldn't believe what she was hearing. Was there really a chance she could live away from home, practically in Dublin, away from Mrs Magee, Mother Veronica and, above all, Stasia. And living in the same house as boys? What would Stasia think of that?

"Come along now. Let's get you home and settled into Pembroke Street. We shall be off to meet Mrs Fitzgerald at the Maple Academy first thing tomorrow."

And with a wave of her hand and a generous tip for the waitress, Lily swept the girls out to her waiting car.

The next morning, at ten o'clock, Slattery, Lily's driver, was waiting for the three women outside the Pembroke Street house to take them off to Dalkey, to the south of the city. Hannah was fascinated by the endless roads of suburban houses. How big must Dublin be? So many people must live here. Each single street must house as many people as the whole of Rowanbridge.

Eventually, the car crunched into a gravel drive. The wide Georgian front door to the Maple Academy was painted a dark green that matched the Ford motor car they were stepping out of.

"And there are the maples." Lily pointed out the two trees growing either side of the front door, not sycamores as one might have expected in Dalkey, but more refined blood-red Japanese acers.

Lily knocked briskly on the green door. Eventually, it was opened by a frail young man who showed them into a small sitting room at the front of the house. With its deep plum walls, oriental carpets on dark polished wooden floors and huge vase of nearly black dahlias, Hannah imagined she could be walking into an opium den. Or at least what she imagined an opium den would look like from her reading of Sherlock Holmes's adventures.

Lily took the tapestry armchair, at once removing her gloves, and Stasia sat on a side chair clutching hers, but Hannah stayed standing, drifting around the room, noting the writing desk, the porcelain and the paintings and every curiosity on the mantelpiece: an ammonite, a papyrus fan, a lump of rock with yellowish crystals sticking up from it, a small brass pot containing a variety of exotic feathers, and what looked like the skull of a rabbit. That, at least, was familiar.

"Lily, how delightful to see you." Mrs Fitzgerald had walked in very stealthily.

"Letitia, my dearest, it's simply wonderful to see you here in your lair at the Maple Academy rather than in the crush at the bar of the Abbey."

Lily rushed over to Mrs Fitzgerald to kiss her on both cheeks, which the older woman accepted calmly.

"Letitia, let me introduce you to my McDermott nieces. This is Anastasia."

"How do you do, Mrs Fitzgerald. My aunt has told us a great deal about you." Stasia offered her hand and Mrs Fitzgerald took it in her right hand and clasped it tightly with her left.

"Anastasia. Such a beautiful name. And shall we welcome you to the Maple Academy soon?" Mrs Fitzgerald drew Stasia closer to her.

"Oh, no. Not me. I've just finished school now. My younger sister." Stasia pulled away and beckoned to Hannah. "This is Hannah – erm, Johannah. She is the one who needs ... the one who is looking for... the right place to finish her education."

Hannah was staring at Mrs Fitzgerald in awe; a tall woman with a great pile of greying hair held in place by tortoiseshell pins and combs. She was wearing what looked to Hannah like a dressing gown, made of navy silk, with crimson edging to the front and long wide sleeves, over a long satiny dress covered in tiny paisley shapes and the whole tied with a wide crimson silk sash around her waist.

"Johannah. I am very pleased to meet you. I hope you will like what you see of the Maple Academy. Our aim is to provide a stimulating and supportive home from home for young academic and creative minds."

Mrs Fitzgerald glided across the room, gesturing at the three women, before taking the tapestry armchair herself. "Do sit down everyone. We shall have some tea while you tell me all about yourself, Johannah, and I am sure your aunt and sister will fill in any gaps."

Mrs Fitzgerald rang a small bell on the table beside her.

"Letitia, Hannah - that's what we all call her - is very much her mother's daughter. You remember, I told you about my sister Evaline who died in 1912? God bless her soul, she was such a free spirit, you know. Did you ever meet her? No, she would have been married and packed off to the country before we became friends. Well, Hannah, just like her mother, loves to play music – she is a very talented violinist - and to tell stories and to dream of travelling abroad. I think the Maple Academy will offer her just what she needs, surrounded by creativity and some like-minded students who can share her journeys of discovery. Isn't that right, Hannah?"

"Mrs Fitzgerald, Hannah is in disgrace at home, in our village and at school and she needs someone with a firm hand to manage her because she takes no notice of me or her father." Stasia thought she should explain the situation more honestly.

"That's not fair, Stasia." Hannah stood up and approached her sister. "I just cannot abide the nuns and I get so bored at home." Hannah turned to Mrs Fitzgerald. "I do want to learn more, Mrs Fitzgerald. More about literature and art and things, and I think the Maple Academy sounds just right from everything my Aunt Lily has told me."

"Do sit down, Johannah. Here's the tea now."

The four of them sat in silence as a young girl with a pronounced limp carried in the tray and set out the china cups and silver teapot.

"Thank you, Ellen. Ellen is one of our students. She has been with us nearly two years. As you can see, her health is delicate and this makes her attendance at a normal school problematic. But she has quite a good mind and I have been teaching her classical Greek this whole year to which she has taken very well."

Ellen looked over at Hannah, behind Mrs Fitzgerald's gaze, and gave her a friendly wink before leaving the room.

Mrs Fitzgerald poured out the tea and offered a cup to Hannah who rose to take it to her aunt.

"Ellen is the sort of student the Maple Academy is for. We are not for ill-behaved girls and boys but for young people who need a special sort of education, where they can receive more personal tuition and a less regimented environment to allow their minds to expand."

After handing Stasia her cup, Hannah took her own and sat back down.

"My teachers and I are not here to stand guard over our students. We must be able to trust them. We have six young ladies and five young men currently, all living in this house and sharing lessons, mealtimes and the public rooms. So, Anastasia, perhaps you could describe to me exactly how Johannah has 'disgraced' herself at home. I cannot afford to take anyone with any hint of immorality about them."

"Heavens, no, Letitia." Lily didn't trust Stasia to respond. "Disgrace is not at all what Stasia meant to say. Hannah is just a little high-spirited at times and you know how some nuns can be. No sense of humour at all. And Hannah also turned down a proposal from a neighbour's son who is out fighting in France, which embarrasses Stasia and James. So, all things considered, we feel Hannah would do well to be away from Rowanbridge for a while, particularly somewhere that can harness her undoubted creativity."

"Is that right, Anastasia? Is that the 'disgrace'?" Mrs Fitzgerald gave the young woman a penetrating stare.

Stasia paused for a moment and then looked over to Hannah.

"Yes, Mrs Fitzgerald. That's all I meant by it."

"Well, I am pleased we have straightened out that little misunderstanding. If you would like to join the Maple Academy, Johannah, I shall be pleased to accept you. Term has just started but you will catch up. I cannot wait to hear you play. We have one other very talented musician – a viola-player - and it will be one of my great pleasures to accompany you both."

Everyone relaxed a little. Hannah took a sip of tea. It took all her composure not to screw up her face at the smoky taste. What the bloody hell was that?

# Chapter 4 - October 1916

Three weeks later, Hannah found herself sitting on one of four iron-frame beds in the largest of the bedrooms on the second floor of the Maple Academy, which looked out over the lawns and trees at the back of the house. Ranged around her were her three new roommates - Visha, Maisie and Ellen - all firing questions at her from their own beds.

"Did you want to come here yourself or were you sent?"

"Do you snore, like Ellen?"

"Do you like cooking? 'cos you'll have to start whether you like it or not."

"Will you play your violin for us after dinner?"

"Have you got any handsome brothers?"

This last question was from Ellen and sent them all into roars of laughter.

"Yeah, don't be fooled by the gammy leg," laughed Maisie. "Ellen can move at the speed of light if there's a good-looking fella anywhere near."

The three girls helped Hannah unpack, showing her which were her designated three drawers and the scant foot of hanging space left free in the enormous mahogany wardrobe.

"Oh, how beautiful is this!" Hannah gently stroked the vivid turquoise and pink silk sari at the far end of the rail.

"I'm afraid I don't get much chance to wear it these days." Visha took out the hanger and held the sari up to herself as she twirled around the room.

"I can teach you how to do some Indian dancing, if you like. I only know a bit but I've tried to teach these two. Total waste of time. Maisie is too shy to do the moves and Ellen just looks like a puppet with a missing string."

Ellen threw a well-aimed pillow at Visha's head, which was sent back with added force and then all four fell onto their creaky beds where they shared more stories about their homes and families until the gong announced that it was time to go downstairs for dinner.

The places at the enormous dining table were almost completely taken when the four girls arrived. Mrs Fitzgerald was already at the head of the table directing who should sit where.

"Johannah, come and sit by me for your first meal at the Academy. I won't introduce you to everybody this evening. You'll never remember their names. Better by far to get to know each person properly over the coming days. This evening I have seated you next to Sourja, who is Visha's elder brother."

"How do you do, Hannah. I hear you are burdened with sharing a room with my sister." Sourja took Hannah's hand gracefully with his long, elegant fingers and bowed over it. He pulled out her chair, tucked her neatly under the table and then poured water into her glass.

Hannah's head was spinning. She had only been to a formal dinner about four times in her life and only then with her Dada or Aunt Lily by her side. Around the long table were more than a dozen other people busy getting settled and chatting to their neighbours. Hannah recognised Eamonn, the tall, pale boy sitting opposite her, next to Visha. He had opened the door to them on their first visit and was now in an intense conversation with the grey-haired lady on his left.

Visha was valiantly trying to make conversation with a boy on her other side, but Daniel was just staring intently at the table, rearranging his cutlery, glass and rolled napkin into a more precise pattern.

Two girls – sisters unquestionably – with burnished red hair came next at the end of that side of the table. At the top was an empty seat next to Ellen, who was smiling encouragingly at Hannah over the candles. Other than Maisie, seated on Sourja's left, Hannah couldn't see anybody else properly.

Mrs Fitzgerald was talking to the gentleman with the impressive handlebar moustache to her right but seemed very distracted and kept glancing up to the door. After a few moments she rose and tapped the side of her glass with her knife.

"Good evening, ladies and gentlemen. I would like to introduce you all to Johannah - or Hannah as I think she prefers - another new student who has arrived a little late. Please make her feel as welcome to the Maple Academy as you did Maeve. Hannah, one of our traditions here is that every month we ask two of our students to devise and cook our evening meal. Tonight, we are lucky enough to be in the care of Harry and Abigail. I hope I shall still be able to say that at the end of the meal."

The table smiled at a rare joke from Mrs Fitzgerald.

"Abigail and Harry, we are in your hands."

A boy - Harry presumably - stood up and cleared his throat.

> *"For food and for raiment,*
> *For life and for opportunity,*
> *For friends and this fellowship,*
> *We thank Thee, O Lord. Amen."*

A couple of people echoed his 'Amen' though not with the same American twang or quite the same enthusiasm.

"Well, folks, tonight Abigail and I have prepared you an all-American supper. I should say, all-American was where we started out but to be honest Dublin isn't exactly San Francisco so we've had to make some substitutions. But we hope you like it all the same."

Harry and Abigail then wheeled in a trolley from the kitchen and set out a number of serving dishes onto the table.

"We've got some fried chicken pieces with Lima beans, baked onions and some pickled beets." Harry proudly indicated which dish was which.

"We wanted to get some green corn but no greengrocer even knew what that was, did they Harry," Abigail was holding a large basket, "but we did find a shop selling cornmeal so we've made you some cornbread." Abigail smiled broadly as she set down the basket of muddy looking rolls in the centre of the table.

"More like cowpats," whispered Eamonn to Visha.

"Thank you so much, Abigail and Harry, for all your hard work. Let us eat," said Mrs Fitzgerald as she helped herself to chicken before passing the dish to Hannah.

Just as people were near to clearing their plates the door opened and in came a tall, golden-haired man. He slipped quietly into the spare seat at the head of the table next to Ellen, who gave him a welcoming smile.

"Apologies, mother and everyone. I was delayed at the meeting."

"Never mind, John. Make haste and take some food before it all disappears." Mrs Fitzgerald anxiously looked across the table to her son and nodded as he helped himself to a little food. "Say hello to our new student, Hannah."

"How do you do, Hannah. Welcome. I am so sorry to be late for your first Academy dinner, but you'll soon get used to my comings and goings, isn't that so, Mother?"

Mrs Fitzgerald smiled indulgently at her son, shaking her head.

When the main course was cleared away Abigail brought in some chocolate brownies which were greeted with a few cheers and much relief.

"We couldn't get pecans so they've got walnuts in instead."

After dinner, the students gathered in the drawing room for cups of tea and chat. Visha stood up to make an announcement.

"Shush everyone. At first, when we heard we were going to get another roommate, Ellen, Maisie and I were rather annoyed at losing the extra space and having another person to share the bathroom with, but we've decided that Hannah is a very fair exchange. We think she's lovely. So, a proper Maple Academy welcome to her. And, guess what - she plays the violin. I thought that maybe she'll agree to play for us on her first night here if we ask nicely."

There was a little encouraging applause but before Hannah could reply an enormously tall boy with apple-red cheeks and sky-blue eyes stood up and came over. He took her hand, bowed over it and kissed it in a mock-chivalrous manner.

"Honoured to meet you, Lady Hannah. Seamus Flaherty at your service. I don't think it's fair to ask you to perform on your first night. Instead, I'm going to play for you."

Seamus took out his viola, tuned up and began to play "The Last Rose of Summer." By the end, half the room was singing along. Hannah was enchanted; as Seamus gave a final flourish with his bow, she stood to applaud and then curtsied deeply in appreciation.

"Thank you kindly, noble Sir Seamus. That was beautiful."

"Well, there you go, Hannah. You're very welcome. Glad you liked it. Thomas Moore wrote the words when he was staying in County Kilkenny which is where you're from I believe. I hope we'll get to play together soon."

A couple of hours later Hannah and her roommates were sitting up in bed answering all the questions she was throwing at them.

"So, the gentleman with the big moustache opposite me. Who's he?"

"That is Mr Ord-Hume." answered Ellen. "He's a dear. He teaches maths and sciencey stuff to the brainboxes here. Like her." Ellen pointed to Visha.

"I'm not that clever. Not compared to Daniel who is a complete genius and finishes all the calculations before the rest of us have even read the questions."

"Genius, sure. Shame he can't hold a conversation with anyone though," returned Ellen.

"And what about Harry and Abigail? They're both American, so are they brother and sister?"

"No. Harry's from California and Abigail is from Washington. Pacific versus Atlantic," volunteered Maisie.

"They don't even like each other, but I guess they just joined up to deliver their weird American banquet." Ellen pretended to vomit.

"It wasn't that bad, Ellen. More edible than the last thing you cooked up anyway." Visha turned to Hannah. "We're quite an international bunch at the Academy. Abigail is here because her father is a diplomat and Harry's father is something in the military I think. Sourja and I arrived a year and a half ago when our parents returned to India to supervise their factory. They make a lot of the shirts for the British Army so they had to ramp up production, but they wanted us to continue our English education but without the need to attend Christian churches."

"What do you think you'll cook when it's your turn?" Maisie asked Hannah.

"Oh gracious, how often will I have to do that?"

"Don't worry. We only have student dinners once a month so you won't have to do it more than a couple of times a year. And someone will partner you. I'll happily share a turn with you."

"And Maisie is a fantastic cook. Sourja and I had never cooked a thing before we came here, but we wrote to our mother who sent some easy Indian recipes back, and some spices, thankfully."

"Ha-ha. Do you all remember how Miss Murray went scarlet and sweated like a pig when she'd taken a mouthful of your curry sauce?" Ellen mimed being overheated and fanned herself with her book.

"And it was hardly hot at all."

"Well, maybe not for you. I thought it was a bit spicy, but I did quite like it." said Maisie.

"Come on Maisie, you could do with spicing up a bit."

"Well, I can boil an egg, Maisie," volunteered Hannah. "And make an omelette. In fact, I'm comfortable with most egg-related recipes."

"You'll be fine I promise."

"And Seamus. How long has he been here at the Academy?" Hannah realised that she was blushing for no apparent reason. "He's a fantastic viola-player. I shall be embarrassed to get my violin out in front of him. How did he know I'm from Kilkenny?"

"We all knew," said Maisie. "We've been finding out little bits about you for weeks now. But only Seamus thought to find some music for you. He is such an angel."

"Right then. Last question. What's with Mrs Fitzgerald's son arriving so late? I can't imagine she'd let any of us off so easily."

"Ah, he's her golden boy. He comes and goes as he pleases," explained Ellen. "I think she'd rather he turn up late than not at all."

"He's a bit of a mystery, really," added Visha. "He's just wrapped up in his books all the time, when he's not out at his meetings, whatever they are. Apparently, he's only been teaching here for a couple of years. I'm sure he'd rather not have to teach us, but what else would he do? Ellen's always trying to get him into conversation, but with very little luck. I think she might have set her sights on him, poor chap."

"Yeah, I'm not ashamed of that. I can spot a handsome man when I see one. He looks like a bloke in need of a good woman, so why shouldn't that be me? He just needs to open his eyes to my charms. Why else do you think I always sit next to the empty seat at dinner? I'm always betting on him making an appearance. But most times it might as well have stayed empty for all the chat I get out of him."

"Well, maybe if you talked a little bit less…"

Everyone chuckled at Maisie's gentle putdown, especially Ellen herself.

The four girls finished their night-time routines and all settled down in their beds, switching off their bedside lights after reading for a while. Hannah found it impossible to get to sleep in her new bed. Her roommates were all breathing deeply as she ran through everything that had happened on her first day at the Maple Academy. The fact that she had an electric bedside light was a minor miracle. Very different from the oil lamps in Rowanbridge. And an indoor bathroom with hot, running water and a flushing lavatory like at her Aunt Lily's. Such luxury.

More thrilling than these technological wonders was being in the company of so many different sorts of people, from all over Ireland and even other parts of the world. And she had been called 'Lady Hannah' by a lovely, tall boy who had prepared a piece of music especially for her. This was a world she could get used to.

# Chapter 5 – December 1916

It seemed to be no time at all before Hannah was packing up her cases again, ready for the journey home for Christmas. She was looking forward to seeing her Dada and Aggie very much - and even Stasia a little. But she was also going to miss the Maple Academy keenly and her roommates.

The previous three months had given her an intoxicating introduction to the privileged, intellectual, metropolitan life: visits to Dublin's museums, theatre and ballet, lessons in painting and pottery and her first tastes of international cuisines. There were rarely more than six or seven students in any lesson and everyone was encouraged to voice their thoughts about whatever it was they were studying. Was the French Revolution a noble seeking of freedom by an oppressed peasantry or a vicious descent into another form of tyranny? Was Hamlet a cruelly misunderstood victim or a big cissy? Whatever the subject, Hannah started to enjoy forming her own opinions and very quickly enjoyed expressing them too.

She hadn't loved all the lessons equally. French lessons were rather mystifying. She was at least two years behind most of the others and however much time Mme Doucet spent with her alone going over conjugations she just thought it all sounded a bit silly. And when would she ever need to speak French? So, there was no way she was going to join Ellen taking on useless Ancient Greek with Mrs Fitzgerald.

Half of the maths lessons were also a frustrating nonsense to her. She was annoyed at this because she had always been told at the convent that she was excellent at maths. From an early age she had loved to count up the coins in her father's tills and help keep his accounts. Mr Ord-Hume was very patient and he had managed to get Hannah to crack some fairly demanding algebra and geometry. But when he tried to introduce her to calculus and the more conceptual aspects of physics, Hannah had lost patience.

But there were other lessons where she simply flew. Hannah had quickly become one of Miss Murray's best pupils in history and her drawing and painting skills in Mme Doucet's art class compensated for her resistance to learning French, though none of them could approach Daniel's virtuosic artistry and photographic eye for detail.

Then there was literature. Mr Fitzgerald brought all manner of texts to the group: Shakespeare, Austen and Shelley of course, but he would also bring in the front page of the Irish Times and get them to compare it to how the same story had been covered by the Sinn Fein republican newspaper.

John Fitzgerald encouraged all his pupils to find poems or passages of novels that they loved and bring them into lessons. They would have to read them out to the others and then explain what had drawn them to that writing. He also made sure that they were fully aware of the contribution of Irish writers to the glories of literature written in the English language.

Plays, from Congreve to Shaw, were always performed and not just read. Hannah increasingly found herself being given leading roles: Juliet, Lydia Languish, Gwendolen Fairfax. This did not escape Ellen's notice who was not exactly pleased, but even she had to admit that no-one could play romantic heroines quite as convincingly as Hannah and she was too fond of her roommate to let it affect their friendship.

But the lessons Hannah looked forward to above all were for music. These were mostly taken by Mrs Fitzgerald, who was an excellent pianist and teacher, but her son sometimes took his mother's place. If literature classes were where Hannah flashed her wit and charm to her admiring friends, music offered her the chance for more inner gratification. Whether it was analysing the structure of a symphony, learning about a composer's life or just quietly listening to a new piece in the music room as Mrs Fitzgerald played through the score on the piano, music lessons gave Hannah deep joy and fed her soul.

She had been anxious about playing her violin for Mrs Fitzgerald. Her teacher back in Kilkenny was competent enough but had allowed the more casual playing Hannah did - in the pub and at the Rowanbridge dance hall - to erode some of the refinement of technique she had once had.

"You have a good ear, Hannah, and a delightful tone," pronounced Mrs Fitzgerald, "very rich and warm. But we need to get you to a top-flight string teacher who will get those fingers back up and relax your bow arm. And then you must persuade your father to buy you a better instrument."

So, Hannah had been boarding the bus from Dalkey to Rathfarnham, every Saturday since October, for her lesson with Mr Felix Brennan, the leader of the orchestra at the Gaiety, along with lovely Seamus Flaherty.

Mr Brennan was a surprisingly gaunt man, considering how many times he wandered off while his pupils were playing their scales, returning with a piece of toast or a bun which he ate at their shoulders, spitting out crumbs onto the manuscript as he voiced his invaluable advice. Hannah could tell his lessons were working wonders – her scales positively slid through her fingers now - and she vowed to practice every day of the Christmas holidays.

As Hannah went through her wardrobe, choosing clothes to take home for the holiday, she realised that she hadn't been in trouble once all term. She hadn't even thought about misbehaving or trying to humiliate her teachers. She and Ellen had made an apple-pie bed for Visha on her birthday last month, true, but that had been funny for everyone. Stasia just wouldn't believe that Hannah had earned no punishments for a whole term. Hannah couldn't even imagine anyone being punished at the Academy.

Hannah stuffed the last pair of stockings into her case and called out to Seamus and Harry's bedroom.

"Seamus, could you come and give me a hand please to shut my case. It's a bit full and I don't want to have to take another."

No response. Hannah walked out of her bedroom, crossed the landing to the boys' door and knocked on it.

"Seamus? Are you there? Or Harry? Could you help me please?"

The door behind her opened.

"I don't think you're going to have much luck there, Hannah. I believe my mother has sent them down to fill up all the coal scuttles and to stack up the log store by the back door." John Fitzgerald stood at his bedroom door, shirt out, dishevelled and, as always, with a book in hand.

"She'll be trying to get as many jobs out of her slaves, I suppose, before you all go off abandoning the six of us left here for Christmas."

With their parents in other countries, Visha, Sourja, Abigail and Harry were staying with the Fitzgeralds over the holiday.

"But can I help instead? I'm not quite as strong as Seamus, I expect, but even I can close a case and carry it down two flights of stairs."

Hannah and John smiled at each other and they returned to the bulging case on her bed, which was quickly strapped and despatched down to the hall.

Hannah waited for John to return to the second floor.

"Thank you so much, Mr Fitzgerald. I shall practice carrying barrels of beer when I'm home to build my muscles. It's a bit pathetic for girls to be so weak I think."

"Not pathetic, it's just the way things are. But yes, we should question everything that is mere convention, and maybe shake things up a bit. And you, Hannah, are just the person to do it."

John gave her one of his rare, broad smiles and went back into his bedroom.

Hannah walked back into her shambolic bedroom and started to put away all the rejected clothes flung on the floor and other beds. Finally, she bent to straighten her bedcovers. John Fitzgerald had left on her bed the book he had been carrying. It was the The Rose, a collection of poems by WB Yeats, whom Hannah knew her Aunt Lily idolised and who was a 'friend of a friend'. Mr Fitzgerald had read out one of his poems to the class only the other day.

Hannah knocked on John's door.

"Mr Fitzgerald, you left this on my bed."

"Ah. I'm so forgetful. I came back in and wondered what I'd been doing before I answered your cries for help." He took the book from her.

"I find I turn to Yeats at many moments for all manner of inspiration and consolation. Do you know his work?"

"No. Well, just the poem you read to us on Tuesday. The one about the white birds."

"Yes. That's a lovely poem. Can you imagine being a bird flying free above the foam with your soulmate?"

John paused a moment as he looked at Hannah.

"Look Hannah, why don't you take this volume home to read and then tell me what you think when you're back next term. You know … you can read them when you need a bit of a rest from carrying all those barrels of beer."

"Ha-ha. I shall Mr Fitzgerald. Thank you. And I promise to take good care of the book."

"Have a very happy Christmas, Hannah."

"And you, Mr Fitzgerald."

"John. Call me John - at least when my mother isn't around." One last smile and the door closed.

Downstairs, as Hannah waited for her taxi to arrive to take her to the station, all wrapped up in her winter coat and hat and with her violin case resting on top of her big case, she tried to make a space for the book in her hand baggage. But she was anxious not to bend it or damage the page edges, so she finally found a home for it, safely tucked inside the left breast pocket of her jacket.

# Chapter 6 – Christmas 1916

James was overjoyed to have his baby girl Hannah back home and wanted to know every detail about the Maple Academy. Stasia was just as anxious to hear all about it too, but she was less forthcoming with questions. Why should Hannah think that all they thought about was her when she was away?

Life in Rowanbridge was very dull compared to everything on offer in Dublin - or even Dalkey. Hannah kept the promise she had made to Mr Brennan to practice her violin every day, and she had plenty of time to read the volume of Yeats several times through, though there were few other ways of nurturing her mind.

But life was full of delicious bodily comforts that Hannah was only too happy to sink back into. Aggie made her bed for her every morning, scrubbed her back, picked up her discarded clothes, prepared all her meals and emptied her chamber pot. Primitive though they were, Hannah thought it was a lot comfier to resort to a pot under her bed in the middle of the night than have to walk along to a cold, tiled bathroom. But the best thing about Aggie was that she could bring Hannah swiftly up to date with all the latest gossip.

"Mrs Magee had pneumonia last month. A shocker of a cough. A bellow more like. You'd swear it was a cow giving birth. I thought she'd coughed her last. But no - that woman has the constitution of a cow too. And the McLoughlins are building themselves a posh new house in their barley field and they say the Byrnes are furious because it messes up their view down to the river. Eileen Pearce got engaged to Jimmy Boyle. He's home from the war for good because he's lost the sight in one eye when some explosion happened right by him. Your Father is relieved to have one of his best boys back at his job behind the bar. Oh, and there was a big hoo-ha when the O'Rourke girls spotted Tricky Byrne fiddling with himself as they walked home from school down the back lane. That's where he hangs out a lot of the time, down by Cromwell's Tower."

"Eurgh, what a horrible thought. Not that I know what a 'male member' - as Stasia calls it - looks like of course. Not like you, Aggie Carroll." Hannah prodded Aggie accusingly in the chest.

"Ha! All in good time, missy. It's true. I've seen my fair share – all shapes and sizes. Funny things they are too. But don't you be telling Miss Stasia any of that. I pray she has no idea how I earn my little treats, my cigarettes and such."

"I think you're safe, Aggie. Stasia wouldn't dream of walking through the yard and the barns, which seem to be where you mostly entertain your gentlemen admirers."

Hannah agreed to pass an afternoon Christmas shopping in Kilkenny with Stasia, but made sure she steered well away from the convent and her nemesis, Mother Veronica. Other than that, there was nowhere to visit.

At the Maple Academy, Hannah had initially attended mass with the small group of students and teachers who were all observant Catholics. But her attendance had dropped off sharply as the term progressed. Harry would disappear off to some Presbyterian church in the centre of Dublin but the remaining students enjoyed their lazy Sunday mornings, reading, chatting, and inevitably talking about their absent housemates. Eventually, Hannah found this had a much stronger pull than the draughty church of The Assumption of the Blessed Virgin Mary and whispering Father Finneran.

Most Sundays, when the churchgoers had returned, the whole school would embark on a bracing pre-lunch walk along Dalkey sea-front. There was always the same vanguard; Harry and Sourja led the expedition - sometimes even breaking into a competitive sprint. At the rear were always Eamonn, with his weak chest, and Ellen, with her limp, and Maisie faithfully keeping them company.

Often the talk would be about religion and the sermon that some of them had just heard; intense debates would begin. These conversations, which would sometimes stretch on through Sunday lunch, had started to work loose Hannah's already shaky faith. It was hard to defend her religion against the persuasive rationalism of Ellen and Eamonn and the alternative Hindu version of spirituality expressed by Visha and Sourja. And, with the exception of Maisie, she was much less fond of the devout students.

But it was Christmas. And Christmas meant singing carols and candlelight and the whole village gathered together at Midnight Mass. And there would be dear old Father Gregory to say hello to. There was no way Hannah was going to miss that. Stasia wouldn't even need to nag.

The little church of St Francis, near the bridge on the way out of Rowanbridge, was crammed to the rafters. Many people were delighted to see Hannah back home. Mrs Magee gave her a warm hug and Hannah said she hoped Mrs Magee's health was now fully recovered, though her frequent coughing fits through the service suggested otherwise. Even Mr Byrne came over to their pew before the service started to shake the McDermott's hands. It was the first time Hannah had seen or spoken to any of the Byrnes since she had rejected Nicholas's proposal, and the tall man's tone was distinctly cool.

"Mrs Byrne and I wish you a happy and blessed Christmas. You are lucky to be all together. We shall observe the holy season, but with our beloved Nicholas off in France it will be impossible to truly enjoy it."

Many of the parishioners, including Tricky Byrne, had arrived well-lubricated after an evening in either McDermott's or McLoughlin's bar, so a rousing rendition of 'Adeste Fideles' was assured.

Mass was about to start. The organist started playing. Hannah turned to watch the priest and altar servers process up the aisle, carrying the cross. She was shocked to see that Father Gregory was not leading the procession but a new priest instead. And even more shocked to see that the new priest was none other than the young man she had encountered at the convent last Easter. Father Stephen was it?

The familiar story of an unmarried pregnant woman journeying to an unknown town, only to be forced to give birth in a stable, still had the power to move Hannah. And she loved to sing the hymns. No singing from Tricky though. Hannah watched him across the aisle; he moved his lips slightly through the hymns but no noise was coming through them.

The congregation filed out into a freezing, twinkling night.

"What happened to Father Gregory? Did he die?" Hannah asked Stasia.

"I would have told you that, stupid. No, he has just retired. He was over eighty and blind as a bat. Couldn't read a word of the gospels anymore. It was beyond time."

The two sisters followed fellow worshippers filing past the new priest standing at the porch, everyone offering him best wishes, a hearty clap on the back or a warm handshake, and, in James's case, a crisp note.

"Well, I hope he spends some of that on a new razor and new shoes. Did you see the state of his chin?"

Stasia tutted loudly.

"Hannah, why would you be noticing such things just after taking Christ's body and blood?"

"Stasia, how could you not see them?" Hannah wasn't sure whether Father Stephen recognised her or not from their Good Friday encounter at the convent eight months earlier. There was no recognition in his eyes as they wished each other a Happy Christmas. Hannah realised she must look very different without a school uniform on and in her normal clothes. And they had only met the once. But she remembered him, for sure. As Hannah walked home, she realised she was blushing at the memory of her tongue's scandalous encounter with the crucifix.

James shut the bar for Christmas Day but it was open and packed on Boxing Day. Hannah was doing her scales in the parlour, while Stasia was meticulously constructing the outer edge of a jigsaw on a side table, when their father popped his head round the door.

"Hannah, will you come and play? Some of the lads are asking after you 'cos they can hear you doing your scales."

"Well, Dada. I would happily, but Mr Brennan told me I shouldn't get back into bad habits."

"Father, you wouldn't want your daughter to be playing for those drunken eejits, surely." Stasia stood up and placed herself in front of Hannah's music stand. "She'll be ogled and will hear foul language. What's the point of spending money to have her educated as a lady when you turn her into a performing monkey?"

"I don't ask for much, now, do I. But the boys are well into their cups and I don't want any trouble. They're saying that McLoughlins have a piano in their bar now and that maybe they'll be switching their custom over there."

"Well, if they're drunk already, who knows what they'll do to her."

"I don't mind. I'll do it for you, Dada. Don't listen to Stasia. I like playing the dances and jolly stuff. And Mr Brennan will never know."

The prospect of playing the traditional songs was only part of the pleasure of agreeing to her father's request, as Hannah pushed past Stasia to follow her father into the bar. There were now only three days left of the Christmas holidays before Hannah would be back on the train up to Dublin, but she wasn't at all sure she could bear even one more dreary dinner with the disgusting soup followed by tedious evenings alone with Stasia, playing Patience or torturing the scrap of embroidery that she had been made to start at the convent.

The sounds coming from the bar were so enticing – her father's booming voice, laughter, conversation, singing - but, much as she wished to, Hannah had stayed away from the bar after her Boxing Day rebellion. It was just not worth being blasted by Stasia's frosty glare.

It did mean that her violin playing had since been confined to the classical repertoire. Hannah hoped Mr Brennan would appreciate her devotion to the cause of refined string playing and that her hours of practice would be noted. Mr Brennan had told Hannah and Seamus that he had entered them both for the Feis Ceoil competition next March so the prospect of public performance and approval was a powerful incentive to Hannah to become as good as she could be.

After a week of cold and drizzle, Hannah woke up to a glittering frost and sapphire skies, and she was determined to get outside as soon as she had eaten breakfast. She walked through the village, turning left at McLoughlin's bar towards the river, then down and along the riverbank where she could see the new house - or 'villa' as Mrs McLoughlin called it – being built, a couple of fields in front of the Byrnes' fine Georgian house. She could see why it might cause some aggravation to them.

Hannah continued walking along the river, then she climbed up from the icy path, turning left to come back to the village by Mill Lane. The stones in the walls sprouted toadflax, and maidenhair ferns sprang out of every crevice. Hannah brushed her gloved hand over the frosted fronds.

The ruined building, known by everyone as Cromwell's Tower, came into view, bathed in a low golden light. Hannah had always been taught that, once upon a time, it had been a very fine castle before that evil English Puritan, Oliver Cromwell, had bombarded it, reducing it largely to a pile of stones but leaving one single tower intact. Most of the stone walls between the surrounding fields had been built from its ruins.

The tower sat on the border between the Byrnes' meadows and her father's potato field and was now home to nothing more aristocratic than the Byrnes' dairy herd when the weather forced them to seek shelter.

Hannah climbed onto the gate into the meadow and called out to the cows.

"Hallo, cows. Mooooo! How are you on this lovely day? Did you have a nice Christmas? Would you like me to sing you a carol? Yes? Yes, of course you would."

Hannah started singing Hark the Herald Angels. A couple of cows turned to look at her, great blasts of steam coming from their nostrils, but mostly the herd took not the slightest notice.

"Crazy."

Hannah jumped off the gate and turned to see Tricky Byrne chuckling behind her.

"Gracious, you gave me a terrible fright, Tricky. That's a bit embarrassing – me singing to the cows."

"Won't tell."

Tricky walked past her and, with his filthy fingers, untied the old rope keeping the gate shut.

"Come on now. Come on wid ya'."

The cows all turned and headed steadily towards the open gate.

"Why are you moving them out?"

"Frost. No grass. Silage in the bottom field."

Tricky wouldn't even look at Hannah but devoted himself to steering the herd towards the lower meadows with a willow wand. He turned back briefly to retie the rope around the gate with a surprising elegance. Then, without another word, he followed the cows away up the lane.

Hannah stood and watched their silhouettes disappear into the low winter sun. She was in no hurry to get back home. Tricky shambled off, looking like the most desperate, ancient vagabond, with filthy trousers, a jacket torn down the back and the pockets hanging off. Not much like the twenty-four-year-old heir to the richest family in Rowanbridge.

A couple of days later, Hannah lay on her bed watching Aggie pack her bags for her return to Dalkey and intermittently reading the volume of Yeats. She wanted to be sure of having something interesting to say about the poems before she handed the book back to Mr Fitzgerald.

"Aggie, what do you make of this? It's called Broken Dreams."

"All dreams get broken, Hannah. Best to steer clear."

Hannah read out the poem.

"What do you think has happened there? Why did Love flee? Is he dead? Or has she gone off with someone else?"

"Oh, don't be asking me, now. I know nothing about poems and nonsense."

"But it's very sad, isn't it?"

"Not really. He just needs to buck up and find the next girl."

"You're not big on the love and romance thing then, Aggie?"

"Dangerous stuff. Stops you keeping your wits about you."

"How about this one then:

"I will arise and go now, and go to Innisfree,
And a small cabin build there, of clay and wattles made;
Nine bean-rows will I have there... "

"Now, this fella has the right idea. Get your beans planted before you start thinking of anything else. That way you won't starve while you waft around getting all stupid and romantic."

Hannah sighed and lay back on her pillow, reading the rest of the poem in silence.

"Oh, I love that one, Aggie. It's so beautiful. I can just imagine the sound of the lapping water and the cricket and the linnet's wings."

Hannah jumped off the bed to give Aggie a great hug which was as warmly returned.

"I'll miss you, Aggie, and not just because you spoil me."

"And I'll miss you too, you cheeky eejit. So will your Daddy, and even Stasia a teeny bit. But don't pretend you'll give us a second thought once you're on that train. You're having a whale of a time up in Dublin, I can see that. Now, enough of the hugs. Give me the book to pack."

"No, don't worry. I'll keep it with me. I might need it for the journey."

# Chapter 7 – January 1917

When Hannah arrived back at the Maple Academy the next day, it was buzzing with all the other students coming back for the start of term. The four who had spent the holidays at the Academy were thrilled to see their friends return and helped unload, carry and unpack.

Various interestingly shaped packages were brought into the house and taken up to bedrooms. Eamonn's mysterious long tube turned out to be a telescope, given to him by a generous uncle. Daniel had brought his easel and paints back with him and before dinner presented Mrs Fitzgerald with a very fine watercolour of the Academy as seen from the driveway.

"That is excellent, Daniel. And all done from memory, I assume. You've captured the colour and shape of the acer leaves perfectly. I shall have it framed properly and hang it on my study wall. Thank you so much." Daniel blushed and mumbled but looked very gratified at Mrs Fitzgerald's genuine praise and pleasure.

Maeve and Roisin were sporting new matching knitted hats and scarves, one in violet and the other in canary yellow which made for a vibrant combination with their coppery hair. Seamus also had a new pullover - in bright scarlet.

"Everyone's mother seems to have been knitting madly for Christmas." A tiny twinge of self-pity passed through Hannah. "Well, at least your jumper matches your cheeks, Seamus."

"You'll like this present I got though." Seamus held out some sheet music for Hannah to see. "Mozart violin and viola duos. We can get old man Brennan to let us play them in our lessons."

Harry had been sent some juggling balls from America and had been practising during the holidays. He insisted on carrying them everywhere, hoping for plaudits, but the regularity of the thuds landing on the table, down the stairs, in the hearth – everywhere but back into his hands – meant that the praise ran out rather quickly.

"Jesus, if he doesn't stop coming into our bedroom to show us his latest pathetic trick I shall ram those balls into his loud Californian mouth," fumed Ellen.

Hannah, Visha, Ellen and Maisie waited to offload all their news until they were in the privacy of their bedroom.

"I couldn't wait to see my Mammy and Daddy and my brothers," said Ellen, "and then, two days later, I couldn't wait to get back. My mother just fusses over my leg all the time and nags me to do my exercises. And then she tells me I need to do my hair differently. So annoying."

"Well, I would have been happy to put up with any amount of nagging if I could have been with my parents." Visha wiped away a tear. "But at least I had Sourja with me. I really felt sorry for Abigail."

"Not for Harry?" queried Maisie.

"Stupid question, Maisie. I'm sorry, Visha. It was very selfish to moan about my family when you couldn't be with yours." Ellen went over to Visha's bed and put her arms around her friend. "How was your family, Hannah?"

"My father was adorable and my sister was a pain in the arse. So, just as usual. In fact, I could swear that everything was exactly the same as last Christmas – even my presents – apart from one thing. We have a new priest in the village."

"I thought you'd decided to give up religion? You big coward." Ellen prodded Hannah in the ribs.

"Not a coward. I just like singing carols. Nothing wrong with taking the good bits and leaving the rest."

"If you ever want to go to Church here, Hannah, you can come with me any time you like." Maisie took Hannah's hand. "Don't let Ellen bully you out of anything."

"Thank you. You are so strong-minded, Maisie, aren't you, despite being just a sliver of a girl," said Hannah admiringly.

The dining table was less crowded than usual with only Miss Murray in addition to Mrs Fitzgerald and the eleven students but the chatter was as loud as ever. After dinner, Mrs Fitzgerald suggested that everyone who could, should perform something to entertain the others, to mark the excitement of rediscovering their friends and the start of a new term.

She started them off with a Schubert Impromptu and then Harry - of course - jumped up first, wanting to perform some juggling but he was prevailed upon to think of something else and, luckily, he could remember a comic monologue by Mark Twain about Adam's problems in the Garden of Eden.

"I didn't think Harry's church allowed him to believe in dinosaurs and the stuff Darwin wrote about," whispered Ellen to Hannah.

Sourja and Visha told some stories from The Mahabharata; the one where Princess Draupadi ended up married to five brothers raised a few eyebrows in the room.

Ellen volunteered next and gave a rather uneven performance on the piano of The Maiden's Prayer, with the sustaining pedal held down throughout. Mrs Fitzgerald looked immensely relieved when she had finished.

Seamus and Hannah raided the sheet music cupboard and found a pile of Gilbert and Sullivan scores. They played some of the most famous duets with Maisie accompanying them on the piano. Tunes from The Pirates of Penzance, Iolanthe and The Mikado were familiar to many and by the end people were tapping their feet, humming along or, in Harry and Ellen's case, even singing out loud.

"Anyone else? Don't be shy. We are all among friends here." Mrs Fitzgerald stood and looked around the room. "Roisin, how about singing us one of your Irish folksongs?"

Maeve gave her sister a little push and Roisin shyly stood up to sing.

"OK then, everybody. This is one of the old Donegal songs that Padraic Colum has been collecting with our father and others. The tune is very old – maybe even medieval – and Mr Colum has written some new words for it, inspired by all sorts of old Irish stories and fragments of forgotten folksongs."

Roisin shook her vibrant hair off her face and began to sing She Walked through the Fair in her pure unaffected voice. The room fell into thoughtful silence at the haunting, modal melody and evocative words.

*As she laid her hand on me,*
*And this she did say:*
*It will not be long, love,*
*'Til our wedding day.*

The song evoked so many images in Hannah's mind; she could imagine herself as the beautiful heroine of the song, drifting elegiacally through the fair as the stars came out, followed by her lover's adoring gaze, then as the supplicant daughter pleading for her penniless suitor and finally as the soft-footed ghost visiting her lover's bed. What a role that would be. But who would be her suitor?

As Roisin finished the song, loud applause came from the back of the drawing room, breaking the trance that had been cast over the room. John Fitzgerald had entered, like a ghost himself, without anyone seeing or hearing him. He was wearing his overcoat still and his face looked grey and weary.

"That was exquisite, Roisin. Well done to you. You have a lovely voice there." He turned to the whole room. "We should all be cherishing our Irish culture like Paddy Colum is doing. Only by singing and playing songs like this and telling the myths and legends of old Ireland can we keep it alive."

"John, thank heavens you're back safely." Mrs Fitzgerald rose as John came forward to embrace her. "How are they up in Connemara?"

"They are all grand and send you their best wishes."

"How is Mary?"

"She is doing well, all things considered."

"Now, John will you play for us, or read us one of your poems?"

"Oh, I'm so sorry mother – and sorry to everyone. I set off at dawn and it's been a hellish journey. I'm dog-tired. And anyway, I think we should all go to our beds with that sad, sweet song in our ears."

John kissed his mother again and headed for the door. As he passed Hannah, he stopped and turned to her.

"Hannah, how are you? Did you have a good Christmas – and did you get to carry many beer barrels?"

"I didn't, I'm afraid. Still as weak as a kitten. But I did do lots of scales."

"Excellent. Felix will be delighted. I missed my Yeats. I hope you took good care of him."

"Oh yes. I read him every day, sometimes with a tear or two, it's true, but always with great pleasure. Don't worry; I didn't get any tears - or beer - on the pages!"

John's smile lifted his exhausted face. "Well, I very much look forward to us having a bit of a sob together soon."

And with a nod to everyone, he was gone.

# Chapter 8 – March 24th 1917

Hannah lay half-awake in her bed. It was only just past six o'clock but the excitement of turning seventeen today was enough to have woken her early, even on a Saturday morning, when the four roommates would normally relish sleeping until nine or so.

She looked around the bedroom. Maisie was invisible, tightly curled under her bedclothes. Visha was also hidden under the piles of extra blankets and covers that she needed in the cold Dalkey air. Ellen, on the other hand, was sprawled on her back, clean out of her sheets, her bad leg resting on a pillow and a faint snoring coming out of her open mouth.

There was no way Hannah was going to spoil their Saturday treat of a lie-in, and it was too dark to read, so she snuggled back under the covers to dream a little longer.

The term had been full of pleasures and pains. The most recent bad memory was from only last Saturday, when she had taken her turn to cook dinner for everyone on St Patrick's Day. Maeve, her co-conspirator, had researched all sorts of traditional Irish recipes, which had looked fine on the page. But when they presented the household with their oaty porridge, served with cabbage and herrings, and a pudding that was just more oaty porridge, with the addition of milk and sugar, it was obvious that Irish gastronomy before the potato arrived cannot have been much fun.

"I told you, Maeve - we should have stuck to eggs."

Then there was Harry. He had become more than a nuisance. Every time Hannah turned around he seemed to be there behind her. He tried to claim the seat next to her at dinner every evening and he had started writing out religious essays and tracts to attempt to 'save her soul'.

Eventually, it became obvious that his close attentions were directed as much to her body as her soul. He would put his arm around her shoulder as he filled her glass with water, take her hand when they all crossed the road to walk along the sea-front, and, last week, outside their bedrooms, he had made to kiss her goodnight on the cheek, but she had ducked and escaped to the safety of the girls' company.

Hannah had shared her growing annoyance at Harry's persistence with her roommates - but also with Seamus, as they had rumbled home on the bus after their string lessons the previous week. Since then, Seamus had done everything he could to thwart Harry's stalking, and last night had even managed to slide into the dining chair next to Hannah the instant before Harry. Harry really hadn't enjoyed being made to look an idiot, sitting on the lap of the amiable giant for all of two seconds.

The pleasures went a long way to divert Hannah from the problem of Harry. Her weekly violin lessons and daily practice were joyful, and the challenge of learning the challenging Mozart duos with Seamus had opened up the new rewards of chamber music. It felt disturbingly intimate to play such wonderful music with Seamus so close to her; his body, his musical line and his emotions so in tune with her own.

Since the New Year, her Aunt Lily had treated Hannah to a couple of Saturday nights out in Dublin. Hannah would arrive at Pembroke Street on the bus or the tram but be brought back to the Academy in Aunt Lily's luxurious car.

In January, she was taken to her first opera, Finn Varra Maa by Geoffrey Palmer, at the Theatre Royal. Not a success. But, last month, Aunt Lily had taken her and Ellen to Man and Superman at the Abbey and the two girls had talked about it for days afterwards.

Her deepest pleasure though had been discussing Yeats with John Fitzgerald. Sometimes, they snatched a few minutes at the end of a literature lesson, or sometimes talked as they toasted crumpets at the fire on a Sunday afternoon. Or they would read to each other in a corner of the drawing room after dinner, before she was chased off to bed by Mme Doucet.

Hannah was fascinated by John Fitzgerald and his interpretation of Yeats's poetry. She felt she was getting to understand more about Yeats but also a little more about her teacher. All Hannah knew about him was that he was Mrs Fitzgerald's son, he was a teacher, he played the 'cello and she guessed he was in his late twenties, early thirties, maybe. That was it.

However, his sensitivity to the poems gave her, she believed, a privileged peek into his mind. His voice would rise as he read out poems about fiddlers, dancing, apple blossom, fishing or horses racing and it was a delight to see him beam and laugh. But Hannah believed this happiness was a flimsy veil briefly flung over a dark well of sadness that he carried around everywhere.

When John read poems to her about old age, crushed dreams and lost loves she believed that he was filling them with his own true feelings: intense, wounded, hopeless... Hannah wished she could take his hand at these moments but guessed such a gesture wouldn't be welcome.

"Wake up, sleepy-head!"

Hannah's reveries were brutally broken by a three-pillow bombardment. Her sleeping friends had woken and crept up on her as she dozed and dreamed.

"Happy birthday, you ancient old thing," shouted Ellen and Maisie started to sing her birthday greetings. Soon most of the occupants of the second-floor bedrooms, including Seamus and Harry, had gathered around her bed to wish her happy returns.

"Blimey. Seventeen, eh? Better look out or you'll be an old maid soon," teased Ellen.

Hannah was treated to double poached eggs for breakfast, her favourite. And, afterwards, everyone moved to the drawing room to present their modest birthday gifts to her:

lavender water from Visha and Sourja, soap from Maisie and some chocolate creams from Ellen.

"Thank you, Ellen, but I'm not stupid, you know," Hannah laughed at her friend, "I know I'll be getting your personal assistance when it comes to eating these."

Maeve and Roisin had each embroidered a linen handkerchief with an exquisite Celtic letter 'H', one in light and one in dark green.

"Good job that the stitching is in green. That way your snot will match it."

"Ellen, you are simply revolting. Thank you so much for these beautiful things, you two. I would never dream of actually blowing my nose on them."

The boys' presents comprised a jar of honey from Eamonn, a pack of playing cards from Seamus and a red velvet ribbon from Harry (of course) and from Daniel a sketch in russet chalk of her playing her violin.

"Daniel, this is brilliant. I've never noticed you sketching me as I've been playing."

"You played on our first evening back." Daniel mumbled.

"And that's it? That's all you need to be able to reproduce this lovely thing? You really are a wonder."

Seamus wandered up to Hannah and presented her with a sheet of music. "Just a little extra." The composer was Percy Grainger and it was a piece called Seventeen Come Sunday. Hannah had never heard of him.

"I know it's Saturday today, not Sunday, but I couldn't resist it and I thought you'd like it. It's a choral piece with brass band." Seamus turned the pages, pointing out to Hannah all the various instrumental lines. "I couldn't quite muster all the forces needed to perform it for you – we are shockingly short of trumpet players at the Academy - but it's based on an English folk song which I shall now attempt to sing for you."

Seamus stood up and cleared his throat.

*"As I walked out on a May morning, on a May morning so
early,
I overtook a pretty fair maid just as the day was a-dawning.*

*With a rue-rum-ray, fol-the-diddle-ay,
Whack-fol-lare-diddle-I-doh.*

*Her eyes were bright and her stockings white, and her
buckling shone like silver,
She had a dark and a rolling eye, and her hair hung over her
shoulder.*

*Where are you going, my pretty fair maid? Where are you
going, my honey?
She answered me right cheerfully, I've an errand for my
mummy.*

*How old are you, my pretty fair maid? How old are you, my
honey?
She answered me right cheerfully, I'm seventeen come …
Saturday!"*

Everyone cheered at this point, but Seamus ploughed on.

*"Will you take a man, my pretty fair maid? Will you take a
man, my honey?
She answered me right cheerfully, I darst not for my
mummy.*

*But if you come round to my mummy's house, when the moon
shines bright and clearly,
I will come down and let you in, and my mummy shall not
hear me.*

*So I went down to her mummy's house, when the moon
shone bright and clearly,
She did come down and let me in, and I lay in her arms till
morning.*

*So, now I have my soldier-man, and his ways they are quite
winning.*

*The drum and fife are my delight, and a pint of rum in the morning."*

By the end, everyone was joining in with the rue-rum-rays and diddle-I-dohs between each verse with increasing hilarity and everyone applauded and cheered loudly as Seamus took a bow.

"Blimey," said Eamonn, "They're a racy lot those English girls. I can't imagine you obliging a man you met on an errand quite so generously, Hannah, even if he did ask politely."

"And I don't think she's looking to marry a soldier-man any time soon, either," Ellen pronounced. "Far too grubby for our Hannah."

Seamus gave the sheet music back to Hannah.

"To be honest, after a pint of rum, you could probably get a girl to do anything you wanted." Harry laughed loudly at his own joke but no-one joined him.

"Not a nice thought, Harry. But thank you everyone. You've all been so kind to me. Best birthday I've had for years. And even though the Feis Ceoil is only a week way, I'm not even going to do any practice today. Don't you dare tell Felix Brennan though, Seamus Flaherty."

The students dispersed but a few of them stayed on to give Hannah a game of gin rummy with her new pack of cards. Then she gathered up all her precious gifts and went back up to her room to put things away before lunchtime.

On her pillow was a small package. It was wrapped in plain brown paper and string but there was a card on top. "To Hannah, on her birthday. A chance to discover some magic. From JF."

Inside was a second-hand copy of Yeats's The Celtic Twilight. Hannah read the card again. She held the book for several minutes before she tentatively opened it. The book had been well-read. It fell open near the end and out floated a handful of pressed rose petals. Were they too meant for her? Hannah dearly hoped so.

# Chapter 9 – June 1917

In the months following her birthday, Hannah looked at John Fitzgerald in a new light. Outside the classroom he said little and spent hardly any time with the wider household, but he was a wonderfully charismatic teacher and Hannah was very aware of her growing fascination with him. She would sit in lessons and study the way he perched on the front desk, a book in one hand and the other in his trouser pocket or occasionally used to brush his long fair hair away from his face. His voice was not loud but it was deep and resonant and drew his students into whatever he was reading to them.

Hannah's private explorations of Yeats' poetry with John had petered out after a few weeks of the spring term and she felt keenly the loss of those privileged dialogues. But, over the Easter holiday, she resolved to immerse herself in John's birthday gift and hoped she'd be able to sustain a discussion with him on the differences between the Merrow, the Leprechaun and the Cluricaun if such an opportunity ever arose.

John usually came down to dinner at the Academy, but as soon as it finished he would escape to his bedroom. Sometimes the girls would come up to bed to hear him still playing his 'cello, and often it was an intensely melancholic piece.

"Look out. Dark clouds over the Fitz again," Ellen would caution.

Ellen considered herself the authority on John Fitzgerald, as far as anyone could be, and she displayed a certain ownership of him. She had been at the Academy longer than any other student and, supplemented by her gossiping with the household staff, she had managed to glean a variety of tantalising snippets. Being Ellen, she was also very keen to share everything that she had amassed with her roommates.

According to Ellen, John had only been teaching at the Academy for the last two years, arriving after Ellen had begun her life there. He had lived in the west before that. She was also sure that he had been married, because one day she had caught a glimpse of a wedding service card in Mrs Fitzgerald's writing bureau with John's name on the front. She thought the bride's name was Aileen - or maybe Alice - but definitely beginning with an A.

"Where's the wife now then?" Maisie enquired breathlessly. "Maybe he murdered her." The other three girls all hooted at the notion of gentlemanly John doing such a thing.

"Killed with kindness more like. I have no idea where she's gone. But I shall find out," promised Ellen.

And, true to her word, a few days later she came back to her friends with the prize that John had indeed been married and had lived with this wife, Ailsa, out in Connemara until she had died just before the war started. Ellen had wheedled this morsel out of Lizzy the cook in return for peeling a bucket of spuds.

"But it's never spoken of. No-one must mention it. Lizzy would only speak in whispers and kept checking that Mrs F. wasn't anywhere in sight."

Then there were the 'meetings' that John disappeared to every week. "I must end the lesson now, I'm afraid. I have to catch the tram into town for my meeting," he would often say. "How was the meeting tonight?" his mother would ask when he returned in time for dinner. But his answers were always vague and shed no light on the nature of them. "Useful," he might say, or "frustrating."

Ellen believed these to be political meetings of some sort, but she couldn't enlighten them further.

All of this did nothing to reduce the mystery around John. Rather the reverse. Hannah became obsessed with knowing more about John Fitzgerald - but she had no idea how to achieve this.

But then a new opportunity to spend time with him arose, courtesy of her Aunt Lily.

"I knew you would win at the Feis Ceoil, darling girl. So proud of you." Hannah and Seamus had both won their categories. "I shall be having one of my literary evenings in July and I'd like my friends to hear you play, maybe with a few others. Nothing too long or involving too many people. And nothing too frivolous. This will be a gathering of serious thinkers," Lily cautioned.

Hannah consulted Mr Brennan who suggested the Mozart duos Hannah and Seamus had now nearly perfected.

"I don't think they are quite – grand enough for what my Aunt Lily has in mind, Mr Brennan."

"You may be right. I know your Aunt well, of course. The Mozart is very demanding and shows off the skills of the pair of you, but I reckon we need something a bit more substantial and more… dramatic."

"Like her you mean?" The pair of them laughed.

"Leave it with me."

At her next lesson, Mr Brennan presented Hannah with a set of sheet music for Beethoven's String Quartet Opus 74.

"This is a quartet from Beethoven's middle period. It's often called The Harp on account of all the pizzicato passages in the first movement. You'll be stretched on every front, but it's a glorious piece. To be honest, it's no harder than the Mozart duos. But this'll do you good. We just need to find you the rest of the quartet. Seamus will be fine on viola. As for a 'cellist, why not ask John Fitzgerald? We're missing a second violin, but I shall have a think."

Hannah found herself blushing at Felix Brennan's suggestion for no apparent reason, but she was also thrilled to have this reason to engage with John again.

She and Seamus looked through the parts on their way back to Dalkey and realised they would have to put in some very serious practice to get this music up to a good enough standard for Lily Murphy's soirée.

"Gosh, it looks tricky, doesn't it. But we can do it. Practice, practice, practice. And it'll be just marvellous to perform with you in front of a proper audience." Seamus squeezed her hand.

The Beethoven quartet was monumental. But they were not daunted and over the following weeks, in their solitary daily practice sessions and shared weekly lessons, the pair started to master the piece.

Hannah agonised about how she should ask John to join their quartet. She didn't want to mess it up and get a refusal. She finally decided that she should ask him in public, at dinner, when she would have the support of Seamus and also his mother.

In the event, it happened quite easily. None of Hannah's pre-prepared persuasive wiles proved necessary.

"Mr Fitzgerald, I wonder whether you would do me a great favour. I have agreed to play a Beethoven string quartet for my aunt's literary gathering in a few weeks' time. Seamus will be playing with me but we need a 'cellist. I wonder whether you'd consider joining us."

"Well, now. I would really love to do that, Hannah. It's been ages since I played in a quartet. And you can't go wrong with Beethoven. Which one is it?"

"The Harp. His 10th string quartet, Opus 74."

"How exciting. That is a real beauty. Thank you for asking me, Hannah. I suppose I'd better get practising. Do you have the parts?"

Over the next couple of weeks, Hannah occasionally heard John practising his 'cello part as she passed by the music room or his bedroom. Eventually, the day came for their first practice session together. Felix Brennan had failed to think of a suitable amateur second violinist so had valiantly agreed to take the chair himself. Clearly, for the prospect of an evening at Lily Murphy's with fine food and wine, it was worth enduring these amateur co-players.

Hannah had tried reasonably hard to persuade Mr Brennan - as the only professional amongst them - to take the leader's chair, but he had said that the whole point of the exercise was for Hannah to be the star at her Aunt Lily's soirée and that, after all, was the truth. So, although full of anxiety at first, Hannah was very excited to take the leader's chair.

Hannah and Seamus set up the music stands downstairs after lunch, a plate of biscuits on hand in case Mr Brennan needed refuelling. Hannah returned to her room and sat on the edge of her bed, cradling her instrument and looking out of the window, waiting for her teacher to arrive. It was a glorious warm June day but that wasn't why her palms were a little clammy.

The doorbell rang and Hannah stood up. Her heart was racing. She went to knock on John's and Seamus's bedroom doors but both were already on the landing, instruments in hand.

"After you, Hannah." John waved to the staircase. "Seamus and I are happy to follow our leader."

Their first session together was a ragged, stop-start affair until Hannah got the hang of being responsible for holding the quartet together. She wasn't used to other players watching and following her so intently, but by the end of the afternoon she had begun to enjoy the feeling of power and control.

Despite the legions of wrong notes from everyone - yes, even from Felix Brennan - it was impossible not to be overwhelmed by this powerful music, which spanned every emotion across its four movements.

"I don't know which movement I love most," mused Seamus. "The first has a cracking viola line for me, but the second is just so tender. I love the way the first violin and 'cello sing to each other." Hannah smiled at hearing it expressed in that way, but yes, Seamus was right, She and John had been 'singing' to each other.

As they packed up their instruments at the end of the afternoon, they made arrangements to meet each Saturday afternoon until the date of the soirée in July. "And I shall be revisiting that third movement before we meet again, I can tell you, and I suggest you all do too," said Mr Brennan as he left the room, picking up a biscuit on the way out.

# Chapter 10 – July 7th 1917

"**Y**ou look absolutely lovely." Maisie sighed, as she sat on her bed after breakfast while Hannah showed off the new dark-blue silk dress her Aunt Lily had bought her for that evening's musical and literary gathering.

"Scarily grown-up, you little minx. Mind you, all those poets and politicians will be far too busy being self-important to give you a second look."

Hannah found Ellen's put-down strangely reassuring. She didn't normally have the slightest trepidation about being the centre of attention, but for some reason tonight was different. Hannah found that playing the quartet produced such heightened emotions that she sometimes found herself in tears by the end of a movement. She didn't want to take her bows with red eyes and a runny nose. She would keep a firm grip on herself.

"It's exquisite silk, but why wouldn't your aunt have chosen something a bit more colourful for you?" Visha stroked the full skirt admiringly.

"Well that's obvious." Ellen threw up her hands. "Why would you let your slip of a niece get all the attention when you're the one who's coughed up for the spread?"

"I like it, though. I like the inkiness - like the sea in Dalkey harbour. And, to be honest, I don't really want to stand out any more than I already have to. I'm worried enough about playing without having to think about what I look like or making conversation with lots of people cleverer than me."

"Well, I'm sure they're just as anxious about meeting the beautiful Miss Hannah McDermott, talented niece of society royalty Mrs Lily Murphy, student of the renowned Maple Academy, virtuoso violinist and the creator of the most disgusting food ever served in Dublin."

With that, Ellen stood up from her bed. "Come on, you two. Seamus and Eamonn are waiting for us for a stroll up Killiney Hill."

Hannah was left alone, looking at herself in the narrow mirror on the inside of the wardrobe door, flexing her arms to check for ease of movement. As she began to remove her new dress there was a sharp knock on the bedroom door. Without waiting for a reply, Harry walked in and, shutting the door behind himself, gave a long admiring whistle.

"My, oh my. The girls said you looked a picture in your new dress and I just couldn't wait to see you in it."

"Please leave Harry. You can see I'm just getting changed."

"No need to worry. You look even more appetising with your dress only half on." And he sidled over to where Hannah was standing.

"Go out now, Harry. Go or I shall scream the bloody place down."

"There's no-one left. Everyone's off taking their constitutional. And all I want is to kiss that beautiful porcelain neck of yours."

Harry lunged at her, making Hannah cry out as she pulled herself away from him to cower in the corner, using her dress as a screen. She heard the bedroom door open, and then a sharp thwack followed by loud groaning. Hannah peeked over the top of her dress to see Harry sprawled on the floor, holding his jaw.

"Get out. Get out now. How dare you prey on a young girl alone in her room." John's right fist was still clenched and his eyes skewered Harry. John dragged Harry to his feet and marched him out of the room.

Hannah could still hear their exchange on the landing.

"That's common assault, Mr Fitzgerald. I won't stand for it. I was doing nothing wrong."

"Sue me then, why don't you? I suggest you pack your bags and leave before my mother hears about what has just happened."

There was more low mumbling. Hannah realised she was trembling. She lowered the new dress that had been used as a shield; the neckline had been torn at the seam a little. She would have to repair that - and her nerves - before the performance tonight. Hannah stood up and waited, expecting John to come in and talk to her about the scene. But she just heard steps running downstairs and John's door shutting.

Later, when everyone gathered for lunch, there was much speculation as to Harry's whereabouts. He had stormed off, who knew where, leaving his luggage to be collected and neither Hannah nor John were of a mind to shed light on the matter. It would soon become obvious that Harry was not coming back.

Five hours later, Lily's driver, Slattery, set down the entire quartet outside her Pembroke Street house, having picked up Mr Brennan on their way through Rathfarnham. The whole house was decorated with lilies – of course – which filled the rooms with their heady perfume. In Seamus's words, it 'smelt like a funeral parlour' but the hostess was very much alive and kicking.

"My darling Hannah." Lily greeted her niece with an extravagant embrace. "And how marvellous to see you all, you divine people. I shall be eternally in your debt. I am so immensely grateful that you have come to grace my modest little gathering. Felix Brennan, how lovely to see you out of the Gaiety's pit for a change. And John Fitzgerald, I can't remember the last time we saw each other. Taking yourself off to the wild Atlantic and then coming back home but living like a hermit these past few years."

Lily swept past them all and beckoned them into the long, high-ceilinged drawing room.

"You all look very smart, and Hannah that dress is perfect for you. See over here, I have acquired four music stands so please set your chairs out as you wish. People will begin to arrive in about an hour, so you have time to have a rehearsal.

After we have drinks we shall be treated to a discussion about Stephen Gwynn and his involvement in the war. D. P. Moran will, I'm sure, be arguing that no Irish nationalist should have anything to do with it. Then we shall ask you to play. You are welcome to listen to the debate, unless you would prefer to stay in the parlour until we are ready for you."

Hannah and Seamus opted to stay out of sight until their performance came around, but John and Mr Brennan wanted to hear what was going to be said so left their instruments in their students' care.

People started arriving soon after seven and, as Hannah and Seamus sat nervously behind the parlour door, they could hear Lily heaping lavish greetings on each new guest.

"Felix, can I introduce you to Eleanor Hull? And gracious me, if it isn't Richard O'Brien. How wonderful of you to come along to my modest little gathering. Have you met John Fitzgerald by any chance? His mother is a great friend of mine. A great educator and inspiration to her special pupils, one of whom is my ridiculously talented niece, whom you will be hearing play later."

Nearly an hour passed. Seamus kept silently practising the fingering of some tricky passages. They could hear the warm buzz from the drawing room of well-educated people making conversation but neither of them was in the mood to chatter. Then the parlour door opened and Felix and John came in to collect their instruments and tune up. Hannah thought her heart would burst out of her chest. They made their way through the groups of guests in the warm drawing room; Hannah feared she might actually faint.

But, as they took their places at their stands, a strange calm fell over her. She looked over to John who was gazing at her intently from his chair and nodding encouragement. They had all decided that Hannah should introduce and explain the quartet, which she stood up to do.

"Good evening, ladies and gentlemen. My Aunt Lily kindly invited me to play for you, along with some of my friends, who are all much better players than me, as you'll hear. No, honestly, they are."

Hannah could see the room smiling at her and her aunt beaming with pride.

"We're going to play Beethoven's 10th string quartet for you, Opus 74 if you're interested. It's often called The Harp Quartet because of the pizzicato effects in the first movement but I don't think they sound anything like a harp myself."

A warm murmur of indulgent amusement spread round the room, which Hannah responded to with growing confidence.

"There are four movements. The first has a slow introduction but then changes to a faster tempo and frankly at the end of it I shall be going demented, struggling to play all the notes. The second movement is slow and sweet while the third gallops along at a raging pace. It has a motif da-da-da daaa," - Hannah sang the four notes and then demonstrated them on her violin, - "which people have connected to the opening of his Fifth Symphony which was composed in the same year. Those four notes are supposed to be Fate knocking at Beethoven's door, but who really knows what anything means in music. It's a funny movement, the third, I think; sometimes angry and then suddenly bouncing along more like a cheeky dance. The fourth movement is a set of variations and altogether more sedate and civilised - just like all of you. I hope you like it."

Hannah sat down to a ripple of expectant applause. She looked around at her fellow players, gathered her thoughts, took a deep breath and then led them into Beethoven's genius.

When they finished playing, there were several seconds of awed silence before warm and generous applause broke out. The four players stood and took their bows; Hannah forgot to count how many times but it was more than enough to convince her they had made a pretty good fist of it. She thought her head would explode with joy, and not just because of the sublime music.

The applause ended and Lily invited her guests to move to the dining room for supper. As everyone started to shuffle towards the door, Hannah dashed through the congratulatory crowd, back to the parlour, avoiding talking to anyone. She packed away her violin and sat thinking through what had just happened. Seamus came in.

"Well, that was great, wasn't it? You were amazing, Hannah."

Hannah smiled and nodded in silence.

"Well, I'm off back to Dalkey on the tram. I don't fancy staying and having to talk to any of those scary bigwigs. John and Felix are in their element, chatting away. They've gone into supper. Are you going in … or … do you want to come back with me?"

"No, you go on without me, Seamus. I must stay to the end for my Aunt Lily."

Seamus quietly put his viola away and put on his coat.

"Well, if you're sure, I'll be on my way." He stood in front of her and bent to kiss her cheek. "Seriously, that was great playing, Hannah."

Hannah was barely aware of Seamus closing the door behind himself. All she could think of was that she was in love. She was in love with John Fitzgerald and she was sure he loved her in return. The realisation had hit her in the second movement as she played its third subject, the swooning melody for the first violin. When she had come to the end of her song-like passage, she looked up and saw John's kind eyes intent upon her. As the 'cello sang out in reply, he had kept up his gaze, not looking at his music once, and she had held that gaze unswervingly. It was not a night to back away from strong emotions.

The rest of the quartet had been fuelled by a huge injection of excitement and anticipation. She had been carried over rapids in a boat, unable to stop or alter course, surrendering to the force and exulting in its energy.

But what now? The door opened and John and Felix entered.

"Brava, Miss Hannah McDermott." Felix gave her an exaggerated bow. "A new star has entered the world of chamber music - and all thanks to me. Well, mostly thanks to me anyway."

"Yes, congratulations, Hannah. That was very special." John spoke softly as he packed away his 'cello.

"Now you two, come on. Let's go and eat and drink with abandon. I am absolutely famished." Mr Brennan had, after all, been without nourishment for two whole hours. "And we'll need plenty of wine inside us. There's to be readings from some young poets after supper and I'll need to be prepared for that. I'd take myself off home after the nosh to be honest but how often do I get a chance to be driven around Dublin in a fancy car?"

"Are you coming, Hannah?" John turned to her at the door, holding out his hand.

"No. No, I'll be fine here. I couldn't eat a thing."

Hannah sat alone and relived every note of the quartet and each exquisite sensation it had provoked. Eventually she began to hear valedictory voices in the hall as her aunt sent her grateful guests on their way and she knew it was time to prepare for the journey home. She collected all her belongings and opened the parlour door to the hall.

"My darling girl, you were simply wonderful tonight. I've had so many compliments about you – and of course about the whole quartet." Lily gave a cursory nod towards John and Felix who were collecting their instruments.

"Let me embrace you. Evaline would have been so proud of you tonight and you looked so like your mother at times. You must be exhausted. Slattery will see you all home safely now. Come back and see me soon, Hannah. There's a lot to talk about."

Soon the three were tucked up on the Ford's leather seats, Felix up front alongside Slattery, Hannah and John in the back, the car trundling through south Dublin on their way to drop Mr Brennan in Rathfarnham.

"Evenings don't get much more glamorous than that these days, what with the war on. I tried to consume enough caviar and champagne to last me until the wretched thing ends. Where on earth does Lily Murphy get all that stuff from, I wonder? It's amazing the secret supplies that money can magic up."

When they arrived at Temple Ogue Road, John got out of the car to help a swaying Felix navigate his garden gate and find his front door keys. Hannah held her breath and wished hard as he returned to the car. John resumed his seat in the back with her rather than beside Slattery up front. She felt that she had willed it so.

There was no conversation between them as they continued home to Dalkey. Hannah thought she could sense an actual physical entity - something she would be able to feel if she just put out her hand - linking them together on the back seat though their bodies remained separate. Hannah looked at her hand, deliberately ungloved, resting on her left knee and at the proximity of John's hand curved around his right knee. Surely, surely, he would take her hand in the next moment and make his love known, albeit in passionate silence.

After another thirty minutes or so of intense hope, the car drew up to the Maple Academy and they left the haven of the car.

"Good night, Slattery. Many thanks for bringing us home." John waved the car out of the drive and turned to the front door. It was nearly eleven o'clock and few lights were still on. This is the moment, Hannah thought. He will take my hand and confess his love. Maybe he'll even kiss me.

John held the front door open for Hannah. As she brushed by him she turned and paused for a moment. John's eyes were fixed on the doormat.

"Thank you so much John. I have had the most magical night of my life, and a lot of that is because of you."

John looked up. "Goodnight Hannah. It was a very special night for me too." He shut the front door and began bolting it. "You get yourself off to bed. Back to studies as usual in the morning."

# Chapter 11 – Late July 1917

The days following Aunt Lily's soirée were bitterly frustrating for Hannah. Soon, everyone would disappear for the holidays and she was desperate for John to show her some sign to treasure back in Rowanbridge. She was certain she had not imagined the feeling – the love – that had been expressed through their playing. But John had offered nothing at all that would sustain her over the next six weeks. In fact, he seemed more distant and distracted than ever and had barely looked at her in their last couple of literature classes.

The end of term would also bring some sad goodbyes. Sourja was leaving school to join the Royal Navy. "My parents are out in India, working hard to support the war effort, so I should at least do what I can. I might even find myself protecting the ships carrying the uniforms from their factory."

And Roisin was also leaving the Maple Academy. Her parents were pacifists and had a deep objection to the war, but Roisin was thinking seriously about becoming a nurse. "They must let me do that, surely. I'll be trying to save people's lives after all."

Both Roisin's and Sourja's plans cast a melancholy shadow over the final week. Hannah looked at the pair afresh and saw them as proper adults now. She wasn't sure that she was ready to be so grown-up herself. The students had hardly thought about the war over in Europe for the last year but it suddenly became very real to everyone.

At breakfast on Thursday, the final day, the conversation was laden with farewells and good lucks and promises to write or visit. Mrs Fitzgerald seemed weighed down with grief as she gave a little speech about how proud she was to be sending Sourja and Roisin out into the world and what a joy they had been to have at the Academy. Everyone shook the teachers' hands and wished them a happy holiday and up in their bedrooms many hugs were exchanged. But there was no sign of John.

"He's gone off somewhere. He got a telegram yesterday evening." Ellen had managed to squeeze this morsel out of Lizzy. But who the telegram was from or where John had gone to was a mystery to the cook and hence to them all.

Hannah finished packing and walked downstairs to find a friendly pair of hands to bring down her cases. On the first floor she saw that Daniel and Eamonn's bedroom door was ajar, with Maisie's gentle voice coming through it.

"Now make sure that you don't exert yourself too much at home. And, of course, I shall write every day."

There was a short pause, during which Hannah was certain she heard some seriously squelchy kissing going on.

"You're so lovely, Maisie." Eamonn's voice. More kissing noises.

Hannah moved swiftly and silently past the door, and down the staircase. So, even Maisie and Eamonn had managed to find love in each other's arms, but she, the supposedly enchanting and talented beauty, Hannah McDermott, could not elicit a single adoring word from the man she had fallen for. Life was so cruel.

******

Stasia was waiting for Hannah at Kilkenny station later that afternoon, but she had no words or smiles of welcome and moved aside as Hannah made to embrace her.

"Get yourself a porter. Jimmy's outside with the pony and trap."

The six miles to Rowanbridge were a glum affair. Every question that Hannah posed was met with a single word; "Later" "No" "Maybe" or a nod towards Jimmy Boyle's back as if to indicate that it wouldn't be appropriate to talk about that particular subject within the barman's hearing.

But her Daddy was thrilled to see her. James plied her with tea and kisses and a bundle of questions about school,

Lily and the musical soirée as they sat cuddled up in front of the parlour fire. Stasia listened in silence until she rose to go and give Aggie instructions about serving dinner.

"What's wrong with Stasia, Dada? You'd think someone had died. She barely even said 'Hello' to me when I got off the train."

"Oh dear. You must forgive her, my love. Your sister has had some very upsetting news this week. Nicholas Byrne came home on leave for two weeks and announced his engagement to some girl from Kilkenny. Louisa something or other. Her father's a bank manager, I believe."

"Louisa Nevin? She was in Stasia's class at the convent. She's awful. Full of airs and graces and a stupid whiney voice."

"Aye, I think that's the name. Anyway, Stasia has taken it very badly indeed, though she's said nothing about it as such. She's a trooper. But I know what's eating her up. Mrs Byrne told us at Mass last Sunday, all excited, and Stasia has hardly said a word since."

"Good riddance, I say. If Nicholas Kennedy thinks Louisa Nevin will make him a better match than our Stasia, she's better off without him. Conceited idiot."

"Well, I'm not sure your sister would agree, but in a way it ends any hopeless wishing she might have been doing. Shuts things down, once and for all. But just you be kind to her, OK, and try not to get on her nerves."

Later that evening, as Hannah sat on her bed watching Aggie unpack her bags, she took out the Yeats book John Fitzgerald had given her. Neither of the McDermott sisters were doing very well in the love game it seemed.

"Aggie, how do you make a man fall in love with you?"

"Jeezus, Hannah, you are joking, I hope. Why would you want to be doing that? Do you really want to be tied to one old fella, churning out babbies year after year when you could be up in Dublin having fun and playing your fiddle to the adoring crowds?"

"Well, if you were in love with him…"

"Don't be an eejit. Stop reading those bloody poems and dreaming yourself into a state. Get yourself something useful to do. Just look at Miss Stasia. She's had her heart broken, I reckon, but she's not moping around. She's busy every day helping your father on the accounts and the orders and almost taking charge. That's the way to block out any feelings you have for any boy."

"Man. Definitely a man, not a boy."

"Well, that's even worse. They're only after one thing. Make sure you don't get led on by their clever words. Whispering lovey-dovey nonsense when they just want to get into your knickers."

"You don't understand, Aggie."

"I understand everything there is to know about men. I am a world authority. I've come pretty close to having to settle down with one of those bastards a couple of times but I got myself sorted and now I know how to avoid any trouble."

"He's not a bastard. More like a saint."

"Well, that's just creepy. Look, have yourself a couple of days swanning around and then you can start helping a bit. There's loads of spuds need picking – if Stasia allows you to work in the field, of course, and if your precious fingers can take the strain."

Aggie stood up, stretched her back and closed the wardrobe door.

"Goodnight, Hannah. It's good to have you home for a while. Your Dada will enjoy having a smiling face around. Me too for that matter."

"Night night, Aggie." Hannah leapt off the bed and gave the maid a fierce hug - reciprocated just as fiercely - before she popped her legs under the sheets and turned out the oil lamp, hoping for dreams of John Fitzgerald.

# Chapter 12 – August 1917

Predictably, Stasia wouldn't hear of Hannah picking potatoes, nor hay-stacking, nor helping with the barley harvest, though she had relented for a few outdoor jobs around the house and garden - hoeing the lettuce or watering the tomatoes - in addition to Hannah's favourite daily task of collecting eggs and feeding the hens.

Instead, Stasia set Hannah to work on her father's accounts ledger most mornings, entering the previous day's takings from their two pubs and the little grocery store they owned in the middle of Rowanbridge. Hannah had fancied working behind the counter in the shop but Stasia wouldn't hear of it.

"What if Mrs Byrne were to come in and see you there, weighing out tea in a pinny."

"Who cares? And why on earth should you care what the Byrnes think any more?"

"We have standards, Hannah. We have to preserve some propriety, even though we need to do more ourselves in the business now that Father's health is failing. I just wish I could get him away from living here next to the pub. He's drinking far too much Guinness every night and staying up far too late."

"Yes, but he enjoys it."

"That's not the point."

So, here was Hannah, on a muggy August morning, sitting at her father's desk with the big ledger open, dipping her pens carefully into the black and red inkpots, entering pounds, shillings and pence into columns, blotting the figures carefully, and then adding or subtracting them with ease and no small satisfaction. In fact, she rather enjoyed seeing the sums steadily mount up to make the weekly and monthly net profits.

The front door crashed shut. Stasia was back from her shopping trip to Kilkenny.

Hannah went to the kitchen to peek at what Stasia had bought in town. Hopefully something more fun than yet another plain white linen blouse or black skirt.

"How was Kilkenny? Did you see anyone?" Hannah flopped onto the old sofa.

"Hannah, it would be extremely difficult to get on a bus in Rowanbridge and go into town and not see anyone."

Stasia bent to place her Monster House shopping bags by the sofa.

"Argh. Stop it, you. You know what I mean." Hannah jumped up and snatched Stasia's straw hat off her head and put it on Aggie who was elbow deep in flour, kneading bread at the kitchen table.

"I did indeed see someone. More importantly, I heard something very interesting from this someone."

"Go on then, spill the beans."

"Not now. I'll tell you when Father is back from Thomastown." That morning, James had gone to pay his weekly visit to their other pub in the next village to go through business with the manager there.

"Oh, for heaven's sake. You're power mad, you."

"Go on, get yourself back to the study and finish those accounts."

"Hey, take this bloody hat off me before you go," shouted Aggie at Hannah's back, blowing a strand of hair from her dusty nose.

James didn't return until late afternoon, so they did not sit down together until that evening's supper. Hannah was delighted there was no soup to swim through and took it as a sure sign that Stasia was starting to reject all that the Byrnes stood for.

"Dada, Stasia went to Kilkenny today and came back with some juicy gossip that she has refused to tell me until you were here too. Please, can you now make her stop torturing me?"

Stasia was ladling out stew for the three of them. "Don't be so ridiculously dramatic, Hannah. But yes, Father, I came back on the bus with Mrs Magee who had heard from Paddy in the Post Office that the McLoughlins have run into trouble finding the money to finish building their house."

"Oh dear, that's a shame for them."

"Yes, a shame for them maybe, but also an opportunity for us. We could step in and buy the house off them and finish it ourselves."

"Now, why on earth would we be wanting a grand villa on the other side of the village away from the pub and the shop?"

"Stasia has always needed a grand villa, Dada."

"Shush, Hannah. It's not a 'grand villa' Father. That's just what Mrs McLoughlin has been calling it. It will be a very nice house with a lovely view down to the river. But, most importantly, it would mean you could get away from being right next to the pub every night and being dragged in to drink with the men."

"I don't want to get away from the pub."

"Father, you need to ease up and drink a lot less, like Dr O'Connor has warned you."

"How come you want to live in a house that would be slap bang in front of the Byrnes?" asked Hannah. "Oh, I get it. You want to be slap bang in front of them in the very house has that spoiled their view. Everyday Nicholas Byrne would have to ride past the windows – the very windows that have stolen their view - and see you swanning about inside looking out of those lovely windows. You are actually evil, Anastasia McDermott."

"Don't be ridiculous, Hannah. We aren't the people who chose to start building the house there. I am just thinking of Father's health. And I think it will be a good investment.

There is plenty of money sitting around in Father's bank accounts doing no good at all."

"Ah, I've never liked those risky investment things, bonds, shares and the like. I like to put my money in things I can touch: a nice shop, a good field. And I like to be able to get my hands on my cash without any fuss if I need it. Pass me the spuds please, my lovely."

"Well, that's exactly what this would be, Father. Property. A good solid investment. Though it's mainly somewhere for us all to live. Just promise me you'll think about it."

James was deftly peeling the potato, skewered on his fork. "We'll see."

******

The following Sunday, Hannah was eating boiled eggs alone, as her father and Stasia had gone off to early Mass.

"They were scrummy. Thanks, Aggie."

Hannah put down her spoon and turned the two empty boiled eggshells upside down in the eggcups.

"Go, on. I dare you to give these to Stasia for her breakfast when she gets back from Mass."

"I don't think she's going to fall for that again this week. And she was very sharp last Sunday. If you want to play tricks on your sister, do your own dirty work."

Aggie opened the big oven door and put a shoulder of pork in to roast.

"Right, now I can have two minutes to myself for a quick fag and a cuppa before they get back."

Hannah followed Aggie out onto the back-kitchen steps. The hens ran towards them expecting some breakfast themselves.

"I reckon that little brown hen lays the biggest and best tasting eggs of all. You wouldn't think it, would you, to look at it."

Aggie took a long drag on her cigarette. "Never judge anything by its appearance."

"Blimey, you're in philosophical mood this morning, Aggie. Has your latest fella been cheating on you or something?"

"I am simply giving you the benefit of my ten extra years on this shitty planet, Hannah McDermott. Please yourself whether you take my advice or not."

Aggie sat and held up her face to the sunshine while Hannah relented and threw some corn to the hens. After a few minutes, they heard the front door close.

"Quick. They're back." Aggie delicately extinguished her cigarette on the back wall and put the remaining half back in her apron pocket to be enjoyed later.

Stasia walked into the kitchen and surveyed proceedings.

"Well, at least you're up."

Stasia took off her hat and gloves as James slumped into his fireside chair. Aggie busied herself making a fresh pot of tea, cutting the soda bread and popping four fresh eggs into boiling water.

Stasia cleared the remains of Hannah's breakfast.

"I see you've prepared your empty eggshells for me again, Hannah. You need to come up with some original ideas I'm afraid. Father Stephen was asking after you again. He's still hoping that you'll come to mass at least once while you're home."

"I've told you. I don't think I can honestly be part of that mumbo-jumbo anymore. I'm not saying I don't believe in God at all but am I really supposed to believe that I'm eating Christ's body and drinking his blood. It's just nonsense."

"He's just trying to save your mortal soul, Hannah. Every single person is precious to God."

"Then why is God letting so many souls slaughter each other in the trenches? Both sides can't have God behind them."

"Ah now, my lovely. That's too hard a question for any of us to answer." James held out his hand for Hannah to come and sit on his knee. "Oof. You're getting to be a big girl now, aren't you."

"I'm still your babby though, Dada, aren't I? I'll always be your babby."

Stasia gave her freshly boiled eggs a brisk crack. "Hannah, could you please go and get dressed as soon as possible. We're expecting visitors."

At ten o'clock, Hannah was sitting on the kitchen table watching Aggie slice carrots, popping any piece that rolled across the table into her mouth, when there was a faint knocking at the front door.

"It's them." Hannah jumped down and ran to the hallway, but Stasia was already there, opening the door to Mr and Mrs McLoughlin, whom she showed into the study. Stasia waved Hannah away, followed their guests into the room and shut the door behind her.

"I'm off out. I don't want to be around if Stasia doesn't get her way."

Hannah picked up an egg basket and walked through the farmyard. But, instead of collecting eggs, she went through to the back gate and out into Mill Lane to pick blackberries.

It was a prickly task picking off the jewel-like fruits without being scratched too much, which Stasia would immediately notice and disapprove of. She took one berry and pressed it against her lips to colour them, as if she were still eight years old. But this time she also imagined the juice being kissed off by a golden-haired 'cellist.

As she got near to Cromwell Tower, she could see Tricky Byrne sitting on the top of the five-bar gate looking out at the grazing herd. He was dressed in rather more respectable clothes than his normal outfit.

"Look at you in your Sunday finery, Tricky. I'm guessing you've been to Mass."

"Clever."

"Are you looking forward to having a beautiful young lady come to live at yours once Nicholas marries Louisa?

Then there'll be babbies soon after I guess, all wanting to play with their Uncle Patrick."

"Nope."

"Go on, you'll enjoy it. It must be a bit lonely up there in the big house with Nicholas away and your parents not going out much."

Tricky said nothing, but just sat and wove the gate rope into ever more intricate knots.

"So, what's happening with McLoughlin's villa? Do you know anything? And how's the view from up at yours?"

Tricky shrugged as if to say he didn't know or care.

"Do you fancy a blackberry?" Hannah held up her basket and Tricky took one which he then squeezed between his barely clean fingers.

"Not ripe."

"Suit yourself." Hannah took a berry, cautiously put it on her tongue and swiftly spat it out. "You're not wrong."

Hannah tipped out the contents of her basket into the nettles by the gate.

"So then, Tricky. With Nicholas off and engaged, what about you? Has any young lady taken your fancy? You'd be quite a catch, you know."

"Funny."

Tricky jumped down from the gate, knotted the rope around the post and set off up the lane. He beckoned Hannah to follow him. About half a mile further on he turned to her and pointed to some blackberry bushes on the right.

"South-facing. Ripe."

And then he trundled off leaving Hannah to strip the laden hedgerow.

******

A couple of days later, Hannah, tired of practising her scales, wandered downstairs looking for something to eat.

"Can I have this, Aggie?" Hannah was in the larder holding out the remains of a blackberry-and-apple pie with one hand and her violin in the other.

"Greedy guts. It's twenty to twelve and you'll be having your lunch soon."

"But Dada and Stasia are still out and I'm starving. I didn't have any breakfast, did I? And I've been practising hard."

"Well, if you will stay in bed until gone ten. Good job your sister wasn't here to see you drag yourself down like a slut. Ah, go on then. You can scoop some cream off the top of today's milk if you like." Aggie nodded towards the small churn sitting in a bucket of cold water on the marble slab as she squeezed out her floor cloths at the sink.

"I wonder what's happening. I don't want to go and live in a posh villa away from everything. Away from the pub and the chickens and all the gossip."

Aggie laughed. "You don't need to worry about that for as long as I'm still working for you. The gossip comes to me as you know. And I'm sure your Dada will let you take your favourite chucks up to the house, as long as they're kept off of Miss Stasia's smart lawns. Assuming they can get old McLoughlin to do the deal of course."

Hannah carefully laid down her violin and bow onto the kitchen table, spooned some cream into the dish and went to sit on the back steps in the sun to eat her very late breakfast. It was hard to believe that they might soon be leaving this house where she had grown up, where she knew every beam in the barns and hen house, and every bump and hole in the back wall of the house.

Why did she care so much when, at the same time, she was desperate to get back up to Dublin to see her friends, start her violin lessons again, learn new poems, see new plays. She, Ellen and Maisie had exchanged a few letters and it seemed they were having as tedious a summer as she was.

But mainly it was thinking about seeing John again that gave her stomach a sick lurch. She had tried to stop thinking about him so much but, unless she was in company, it was hard to prevent thoughts of him delighting and tormenting her in equal measure. He was especially present whenever she played her violin.

Hannah had contemplated writing a letter to him, to declare her love, but had rejected the idea, knowing that John would not respond well to such a direct approach. But now there was only a fortnight more to wait.

"Hannah!" Aggie hissed to warn her that the front door had just opened.

Hannah scooted back to the kitchen table and took up her instrument just as James entered the kitchen.

"Where's Stasia, Dada?"

"Good afternoon, my lovely." James kissed the top of Hannah's head. "The great hunter has returned with her kill and is now in the study slicing it all up. Poor old Willy McLoughlin didn't stand much of a chance once your sister had him in her sights. To be honest, I think both parties got a fair deal in the end."

Stasia walked into kitchen and nodded towards Aggie. "Father, please don't talk about our affairs in public." Aggie shot Hannah a sideways look and raised her eyebrows.

"How soon can lunch be ready, Aggie?"

"I can have it on the table in about forty minutes, God willing, Miss Stasia."

"Yes, please." Stasia turned to leave. "And Agnes, why is that dirty dish out on the kitchen step?"

Over lunch, Stasia outlined the bones of the deal they had struck with William McLoughlin that morning. The uncompleted villa and the two fields around it would pass to James McDermott in exchange for the pub in Thomastown and a small cash sum.

"This way the McLoughlins get a lump sum to pay off their debts to the builders and a going concern with the

Thomastown pub. We get a fine new property – yes we have to spend a bit to get it finished - which gets Father away from living next to the pub here, and we also put more of our money into land and out of running pubs." explained a very satisfied Stasia.

"What's going to happen here? Are we going to sell this house and pub?"

"Well, I would very much like to do that, but Father won't hear of it."

"No, I've gone along with most of what your sister wants. But this is the house where I was born, my father was born and both of you. It's more than just bricks and mortar. I couldn't bear for it not to be in the family."

"We're going to install a manager here. Jimmy Boyle maybe if he wants it. He wouldn't be my first choice but, with so many good men away fighting, beggars can't be choosers."

"He and Eileen will be getting married soon so she'll try to stop him drinking away all our profit."

Stasia speared a slice of gammon, "Eileen will certainly help, Father, but for as long as I am around you can be assured that Jimmy Boyle will do his job properly and behave himself."

# Chapter 13 – September 1917

Lily, in a swirl of chiffon, was on the platform, all ready with a porter to meet Hannah from the train.

"My beautiful girl. How marvellous to see you. And I see you've been out in the sun this summer. You need to be a little careful of that. Pale and delicate is a more fashionable look, I think."

Hannah linked arms with her aunt and they strode off, leaving the porter to load up the cases and follow them out to where Slattery was waiting in the car.

"We shall have tea and cakes at Pembroke Street before we take you out to Dalkey. That way you can tell me all the news from Rowanbridge. I cannot believe you are moving out of the Main Street house."

"I know. It's Stasia's big plan to get Dada away from the pub and to stop him drinking quite so much. I also suspect thumbing her nose at Nicholas Byrne has something to do with."

"Yes, she has an extraordinarily strong will. Most young women would want to go as far away as possible from a man who has spurned them. Who knows what she has in mind. I await developments with interest."

Part of Hannah was frustrated to have her arrival at Maple Academy delayed for another hour or so, but it meant that the exquisite anticipation she had been enjoying all journey was extended too. And the little raspberry tarts were scrumptious.

"You and your playing are still being talked about in my circle." Lily poured out her special blend of Bewley's tea from the silver pot into the translucent china cups. "You must all come back and play again soon. Start practising now. Maybe some Mozart this time. Something a little more elegant than Beethoven I think. What about Ravel? I would love to feature a living composer and his quartet has been much praised. Mind you, you might have to find yourself a new 'cellist."

Hannah's heart jumped.

"I went over to see Letitia for dinner a couple of weeks ago and there was no sign of John. She said he was out on the west coast dealing with important 'business affairs' and she wasn't sure he would be back for the start of term even. Now, what sort of business would he be having in Connemara, for heaven's sake? I don't believe a word of it."

Hannah drank her tea in silence.

"Now, I'd be more likely to believe he was off hiding from the police among the bogs and lakes, because I've heard from one of my friends that he's quite the Fenian, that man. Though I can't believe he'd be capable of any actual violence - not that the constabulary makes a distinction. They're happy to round up anyone they think supports the Volunteers."

Lily brushed an errant pastry crumb from her skirt and wiped her mouth with the embroidered napkin.

"Anyway, there'll be some changes at the Academy for you. A few friends gone off into the big wide world - and a few new arrivals I dare say."

****** 

Hannah watched as Slattery drove away and turned to knock on the familiar green front door of the Academy. Five seconds later the door was opened to reveal the beaming face of Seamus looking down on her.

"Hurray, it's Hannah." He gave her a massive bear-hug. "I hope you've been practising plenty. I've been given a score of the Mozart Sinfonia Concertante which we'll just have to do together if we can find ourselves a little band to accompany us. It's absolutely terrific."

All her other friends were already back, plus there was a new pasty-faced girl called Morag and a boy - who looked about twelve but was actually sixteen - called Angus. Hannah didn't have the slightest interest in either of them.

Up in their bedroom after dinner, the four friends exchanged stories about their summer holidays.

"Oh my God, the boys in Tramore were so handsome."

Ellen had been to the seaside with her parents.

"And, I tell you, when they got down to their bathing suits on the beach, you could tell which ones had the biggest... thingy."

The girls roared with laughter.

"Not that I had any luck with any of them, what with my attractive limp and all, plus my Ma and her beady eyes. But there was one young fella who'd clearly just come back from the front. He'd lost a foot and he was doing his best to walk with his crutch in the sand. I'm telling you, he had the biggest bulge of them all. I'd be perfectly happy to settle for just the one foot but a mighty do-da. In fact, we could hobble along together quite happily. And once we were horizontal, no-one would know we weren't quite perfect."

"Well my holidays had nothing romantic about them at all," bemoaned Visha. "But it was wonderful to see my parents again, back in Dublin for a while, though terribly sad knowing that they were only here to get Sourja ready to go off to Portsmouth to join his ship. He looked so dashing in his uniform but they must have been wondering if they'd ever see him again."

Visha wiped away a tear and Maisie put her arm around her friend. All four were quiet for a few minutes contemplating the reality of the war, realising that they and their friends were now at the age when they would be expected to fight or be directly involved in the war effort. Who would be next to go off to the trenches or the fighting ships?

"Well, my darling girl, at least you have some comfort." Ellen stroked Maisie's hair. "The love of your life is not going to get called up any time soon is he? He'd be about as useless as me." Ellen looked up. "Did you know about Maisie and Eamonn, you two? They've written to each other every single day of the holidays and they couldn't wait to get back here, I bet."

Maisie blushed and giggled.

"I had worked it out, but only on the last day of term," admitted Hannah.

"I had no idea, but I'm not surprised," laughed Visha. "You've always been so kind to him. I mean, even kinder than you are to everyone, Maisie."

"Please don't say anything to anyone else. Mrs Fitzgerald would be appalled. She'd probably make one or both us leave. And anyway, who knows what will happen. We're not in any position to get engaged yet and maybe it's just a schoolgirl/schoolboy crush."

"Now that's what I need. A decent crush in my life." Ellen threw herself back on her bed. "Someone to think about as I'm touching myself ... you know... like that. Now, don't pretend you lot don't know what I mean. I did have a darling crush on John Fitzgerald of course, until someone stole him away from me." Ellen rolled onto her side chuckling and pointing at Hannah. "Mind you, where is he now? The word in the kitchen is he hasn't been back since the last day of term. I reckon you've scared him away, Hannah McDermott."

The first week back at studies felt very flat indeed. How could the absence of one very quiet man make such a difference to the atmosphere of a place? And Mrs Fitzgerald was clearly missing her son, even though nothing was said and no routine went unobserved. She had taken John's literature classes herself – Paradise Lost this week – but everything she said sounded empty. Contemplating man's original sin seemed fitting enough when the newspaper front pages recounted daily the horrors of Passchendaele.

At the first Friday-night dinner, Hannah took pity on the baby-faced newcomer and sat next to him. Angus from

Glasgow had only recently lost his mother and, with his father away fighting, he and Morag, his whey-faced sister, had come over to Dublin to be close to his mother's Irish Catholic relatives. Both of them had been wandering around the Academy with vacant looks all week, as shell-shocked as if they had been at the front themselves. Hannah was rather touched at his plight and decided to do her best and make conversation.

"Do you play any instruments, Angus?"

"Yes, I play the bagpipes. Not very well, mind. But I haven't brought them over with me, I'm afraid."

Hannah hoped her profound relief didn't show.

The sound of walking on gravel came from the drive.

"Seamus, could you please go and see who that could be at this hour of the night," asked Mrs Fitzgerald. She obviously thought that, of anyone round the table, Seamus's great height would present the most daunting welcome.

They all strained to hear the front door open and then the animated conversation that ensued. It was obviously not a ruffian or a tinker.

"It's John." Mrs Fitzgerald dashed - in as dignified a way as she could - out of the room and the welcoming noises of relieved greetings grew louder.

Hannah wanted to dash to the hall too but could only sit and wait as the conversation grew gradually quieter. Seamus came back to the dining room and helped himself to another piece of treacle tart.

"It's Mr Fitzgerald back home."

"You eejit. Do you think we couldn't hear?" Ellen flicked her napkin at Seamus as he poured the now cold custard onto his second helping.

"Where's he been? That's what we want to know."

"Sorry, I have no idea."

They all waited for a while but Mrs Fitzgerald did not return. After cups of tea in the drawing room, people started to make their way to bed. Hannah hung around for as long as she could, hoping that the Fitzgeralds would finally put in an appearance. Finally, only she and Seamus were left sitting either side of the unlit fire.

"Have you started looking at the Mozart yet?"

"Seamus, I have hardly picked up my violin this week. Haven't felt like playing at all for some reason. This place just feels – different. Like it would be wrong to play such joyful music. We can take it along to our lesson with Felix tomorrow. How would that be?"

"Yes, sure. But I just can't wait to start playing it with you."

"Yes, and I bet you've already practised loads at home. It'll take me a while to catch up."

Seamus stood up.

"I can wait until you're ready, Hannah." He looked down at her reclining in the chair. "I'll always wait for you."

Hannah sat for another twenty minutes or so until all the noises of bedtime routines had subsided. As she climbed near to the top floor she could hear faint groans coming from John's room. Hannah crept up to the door and listened harder. Oh God, was he ill?

She hesitated for several minutes then knocked lightly on the door. No answer, but the groaning stopped. She knocked again a little harder and whispered, "John, it's Hannah." Still no answer.

She waited for what seemed like minutes and then gently opened the door. John was sitting at his desk, with his forehead resting on his two clenched hands. In front of him was a small photograph and a long lock of golden hair tied with some cream wool. He leapt up as he saw her enter.

"Hannah. I'm sorry I didn't answer. I am … not good company right now."

"I was worried. You sounded in great pain. I thought you'd had an accident"

"Pain? Yes. But there are different sorts of pain, Hannah."

She stepped over the threshold of the room. "Can I help at all? Would you like to talk about it?"

"Thank you, Hannah. You are very sweet but I cannot talk about this. Not yet." John shook his head. "Maybe some time, though."

There was a long pause as they looked at one another. "You need to get yourself off to bed. Won't you be seeing Felix tomorrow for your first lesson this term? He won't be very forgiving of any fumbled scales, you know."

"Yes, I should go to bed now." Hannah turned to leave but at the door she turned back. "I care about you John, and I hate to think of you in any sort of pain. Please know that I want to help. I'm always ready to listen and to understand."

"Yes, I know that Hannah. Thank you. You are a dear, kind girl and a trusted friend. I know you care about me. Goodnight now."

As Hannah tried to make herself sleep, she kept returning to the photograph, the lock of hair and John's tortured face. Had he been rejected by his golden-haired lover? If so, then that would explain his reticence to declare his love for her. But if the affair was over now, once the wound of rejection had healed, he would come to see that a better lover was sleeping only across the landing. And she was waiting for him.

# Chapter 14 – Early October 1917

Hannah was sitting on her bed, re-reading the letter from Stasia that had arrived yesterday. Her sister's glee at the progress of the 'villa' was palpable. Stasia detailed every building decision she and Dada – but mostly Stasia – had made and how they were improving the McLoughlins' original plan to make it a dwelling to rival the Byrnes' imposing Georgian farmhouse that was now rather obscured by it.

Mr Byrne had come to see James and Stasia the previous week to ask that they plant some trees to screen the back of the villa and their outbuildings. Stasia was 'thinking about it'. Hannah guessed she didn't want her view over to the Byrnes' house obscured to impede any future spying.

"We should be able to move in before Christmas. Isn't that exciting?" her sister had written. Hannah thought differently.

"Are you coming, Hannah? We're off now," Seamus called up from the hall where the regular Sunday walkers had gathered for the off. "You need to wrap up well. It's blowing up strong out there."

Hannah loved to see the wild sea when the weather was like this. It was so much more dramatic and stirring when the waves were huge and fringed with foam.

"Wait for me." And she grabbed her outdoor clothes plus an extra scarf and raced downstairs to join them.

"Come on, slowcoach." Ellen was holding the front door open. "If we don't start now we'll never be back for lunchtime, given the pace that some of us walk at. And that would be a disaster."

"Me, the slowcoach? That's rich."

It was certainly breezy and yellow leaves were swirling on the pavement outside the Academy.

"It's really feeling like autumn's set in now, doesn't it?" Seamus came up alongside her and, without any fuss, took her hand to help her across the road over to the promenade. He didn't let go as they walked along behind the group in front with the usual stragglers at their back.

"I'm glad to see these precious hands are well covered up. We don't want any excuses for you not to do some practice with me this afternoon on the Sinfonia."

The Mozart was coming along well but Hannah had still not caught up with Seamus's competence. The piece made her very happy though and she had been rediscovering the joy of playing. Hannah remembered how thrilling it had been to play in the Beethoven quartet with John, but he hadn't touched his 'cello yet this term.

Seamus lifted Hannah's gloved hand to his lips momentarily.

"We need to get on with it. I want us to try and perform it before the end of term. Mr Brennan has said he can get us a small band of players together and maybe we can do it in The Assumption as part of their Christmas concert. That is, of course, assuming Father Finneran will allow us two wicked heathens to set foot inside his church."

"I'm not exactly a heathen, like you. And anyway, wouldn't it be better to wait until spring-time rather than try and play in a freezing church?"

"Probably... but I won't be here, Hannah."

Hannah stopped walking and took her hand away.

"What? Why? Where are you going?"

Seamus walked on to prevent the rear guard catching them up and Hannah ran after him.

"I wanted you to be the first to know. I'm going to be eighteen in January and I'm embarrassed not to be doing my bit in France. Plenty of lads have been fighting since they were fifteen. So... I shall sign up after Christmas." He turned to look at her. "Then you'll see how much you miss me, Miss Hannah McDermott. And how handsome I shall be when I'm all decked out in my military finery. Race you down to the beach."

Seamus pulled her hat down over her eyes and charged off, but Hannah was not going to let that stop her.

Chasing after Seamus was easier than trying to find some words in response to this news. Her Seamus, always there to run errands, carry violin cases, pour her water, share musical triumphs and fight her corner. But soon not to be there at all.

They rarely went down onto Killiney beach – Mrs Fitzgerald disliked them trailing sand into the house – and the rest of the party continued their walk along the road. But today, Hannah and Seamus picked their way along the edge of the crashing sea, scattering the gulls who were scavenging among the shells.

Seamus tried to speak but the wind snatched the words out of his mouth and threw them out over the cliff. The noise of the waves was unconquerable. He bent down and picked up something; it was a barnacle shell that had been worn away to just a skeletal circle. He took Hannah's left hand and tried to slip the shell over her ring finger but her gloves were too bulky. She took it from him, put it in her coat pocket and squeezed his hand. Above them, two white birds were circling and swooping.

"Last one back's a sissy," Hannah hollered, as she charged off the beach back towards the Academy, but whether Seamus caught her words it was impossible to tell. It didn't take him long to catch her up though, and they arrived back together in time for lunch.

Since his return, Sunday lunch was the one time in the week when John had chosen to eat with everyone else. At other times, he took a tray to his room, and Hannah often saw how little had been eaten when the tray was left outside his door. It made Hannah smile to see Mrs Fitzgerald fuss over her son, making sure he had enough on his plate and that it got eaten entirely. And she was happy too to see John starting to re-enter the life of the Academy properly.

Hannah looked around the table. Big, strong, decent, confident, uncomplicated Seamus was sitting opposite her, only one seat from tortured, intriguing, taut, lean, damaged John.

It was impossible to misinterpret the gesture Seamus had made on the beach but, when they had arrived back at the Academy, there was no opportunity for Seamus to be alone with her. Hannah knew the moment would come soon enough though and she would have to find the right answer. On the face of it, Seamus was a much better catch than John. Why couldn't she make the older teacher feel for her what Seamus clearly did.

After the pudding was cleared away, Seamus tapped his glass.

"Dear friends, I should like to say a couple of words. In January I shall be eighteen, so I have decided to join the war effort. That means this is my last term here at the Academy and I wanted you all to know so that we can make the most out of every day we have left together."

Hannah sat up, terrified that Seamus had taken her pocketing of the shell as agreement to some sort of engagement which he was now about to announce.

"These last two years have been the happiest of my life and so much has happened. Who knows how long any of us has left. You churchgoers have the comfort of looking forward to everlasting bliss but we sinners can only make the most of every moment. So, here's to us."

Seamus gave everyone his biggest smile and raised his glass of water in a toast which everyone copied. Any other thoughts he might have had were kept to himself.

****** 

The following Saturday, Seamus and Hannah were sitting side by side as the tram rumbled through the southern suburbs of Dublin taking the two apprentice soloists back to Dalkey. They were talking about the niceties of the Sinfonia Concertante they had just been practising for Felix Brennan and discussing whether they agreed with all the refinements and nuances he had suggested.

Hannah had expected Seamus to use their first time alone together on their journey into Dublin to talk about important and serious things. Love things. Marriage things even. She slipped her hand into her left coat pocket. Yes, there was the shell ring still. It had really happened. But Seamus was just chatting cheerily about the week they had just shared: Miss Murray's ghoulish stories about the Black Death, Mr Ord-Hume's musings on the likelihood of other life forms in the universe and John Fitzgerald reading Thomas Hardy's heart-breaking Jude the Obscure.

Surely Seamus must bring up the subject now, their last chance to be totally and safely alone together until next Saturday's lesson.

"I love autumn. I think it's my favourite time of the year. Just look at those trees. They look like there's a fire raging inside them." Seamus was pointing to a row of three Sumac trees in the front garden of a house in Blackrock.

"They are gorgeous. Some people call them the Tree of Heaven. We used to have one in our back yard until my sister had it dug out. She complained that it kept sending up suckers everywhere."

"Fancy complaining about that. Isn't it grand to be getting new beautiful trees all the time – and for free."

"Ah, Seamus, you don't know my sister, Stasia. Nothing is allowed to behave in such a random and promiscuous way. They would need her written permission to start spreading out like that."

"You're not like her then. No-one could be more open and generous than you." Seamus took her hand.

Hannah wasn't sure what to do. How could she take her hand away now when she had been called generous by the loveliest student at the Academy. She didn't think of herself that way at all. In fact, Stasia was always telling her she was a 'selfish little madam'.

"That's sweet of you, Seamus, but I think you're confusing me with yourself."

After about five minutes, as Seamus's grip relaxed, Hannah slid her hand from his and put it into her pocket to feel the shell ring again. Should she take it out? Maybe it would help him start the conversation that she felt was lurking just inside his lips. But Hannah was not at all sure she wanted the conversation to start because that would require her to respond and she had no idea what she would say.

When they arrived back at the Academy, Hannah went up to her bedroom to hang up her coat. She fished inside the pocket for the shell ring. She slipped it onto her ring finger and held her arm out, the better to admire how it looked. Charming, but gold and diamonds would definitely look better. She removed the ring and went to throw it into the bin. She looked at it and stroked the smooth translucent circle, then opened her violin case and popped the shell in her rosin box.

After lunch, Mrs Fitzgerald asked to hear how the Sinfonia Concertante was progressing and offered to accompany them. Hannah and Seamus were only too happy to oblige; it would be a treat to play with an accompanist away from the forensic attentions of Felix Brennan.

As they started the slow second movement, the door to the drawing room opened softly behind them. Hannah didn't need to turn around to know that John had come into the room. Was it a particular smell or the soft shuffle of his shoes on the wooden floor? Her heart raced. Seamus couldn't make that happen to her.

Knowing John was there, watching and listening intently, inspired her to dig deep inside herself for her very best playing. She tried to load every note with meaning hoping that John would recognise the messages and sense the passionate intent behind them.

When the movement ended John applauded and came to stand behind his mother at the piano.

"That is sounding splendid. You will be more than ready to perform this in public by December, don't you agree Mother?"

Mrs Fitzgerald nodded her smiling approval.

"I just hope Dalkey will be ready to welcome our two gifted young performers. We don't want you performing to a half-empty church of Father Finneran's devoted parishioners."

"John, I shall be inviting various friends and Hannah's Aunt Lily has also promised to drive some of her Dublin circle out to hear them."

"Did you know the piece before, Seamus? I've never heard it. It's an absolute jewel."

"I found the music in a second-hand shop in London, sir, when I went over in the summer and the shopkeeper tried to play bits for me on the piano. I knew instantly that I had to play it - and play it with Hannah of course." Seamus beamed at her. "We viola-players don't often get such a wonderful chance to show off."

"Yes, you are the unsung heroes of the orchestra. It's good to see you cast off your modesty and take centre stage for once." John put his arm around Seamus's shoulder. "We've never had two such talented players here at the Academy at the same time, have we Mother? And you play so beautifully together and make such a very handsome couple. We're very, very proud of you both."

# Chapter 15 – Late October 1917

Most days, when lessons were over, Hannah and Seamus would squeeze in an hour or so before supper rehearsing the Sinfonia together in the music room. Still Seamus said nothing about any romantic feelings and Hannah was starting to think that she must have imagined the whole scenario.

As they came to the end of the third movement, there was a knock at the door and John poked his head around.

"Well done, you two. It's all coming along beautifully. I think you could both make your living as performers you know. Sorry to interrupt, but I just wanted to say, Hannah, that I've managed to get my hands on a new poem from WB. It's not yet published properly – and may never be, given it's about the Uprising. He is on the side of the angels, of course. Maybe you'd like to borrow it some time. Only if you're interested."

With the weekend came some fierce weather; wind and rain lashed the front bay windows of the Academy. Angus had made the mistake of announcing that he had been the chess champion at his previous school. Since then, Daniel had attached himself firmly to the younger boy and, whenever any spare moment opened up, he would corner Angus in the drawing room wielding the board and pieces box in gladiatorial manner. There was no escape for Angus this Sunday afternoon.

Eamonn wandered over to watch the contest, Angus's mouth open in concentration and Daniel's left heel bouncing his knee at high speed, impatiently waiting for his next go.

Eamonn slapped Angus on the back. "Good luck, old chap. It used to be me, sitting there in agony, screwing up my brain to get one over on this chap." Daniel's mouth gave the hint of a smile without his gaze leaving the board. "But there's only so much humiliation a man can take."

Eamonn wandered back to the window seats where Maisie was watching Visha do a jigsaw, while next to her Maeve was crocheting something formless in sludgy brown. Ellen was stretched out on the sofa, half-asleep. The faint strains of the Sinfonia were coming from the music room at the back of the house.

Ellen suddenly sat up and gave a manufactured scream." If we have to listen to that bloody Mozart any more I can't promise that blood will not be spilled."

"Aww, Ellen. It's beautiful. I could listen to it all day." Maisie was nothing if not loyal.

"Well, that's good, because I think we might have to." Eamonn surreptitiously stroked Maisie's back. "But cheer up, Ellen. It's only for another two months."

Ellen squealed again, threw herself backwards and covered her head with a tapestry cushion.

"Now, don't let Mrs F catch you with your feet on her sofa and manhandling her petit point."

Ten minutes later in the music room, Hannah was kneeling, packing away her violin case, when she became aware that Seamus had knelt down beside her. This was it. This was the moment.

Seamus took her left hand and kissed it.

"Hannah, I want you to know that playing music with you is the nearest to heaven I shall ever get. Music is the only heaven I can believe in. When I am gone away, up to my eyes in mud and bullets, just remembering these times will get me through."

Seamus stood up. "Let me carry your violin to your bedroom. I'm going up there anyway."

He left carrying both instrument cases. Hannah rose, utterly perplexed. Why couldn't people just come straight out with what they were feeling?

Hannah joined her friends in the drawing room just as the afternoon tea trolley was wheeled in. There was a rush for the scones and the jam tarts. Angus speedily conceded defeat by knocking over his King, fearful of losing out on the baked goodies and Daniel meticulously notched up another win in his pocketbook.

Hannah held back until others had served themselves. But there was plenty and she was just piling blackcurrant jam onto a scone when Seamus came in.

"Hey, everyone. John is upstairs playing his 'cello. And something quite jolly too."

"Hurray. That's the first time this term." Ellen grabbed Eamonn's hands and did a little lop-sided dance with him.

The mood of the entire room changed from heavy ennui to cheerful excitement.

"Thank heavens," said Abigail. "Maybe we'll start doing some happy books now. It's been doom, doom and death all term."

After the tea things were cleared away, Hannah went to fetch her book from her bedside. On the top landing, she stood outside John's door. He had finished playing. She hesitated for a moment, but then, recalling her irritation at Seamus's inability to get to the point, she knocked quite firmly on the door.

"Come in." John sounded quite bright. He smiled when he saw Hannah come into the room. "Ah, Hannah! Have you come for the Yeats? It's in this pile somewhere." He went over to his desk. "Have a seat for a minute. Let me talk you through it and what I can make of it."

So here she was, invited to sit in John Fitzgerald's bedroom, waiting to listen to him read through the poem and then give his verdict. She breathed in the air of the room: vanilla soap, old leather, dusty rugs and an undertone of tomato-smelling sweat. As John sorted through the piles of documents, newspapers and books on his desk, Hannah looked around at his lair, until now only glimpsed at through a half-open door.

A monolithic oak wardrobe occupied the far wall with the desk opposite it, side on to the sash window, to capture the maximum daylight, though at five o'clock on an October afternoon the light from the brass desk lamp was essential. Two ancient leather armchairs, one now occupied by Hannah's slight frame, faced each other on the Turkish rug next to the bed. John's bed. Hannah would have had to turn her head to study the bed properly but that was what interested her most. Oh, why had she chosen this chair and not its twin? She could see the footboard at least and could ascertain that it was a double bed covered in a thick satiny counterpane.

"Here we go." John held the small pamphlet aloft in triumph and then brought it over to her. "You have a read while I finish this marking."

Hannah did her best to concentrate on the text. After ten minutes reading and re-reading, she ventured a comment.

"This is about the Uprising of course, and there are names of the rebels included. But I'm not sure what he thinks of it all. He doesn't seem very enthusiastic about it, even though he seems to admire the brave people who are clearly inspired by their strong political principles."

"Yes, I think you're right." John rose from his desk and came to join her in the matching armchair. "His repeated phrase 'A terrible beauty is born' captures his ambivalent attitude."

"But Yeats is a republican, isn't he?"

"Indeed, but, like me, he's fine with the nationalist politics – the theory and the debates - but can't bring himself to endorse the violence that is always needed to overthrow oppression and colonialism."

"So, the constabulary won't be coming after you then. Ellen was trying to tell us all that you had disappeared at the end of last term because you were a known Fenian and about to be arrested for conspiracy."

John laughed. "Sadly, I am not nearly brave enough. I like to go to meetings, hear fierce arguments and chew things over with my friends, but that's as far as it goes. I am a fake and a lousy coward and I'm waiting for my betters to do the hard work of freeing Ireland. But it's amusing to think you all thought I might be capable of taking up arms for my beliefs."

"What would you fight for, John?"

He thought hard and looked out towards the window.

"I would fight and die for the people I love. That's not saying much though is it? Who wouldn't say that?"

"I can think of plenty of young fellas who wouldn't get out of bed to save their mammies. Would you have gone to fight in France if you weren't... too old?"

"That's a tricky question. Thankfully, I haven't had to confront it. Not yet anyway."

John buried himself in the poem again. Hannah was able to study his face at close range: the fine lines at his eyes, the long eyelashes that were nigh on invisible at normal range, the few grey hairs within the mane of gold. And the lips. Exquisite, full lips, now slightly apart.

"John, can I ask you something?"

"Give it a go, Hannah."

"If your absence over the summer was nothing to do with the cause, was it to do with the great pain you were going through – maybe are still going through?"

His eyes met hers. "Yes. My time over in the west was very ... unhappy."

"You can tell me about it, John. I would never breathe a word to anyone else. And I want to be a loving friend to you – your best friend even."

John stretched over and took her left hand with both of his and cradled it gently.

"It's not that I don't trust you, Hannah. I do and I know we are great friends. But I couldn't tell you about it without breaking down, and that would be awful – for you and for me."

"Why? Why shouldn't men weep when there's something to weep over?"

"Hannah, I promise that I will tell you as soon as I am ready. Only my mother knows in Dublin and I'd like it to stay that way for now. I'm sorry."

John stood up and went to the door.

"Why don't you take the pamphlet away with you and we can talk about the poem when you've had more time."

Hannah understood that she was being dismissed and obediently rose and left John alone with whatever the agonising thoughts were that she had clumsily managed to reawaken.

# Chapter 16 – November 1917

Slattery was driving more slowly than usual. Lily Murphy was in the front seat alongside him and that made him nervous. And in the back were three very lively and noisy young women, bristling with excitement after seeing the matinée at The Abbey.

"Good day there, peasants." Ellen gave an imperious wave to the shopkeepers and shoppers in Exchequer Street. "Oh God, Mrs Murphy, I'm so sorry. I was just having a joke, there. I've only been in a car twice before and it was nothing like this. I feel like a princess you see."

"Dearest Ellen, please don't concern yourself. I like a joke as much as the next person. Though, of course, this car will never carry any princesses, duchesses or such parasites while it is in my possession."

Over fancy tea and cakes back at Pembroke Street, the chat turned to the December concert that Hannah and Seamus were still practising hard for.

"You're still intending to perform in that horrid church in Dalkey I assume. Who on earth is going to come and see you there? Apart from me and your school friends – and maybe the odd parishioner. Surely, we can do better than that. I would hold it here in the drawing room, but there simply isn't enough room for the orchestra and an audience. How many are playing, did you say?"

"Mr Brennan has organised about sixteen players from the Gaiety, plus John Fitzgerald and, of course, Seamus and me."

"Right. I have an idea. Why don't I get my friend at Trinity to loan us one of their spaces – the Long Room, or the Chapel or even the Dining Hall, frankly – and then we can publicise it properly. I'm happy to buy a couple of newspaper advertisements for it. And it will be big enough to accommodate all your school friends – at the back."

"What will it all cost, Aunt Lily?" Hannah's accounting instincts were provoked.

"Don't you worry about that. I know - let's hold the concert to raise money for the poor widows and families of the victims of the Uprising who are suffering so much. That's how we'll get the room for free. I just need to get a little something quaffable for the players and we're done"

Visha stiffened. "Mrs Murphy, I doubt that Trinity would wish to support a nationalist cause and I'm not sure that everyone who is playing would be happy to support that either. And not even all the students of the Academy should be assumed to be Nationalists." Visha had received a letter only that morning from Sourja detailing the sinking of various merchant ships so she was feeling more than usually patriotic.

"Maybe you're right. Still, there must be a good cause we can espouse to get us somewhere in Trinity for free. I'd love to support the Women's Suffrage movement."

"We'd all be very happy with that, wouldn't we?" Ellen and Visha nodded their agreement. "But I don't think it would be widely popular, Aunt Lily."

"Perhaps The Red Cross would be acceptable to everyone then."

The three girls all agreed with Lily that no-one, whatever their political affiliations, could possibly object to raising money for The Red Cross.

"Aunt Lily, it's getting rather late isn't it, to be organising a concert in the middle of Dublin, when it's only a month away? December 16th. It has to be a Sunday to get all the players from the Gaiety. And we can't just play the Sinfonia Concertante. It only lasts about a half hour."

"Well, you can play The Harp Quartet again, can't you? And I can easily drum up a few other acts. What about other students at the Academy?" Lily looked hard at Visha and Ellen. "Is no-one else talented … in any way?"

"Don't look at me, Mrs Murphy. I can just about play The Maiden's Prayer but when I do everyone looks like they wish I hadn't."

"Ellen is being rather hard on herself, but no, I don't think her playing would be a match for Hannah and Seamus." Visha was always direct.

"Well, it's really no problem. Letitia can play us something lovely. Or she can accompany my dear friend Richard McKendrick, who has an amazing voice. Or both. And then we can have some poetry readings. I'd love to do some. Yes, yes, I can see it all now."

Lily leapt up to go out to her study to start writing notes to all the people she needed to galvanise into action. A new project. How wonderful.

Lily popped her head back round the door. "Stay as long as you like, girls. Slattery will take you back to Dalkey when you're ready. But Hannah, make sure you don't go without the letter I'm just about to write to Letitia."

The girls arrived back at the Academy just in time for supper. Eamonn and Seamus were on cooking duties and had made a chunky beef stew with dumplings. For pudding, there was a cold apple mousse.

As the two young men put the dishes on the table, the tall, ruddy-cheeked one towering over the pale, slight one, Ellen looked around the table. Mrs Fitzgerald had not yet arrived.

"What's the betting that Seamus made the stew and Eamonn the mousse?"

"Well, how wrong could you be, Miss Clever-Clogs." Seamus held out his massive hands for inspection. "I - with my famously delicate fingers and refined taste buds - concocted this fluffy confection of a pudding, while my muscular pal here didn't just cut up the meat and onions, he actually went out into Dalkey and hunted for his own ox which he wrestled to the ground with his bare arms."

Seamus put his arm around Eamonn's shoulders and squeezed hard. "Isn't that so, pal?"

"Not a word of a lie, young Seamus."

"This man has hidden depths, Ellen McPartlin."

Maisie smiled up at Eamonn. She knew exactly how deep they were.

Mrs Fitzgerald arrived and more serious conversation followed. She questioned the three theatregoers all about The Cobweb, which she had been sorry to miss, before leaving for her private sitting room.

"Why don't we play something tonight? There are no grown-ups around." Ellen was always up for some fun and games. "How about charades?" Visha and Morag groaned but everyone else seemed willing.

It was gone half past ten when Hannah, Ellen and Maisie joined Visha in their bedroom. She was sitting up in her bed writing to her brother.

"I have told him every stupid detail about this place. Anything to try and help him remember the happy times."

"We don't know how lucky we are, you know." Maisie wriggled into her nightie.

"Maisie, you are so sweet. You didn't even get to come to the Abbey with us." Hannah sat on Maisie's bed and kissed the top of her head.

"Yes, but Maisie is in love and that makes everything just perfect." Ellen pulled up her eiderdown.

Hannah wasn't so sure. It was all fine and dandy to be in love if the person you loved reciprocated that love. But being in love with someone who barely registered your existence wasn't fun at all.

All the lights were now switched off. Hannah stared into the blackness and conjured up a gallery of images: first John, then Seamus. Then John and Seamus playing together at the nightmare of a Christmas concert that her Aunt Lily was surely going to make of it. She closed her eyes and turned to her favourite sleeping position, on her left side with her hand under her pillow. She felt something there. Some card? No, it was an envelope.

Hannah knew it must be from John; it was hard to sleep knowing the letter was waiting to be read… but sleep came eventually.

# Chapter 17 – November 1917

Hannah woke just after six, her hand still under her pillow resting on the envelope. She slid out of bed, put on her slippers and dressing gown, slipped the letter into her pocket and crept out of the bedroom to go and sit on the lavatory. Her hand shook as she tore open the envelope, and not just from the cold.

"My dear Hannah,

I hope you will forgive me for resorting to pen and paper. I want to share with you some important parts of my life – and I think you want that too – but I don't have what it takes to tell you in person. I know that makes me an emotional coward. But this way you will at least get the whole story without me breaking down in the telling of it. I want you to understand because you are a special friend.

I was just twenty-one when my father died in 1907, in my final year at Trinity. My mother was left with this huge house and some money but not nearly enough to live on to the end of her life. So, in her determined and practical way, she set about establishing the Maple Academy.

I hated that. This had been my family home. I was moved out of my spacious bedroom and banished to the second floor. The drawing room where I had sprawled in front of the fire reading poetry was now full of silly teenagers. All our mealtimes were shared with a dozen strangers. The scullery was full of other people's undergarments drying on the rack.

I had lost my father and was missing him terribly. But I felt I had lost my mother too. We hardly ever had the time or the space to talk as we had used to.

Of course, as I now look back, I am embarrassed to remember what an egotistical, selfish idiot I was. My poor mother was working herself half to death to turn this place into a viable business and all I did was mope and moan.

I began to hate life in Dalkey and everything about polite Dublin society. It felt so sterile: pavements, trimmed hedges, 'civilised' conversations, Anglicised accents. I yearned for something more real. Something raw and honest.

I found myself turning to what I hoped was true Irish culture and I also began to interest myself in the Home Rule movement. I wanted Ireland to find its own voice and shake off England – politically certainly, but also culturally.

I became obsessed with needing to learn Gaelic. I thought it would magically imbue me with the wisdom and peace of the ancients. I would be blessed with understanding. I bought myself some books but they were impossible to learn from.

Ten months after we had buried my father, I announced to my mother that I wanted to leave Dublin to go to the west coast to learn Gaelic among some native speakers. This must have been a dagger into her heart. I cannot now believe that I was so callous. How could I have thought of just abandoning her to cope alone? But young people's self-absorption knows no limits and, of course, she would never have shown me her dismay.

I don't know how she managed it, but she scraped together a couple of hundred pounds to fund my trip and she watched me walk out of Maple Villa the next May. When the train set me down in Galway, I found myself some accommodation but I soon realised that I needed to go further west. I hadn't yet shaken off Dublin. So, after a few days, I got myself right out to Clifden on the far west coast of Connemara. It was about as far away from Dublin as I could have gone and still stayed on Irish soil.

Clifden is quite a thriving little town. Plenty of traditional farmers and fishermen but also many people were finding jobs with the new Marconi telegraphy station. After a couple of weeks, I got myself a job there as an accounting clerk. Don't laugh. I can, in fact, add up pretty well when I have to. It wasn't at all what I had wanted to fill my days with but I knew that the money my mother had given me would not last forever.

I coped by not living in Clifden itself. I found lodgings in a little village a few miles north, right by the sea. I took my time to find somewhere that offered me the escape and freedom I was searching for. Yes, from nine to five I had my nose buried in my ledgers, but then I was free to cycle home to the vast sea where I could wash all dreary thoughts away. And I had chosen not just the place carefully but the people too. The family I boarded with were fluent Gaelic speakers. They did speak English perfectly well and could converse with me happily enough, but they talked to each other in their native tongue.

Ruari and Shawna De Bhailis are the hardest working people I have ever met. Shawna would bring me a jug of hot water at seven am every morning having risen herself at five o'clock to make bread and to pack food for Ruari before he set out in his small fishing boat soon after that.

After I got home from work, at about six o'clock, we would eat supper together and then Ruari would start on mending his nets and Shawna would take up her lacework or her knitting. These she would send off to the big shops in Galway where they would be sold for a fine price. But she only received a pittance for them.

I never saw them sitting down without some task in their hands. Except on a Sunday maybe. Maybe for just an hour they would allow themselves to sit and chat, in Gaelic of course. Or maybe they'd sing, or Ruari would play his penny whistle. But it wasn't long before they would get up to go and cut some turf or to salt some herring or dig some potatoes.

The De Bhailises were so kind to me. After only a couple of months I felt as if I had been adopted. I even began trying out a few phrases in Gaelic having listened to them repeat words again and again for my benefit. Ruari and

Shawna were very encouraging but my attempts at Gaelic would send their two daughters into gales of laughter.

Yes, they had two daughters. Two beautiful daughters. Aoife and Ailsa. And yes, I fell in love.

I fell a bit in love with them both for a while. They had hair as dark as forests but with eyes as green as the sea all around us. As time went on, I found that one of them, the elder daughter Ailsa, would spend longer listening to me read, or would serve me extra portions of my favourite food or come with me on walks along the waves without needing an invitation.

Ailsa and I never needed to say very much to each other; we loved just being together in silence. And we understood each other. As the leaves turned from green to gold with every passing autumn day, Ailsa and I found ourselves more and more deeply in love.

Ailsa taught at the local primary school and she was an excellent teacher if my progress at Gaelic was anything to go by. She loved to be surrounded by happy children. She delighted in sharing traditional Irish fairy tales with me and I would reciprocate by reading Yeats to her.

One night, there was a wild storm with lightning and thunder. I awoke with a start at the noise of my window banging shut. There, on the end of my bed, was Ailsa, just sitting watching me. I am sure I don't need to tell you that what followed was the most natural and beautiful thing in the world.

But now that I had taken Ailsa into my bed it was only right that I ask for her hand in marriage the very next day. Ruari seemed totally unsurprised and embraced me like a son. He opened the front door of the cottage and there were Shawna and Aoife on the step, weeping and laughing and hugging Ailsa. It seems that the whole family had been complicit in this romance but no-one could have been happier than me, even if I had been somewhat 'played'.

Now I had to tell my mother that I was intending to marry a fisherman's daughter on the wild west coast and live the simple life there. I went to Dublin, taking Ailsa and Aoife with me for support, and we showed up unannounced on the doorstep of Maple Villa.

Naturally, my mother was deeply shocked but she voiced no criticism. She just tightened her lips in disapproval. You'll know that look well. She agreed to come out to Cleggan for our planned wedding the next spring, and she was extremely polite to the de Bhailis sisters and even took them shopping for some wedding finery.

Back in Cleggan, I lived through my first winter in Connemara. It was tough cycling to work through gales, rain and the bitter cold, but my life felt clean and right and I earned every mouthful of the simple food and every free moment when I was with Ailsa and out under the sky.

We married the week after Easter. We had maintained separate bedrooms but Ailsa was already carrying our child. The priest didn't seem to notice, or, if he did, he didn't seem to mind. I had had no choice but to agree to marry in the little church at Claddaghduff and it made Ailsa happy. She was a dutiful Catholic along with the rest of her family. The church was very empty; a few neighbours, a couple of cousins, two of my colleagues and then my mother in her Dublin finery.

Máire was born in the July, a month before she was due. She was a tiny, beautiful fairy of a child, and blessed (or maybe not!) with my fair hair. Ailsa and I were in heaven, enjoying the golden summer and the thrill of a new-born daughter who hardly ever cried.

We started to suspect something was wrong when Máire was coming up to nine months old. She couldn't sit up unaided and she didn't seem to hear what we said to her. By the time she was a year and a half, she was still more or less immobile and we accepted the likelihood that she was deaf. We loved her not one jot the less. If anything, her difficulties made us appreciate all the more the wonderful things she could do: her smile, her love of her little woollen rabbit and the hugs and kisses she gave so freely.

We took her as often as we could afford to the hospital in Galway. Eventually they declared that she had a form of spastic palsy and would never develop normally. This was a terrible blow but Ailsa set about making Máire's life as rich and pain-free as she could manage.

When Máire was about two years old I managed to get myself a new job teaching at the industrial school run by the Christian Brothers in Letterfrack, just along the coast. This job came with its own accommodation, so the three of us moved out of the happy cottage at Cleggan, leaving behind all the support that Shawna and Aoife had given to Ailsa in the care of Máire. But we thought that the extra room and privacy was worth it, and, with no time taken up travelling to work, it meant I had more free time to be with my beloved girls. Also, it was back to literature for me - or so I thought - and no more accounting.

It didn't take long for me to realise that I had made a terrible mistake. St Joseph's was run by the Christian Brothers for the benefit of poor and homeless young boys, mainly from the cities. I discovered about two hundred boys there in various states of distress, mental and physical.

Most of the teachers were Christian Brothers but I was one of several lay members of staff employed to teach or provide other services. I had hoped I would be immersed in books. In practice, my job was to teach reading and writing to those boys who were completely illiterate despite many of them being nearly old enough to start working. There were also some local Gaelic-speaking boys. The Brothers tolerated the use of Gaelic but realised that the ability to speak and write standard English was also a valuable skill when it came to finding work.

Any grand thoughts I had had of opening up the minds of these young boys to the joys of novels and poetry evaporated on day one. St Joseph's was not interested in opening up young minds but only in confining them and regimenting them until their owners became submissive potential employees. But I gritted my teeth and set about my task. There was some joy to be had when a bedraggled urchin's chest filled with pride after reciting a page of prose or writing their own name for the first time.

I began to notice that many of the boys were suffering severe physical punishment. I could see the welts and bruises on their arms and I could guess at the punishments that caused them to sit or walk with difficulty some days.

The Brothers were totally unashamed of how brutally they punished the boys. They believed that sparing the rod would spoil the child; that evil had to be beaten out of them so they could grow up to be respectable hard-working citizens. I could just see poor, vulnerable children being ground down by fear and pain.

I did complain - repeatedly. Every time I saw some child who had been dealt blows that were causing him lasting damage I would march into the head Brother's office to express my disgust. This went on for about six months until one day I was called into that very office and given my notice. This would have been just before Christmas 1912. How very Christian. They allowed us to stay in our rooms until the January and we then moved back in with Ruari and Shawna, while I tried to find myself some work.

It was a hellish winter. The three of us were squeezed into one bedroom and there was very little money. But Ailsa never uttered a word of reproach. Indeed, she had seen the state of the boys around the school and was as outraged as me. I used up the last of the money my mother had given us, so, by the February we were totally dependent on Ruari and Shawna for food and clothing, not just for the roof over our heads.

I tried to get my job back at the Telegraph Station but with no joy. I would cycle into Clifden almost every morning to see if there was any casual work to be had but February is not the best time to be looking, with farms and fisheries in their lean times.

It happened quite suddenly. I simply hadn't noticed how tired and drawn Ailsa had become. She had been doing much of the housework to allow Shawna to do more needlework to earn some pennies. She had been making sure Máire and I were never short of food by living on tea and a little bread herself. She had been devoted to giving Máire her special exercises in every spare moment. She had literally worn herself away.

When she fell to the pneumonia she tried to carry on for days, pretending all the time that nothing was wrong. So, by the time she took to her bed she had nothing left to fight with. She apologised for getting ill, for leaving Máire and me, but she was also strangely at peace. The end came fast.

My beautiful Ailsa. She looked like a princess at sleep on the bed. Oh, to have been able to awaken her with a kiss. Heaven knows I tried. Fairy stories are all very well on the page but I could find no magic to breathe life back into her.

Had I not had Máire, I would have just walked out into the cold grey day and on into the sea without stopping. My life had been turned upside down and all joy had gone. But I couldn't let it collapse. I had to look after Máire.

Máire missed her mother as much as anyone. We took her to kiss her mother goodbye and she clung to Ailsa's corpse with a strength and grip that you would not have believed possible in such a frail little body. When I finally untangled her and carried her out she was holding the blood-stained handkerchief her mother had been using and she wasn't going to let it go.

We helped each other through the next few months. I spent as much time as I could with Máire, helping her with her emerging and fractured speech, moving her legs, banging her back to get the phlegm out of her chest. She helped me by simply being there; loving me and holding onto me, with her mother's green eyes and sweet face.

Over the summer I managed to get some work with a local farmer scything hay. I loathed the work but it boosted the household income a little. Aoife had taken Ailsa's place teaching at the little village school a couple of days a week. We were just about surviving. But there was no future for us. The winter would be back soon enough and the casual jobs I was doing would disappear as quickly as they had come. Máire really needed to see the Galway hospital again and where was I going to find the money for that? Ruari was getting no younger. I felt mounting despair.

I suppose I could have asked my mother for money but I had already taken money from her without earning it. I decided that the only solution was for me to return to Dalkey, to start work as a teacher here at the Academy and to send money back to my family so that they could look after Máire properly. Between them, Shawna and Aoife were only too happy to care for my darling girl as long as they had enough income to let them reduce their other work.

My life took on a new rhythm. I would work here at the Academy during term-time, writing every week to Cleggan, tucking a modest postal order into the envelope, and soon I would receive news back. Sometimes Aoife's letter would contain a little drawing that my sweet Máire had done for me: her rabbit, her granny, the hills, her grandfather's boat, the gulls, the great boiling sea itself. They helped me transport myself back to Connemara for a few precious moments.

Then, as soon as term ended, I would jump on that train and get myself off to Clifden. Except for the Christmas break. I always felt an obligation to stay here with mother for the celebrations, but my heart was always in Cleggan.

One Christmas, Aoife brought Máire here for a couple of days. There were no students and only loyal old Lizzy to cook for us. It was a disaster; the journey was far too taxing for Máire and, although my mother initially seemed pleased to see her granddaughter for the first time, she wasn't at all comfortable to allow these two worlds to collide. She clearly found the physical rituals we had to follow for Máire distasteful. Every time someone knocked at the front door, she started up in fear of one of her Dalkey friends coming in upon her less than perfect family. It was a relief to put Aoife and my darling on the train back to Connemara a few days later.

And thus it has gone on for the last few years. But, all the time, Máire has been getting weaker. The change was gradual for everyone around her. But for me, seeing her only every few months, the visible deteriorations were shocking. Not just that, but her lively eyes seemed to be slowly clouding over. Then the telegram arrived just before the end of last term. I had been expecting it. I had been expecting it for months.

We took Máire to Galway Hospital but after a couple of weeks they told us to take her home. They could do nothing more for her. For her last three weeks, we never left her. She was never alone. One of the three of us was always at her side.

But she left us. It was the most perfect August day - with a golden sun and deep turquoise sea reminding us of how our darling had looked in the happy times - when she breathed her last. We buried her with her mother in the graveyard over on Omey Island, across the bay from the church Ailsa and I had married in.

That, Hannah, is my pain. A pain I shall carry to the end of my days. It will be some comfort to me that you now understand why I am such terrible company and always in this dark place. I do try - and will keep trying - to find some joy in life, but it is very, very hard.

Thank you for taking the time to read this long letter. And thank you for being a good friend with only the best thoughts for me.

Your friend John, in love and trust."

Hannah kissed John's signature then folded the sheets, returned them to the envelope and went back to bed for a brief time, thinking through everything she had read until her friends started to stir around her.

# Chapter 18 – November 1917

Hannah read John's letter every day for the next week. She kept it on her person at all times, fearful of it falling into another's hands. Only yesterday, she had been reading it again, sitting on her bed, when in had burst Ellen and Maisie without her hearing their approach. She had managed to fold it away swiftly and fend off Ellen's curiosity by fibbing that it was from Stasia about the date for moving into the new house.

She had taken John's sign-off "in love and trust" very seriously indeed. She and John had exchanged no words on the subject but now looked at each other in a new and more intimate way. At least, it seemed so to Hannah. She hoped that John's dreams were as full of her as hers were of him.

On the outside, life went on as normal. Hannah and Seamus were practising hard for the concert, which, thanks to Lily, had become a rather ambitious affair. Lily had been rebuffed by all her Trinity College contacts, much to her indignation, but Felix had ridden to the rescue. He had arranged for the concert to take place in the Gaiety Theatre itself, on the Sunday afternoon when it would normally be dark. Lily had placed a modest advertisement in a few of the more respectable newspapers and there was a small poster outside the Gaiety itself, promoting the concert as a fund-raiser for the Red Cross. Hannah was delighted to be performing in a proper theatre but Seamus had worried that people would expect a professional standard which he knew they couldn't quite deliver.

Hannah and Seamus were now sitting in their usual seats on the tram back from their lesson with Felix. Hannah wondered what was keeping Seamus so quiet and deep in thought. It couldn't be just anxiety about the concert. Maybe it was the rapidly vanishing term and the different sort of challenge that would face him in the New Year. Hannah couldn't imagine how such a kind and sensitive person would ever bring himself to wield a gun and actually kill another human being. Maybe he was preoccupied because he was wondering about how to broach the subject of his feelings for her, which she knew were as strong as ever. But she was now certain that she would not welcome any declaration of love from him. John was the only love for her. These days, if she and Seamus were ever alone, she tended to dredge up some banal topic of conversation to head off any potential awkwardness.

They arrived at Dalkey and Seamus took both instruments down from the tram and then tucked one under his arm to help Hannah down the steep tram step onto the pavement.

"Only three more lessons before the performance. I'm going to spend the rest of the day on the last movement."

"Yes, but we've also got a couple of rehearsals with the other musicians." Hannah was surprised to hear Seamus's nerves talking.

"But not until the last week. I'll be honest with you - I am totally petrified."

"Well, you're the lucky one, because, if we do disgrace ourselves, you can just disappear off to the trenches, whereas I shall have to face all our friends, Aunt Lily and her entourage, Felix and - worst of all - Mrs F. the next term."

"You're right. It's definitely worth getting my head blown off not to have to live with Mrs F.'s disappointment."

The two friends laughed as they linked arms and headed back to the Academy.

Dinner that night was prepared by Maisie and Morag: a rather delicious fish pie followed by currant sponge. Later, the four roommates were sitting on their beds before lights out, reading, brushing their hair, filing their nails, when Ellen let out an enormous belch.

"What on earth was that?" Visha made her disapproval of Ellen's frequent vulgarity very clear.

"Jeezus. I thought it was the Germans dropping a zeppelin on us," giggled Hannah. Growing up next door to a pub, there were few bodily noises she wasn't familiar with.

"I'm sorry. I love mackerel but it really disagrees with me and repeats on me something shocking. I'll be burping all night."

"Delightful. We look forward to that then." Visha closed her book and got into bed.

"Oh, I'm so sorry, Ellen. If only we'd known. It was just that mackerel was one of the few fish available today. It's not really right for a fish pie, is it?"

"Don't you worry, Maisie, my sweet. It was scrummy. I shall be able to enjoy it again and again until morning comes."

****** 

Hannah realised she had barely slept at all when she heard the church clock chiming two o'clock. The wind was tearing round the outside of the house and thrashing tendrils against the rattling bedroom window. Distant rumbles of thunder followed some spectacular lightning. Everyone else seemed to be sound asleep, with Ellen emitting her usual snuffling.

Hannah gingerly turned back her covers and swung her feet out of bed. She just knew that John was awake too. How she knew she had no idea but, sure enough, when she tiptoed onto the landing, stroking the door shut behind her, there was the tell-tale sliver of light.

Hannah told herself this was simply the right thing to do. Be brave. Be bold. Nothing will happen unless you grab opportunities and make your own future. She gave a barely audible knock on John's door. Silence. She knocked again and then slowly opened the door. John was standing just behind it, fully dressed. As she appeared, he grabbed her arm, pulling her inside the room before shutting the door behind her.

"What are you doing, Hannah, up at this hour?" John whispered.

"I just had to see you John. I've been wanting to tell you how moved and sad your letter made me. But I also want to tell you that there is hope, and there will be joy in your life again. Because… because I am in love with you, John."

They stared at each other for several moments before Hannah moved to within a foot of John. He seemed transfixed.

"John, I think I have been in love with you for almost as long as I've known you, but I didn't know what to call the feeling. I have decided to tell you because I think you care about me too. Maybe not quite the same love as I feel, but as near as dammit. I know you will never act first, because you are my teacher. I understand that. It would be improper. But I just have to tell you. And I think I will die if you don't kiss me. Right now."

Hannah took one more step and John opened his arms to her. After a moment in his embrace, Hannah twisted her face up towards his. She could feel his heart banging against his ribs. Or maybe it was hers. She closed her eyes and placed her lips onto his cheek.

"No, Hannah. No." John put his hands on her shoulders and stepped backwards out of her reach.

"I'm sorry. But this is wrong. God knows I would dearly love to kiss your exquisite mouth and tell you how I feel. But it just cannot be. Please go back to bed. Now. Please." John took her hand, kissed it and then led her to the door.

Hannah decided to retreat, backing out of the door, but she left John's room with a knowing smile of satisfaction. He had said that he would dearly love to kiss her. That was enough – for now.

# Chapter 19 – December 1917

After her declaration of love on that stormy night, Hannah decided that another head-on onslaught was probably not the best strategy. John could be in no doubt about her feelings - and she was in little doubt about his - so now she would see whether he would make the next move.

Over the following two weeks she found any reason to go to his room – to borrow a book, to return a book, to ask for help with an essay – any reason at all sufficed if it gave her access to John when he was alone.

Hannah would merrily breeze into his bedroom after a perfunctory knock - sometimes several times a day - and sit herself down before asking whatever question she had dreamed up, whether invited in or not. Eventually, John seemed to accept that this was how it was going to be and appeared quite relaxed when Hannah claimed one of his armchairs, book or music in hand. Hannah believed that he was even starting to enjoy these encounters. Her obsession grew with every encounter; he was so beautiful and so kind and clever.

"Where were you yesterday?" John asked her, the day after an extended practice session with Seamus at Felix Brennan's had left her no spare moment for John. Hannah heart soared at the realisation that he had missed her as much as she had missed him.

They were studying Jane Eyre in class; John had asked his students to write an essay on the topic of loyalty. Hannah decided to knock on John's door just before dinner to discuss it, her copy in hand.

"I just don't know what to think, John. Rochester can't still love his mad wife surely, and he seems to love Jane. And she obviously loves him very much. So, who is he supposed to be loyal to? He can only be loyal to the memory of his wife as she used to be. Is he supposed to be loyal to his marriage vows – a rather abstract notion - or to his true feelings?"

"That is exactly what you need to explore in your essay, Hannah."

"Rochester is so annoying and not very honourable, is he? He takes forever to tell Jane he loves her and then tries to marry her when he's still married to the mad woman."

"Maybe he loves them both."

"No, that's not really possible, is it?"

"Do you doubt his love for Jane?"

"Well, he doesn't express it very passionately, does he?"

"Must love always speak through words?"

They looked hard at each other. John slid from his chair to kneel at Hannah's feet. He took her face in his hands and kissed her, gently at first but with increasing fervour. She put her arms around his neck and allowed him to open her lips with his tongue, mirroring his movements. She was a fast learner.

Hannah eventually pulled away from him to grab a breath.

"You know that was my first ever proper kiss, John. And it was a pretty fantastic too."

John laughed. "I'm pleased it lived up to your high expectations."

Hannah slipped off her chair to kneel thigh to thigh in front of John; she stroked his face and kissed him again.

Ten minutes later, the dinner gong sounded. Hannah and John were by now lying on the rug between the two armchairs, wrapped in each other's arms. Hannah stood up and brushed her hand over her hair. A fair amount of kissing and hair stroking and soft words had been going on. She held out her hand and pulled John to his feet.

"See you down there in a minute." Hannah opened the door and then ran back to plant a chaste kiss on John's lips. "I love you," she whispered and he laughed in return.

Seamus was standing on the landing as she closed John's door behind her.

"What magic tricks have you been performing in there. Did I actually hear John laughing?"

"Oh, we were just finding the funny side of Mr Rochester." Hannah felt very awkward, speaking to Seamus, mere seconds after her lips had been on John's. She wasn't at all sure that her lips were working properly anymore and suspected they were bright red and swollen. In fact, if she had emerged holding a sign saying: 'I am a slut,' Hannah thought it couldn't have been much more obvious what had been happening.

With a burning face, Hannah preceded Seamus down the two flights and they sat down to dinner. Hannah chose a seat as far from John's usual place as possible, next to Angus. As the young Scot recounted the tedious details of the weekly letter from his Great-aunt in Dundee, Hannah's thoughts drifted away to John. Oh, how wonderful to be finally properly in love with someone who loved her back – though he had not yet said those special words. Never mind. What would happen next? Should they make their relationship public? And what on earth would his mother say?

"Hannah. For the third time, would you like some carrots?" Mrs Fitzgerald was glaring at her and proffering a vegetable dish.

"Oh gracious, I'm so sorry, Mrs Fitzgerald. I was somewhere else entirely."

"And I think we all know where," Hannah heard Ellen whisper to Seamus.

The door opened and John walked in. Hannah thought her face would explode with embarrassment. Ellen threw her a knowing smirk.

"Mr Fitzgerald, there's a seat here, next to me." Ellen patted the chair on her left. "It's chicken stew tonight. I thought you weren't going to make it to dinner, seeing as you've been so wrapped up in whatever it is you've been doing in your room all afternoon."

****** 

Several days passed. Hannah was surprised none of her roommates brought up the subject and she decided not to go into John's room again. Not for a little while at least. In truth, she was a little nervous about what would happen next.

She enjoyed reliving their first kisses in her mind. In the depth of the night, she would kiss her own hand, imagining it to be John's lips. Part of her simply couldn't believe she had made it happen. She and John exchanged the odd smile over the following days and their hands brushed against each other briefly as John had handed out copies of Keats to the class. But nothing more.

When she woke up this morning, Hannah's thoughts did not go first to John but to what was happening later that afternoon: the first rehearsal of the Sinfonia Concertante with the small orchestra. Felix Brennan had managed to assemble a respectable small group of professional players plus a few of his most talented students and had also arranged for them to rehearse in the empty Gaiety Theatre that afternoon.

Hannah was terrified but strangely enjoying the feeling of terror. Nothing good would ever happen unless you pushed through your fear, Mrs Fitzgerald had instructed them after she had accompanied Hannah and Seamus's practice session last night. Hannah wondered if it was possible to become addicted to such feelings.

But, before the ordeal of facing the orchestra, there was the tram ride into Dublin to face, accompanied by Seamus and John. If anything, Hannah was dreading this more.

The three of them made their way to the tram stop immediately after an early lunch, Seamus carrying Hannah's violin as usual. He was not his normal sunny self but locked into his own thoughts. And, of course, John was never exactly chatty, but Hannah couldn't bear to let silence grip them so she kept up a shaky stream of conjecture - "I wonder what Felix will be like as a conductor" - and observation - "Oh look, Seamus, they've finished painting that fence," - during the short walk to the stop.

When the tram arrived, both men let Hannah board first, with Seamus following behind and John lumbered on last, hoisting his 'cello up the step. Normally Seamus would have sat down beside Hannah, but he took the seat behind her. Hannah could practically see John working out how to manage this situation.

"Seamus, would you do me a favour now and you sit next to Hannah, so that I can have my 'cello on the seat next to me." Well-played my man, thought Hannah.

The rehearsal was rather chaotic at first, with people shouting for scores and tripping over music stands as they squeezed to their desks, but eventually there was enough calm for Felix to tap his stand and raise his baton.

Hannah stared out into the black auditorium over the long introduction. In two weeks' time it would be full, with row upon row of people who would have paid to hear them play. Her stomach gave a small hop but a smile also crept over her mouth. She turned to watch as the orchestra began to play. She was taken aback at first by the level of noise; she had never played with such a large group before and there were so many alien sounds - horns, oboes and the rest. And most of the violinists were much better players than she was, even the ones in the back rows. Never mind. It was her stage. Before she turned back to prepare for her entry she caught sight of John, at the second desk of 'cellos, concentrating hard. He was so handsome, but so sad. She would change that.

Hannah and Seamus looked intently at one another as they waited for their cue with lifted bows. And then they were in, soaring over the orchestra, all nerves dispelled.

# Chapter 20 - December 16th 1917

"Now, just take it easy, Hannah. You don't want to be sick all down your lovely blue dress." Seamus filled her glass half-full of champagne and then filled his own right up.

"You hypocrite. You've drunk just as much as me. More maybe."

"Yes, but I'm at least twice your size, and this is nearly my last night in Dublin with my friends – with you – and then I'll be off to get slaughtered by the Hun. I'd say getting a teeny bit drunk on your Auntie's champagne was more than forgivable."

Hannah gave Seamus a generous hug, returned with feeling.

"And we did it. We got through the Mozart without any major mishaps. Everyone keeps telling me we were marvellous."

"I think they are being kind. But yes, I think we were at least not embarrassing."

Lily Murphy was strutting around her festively decorated drawing room, taking total ownership of the successful concert which had finished an hour or so ago, introducing people to each other and frequently calling out to Hannah to come over and meet her very dear friend this or that.

Invitations to the post-concert reception here in Pembroke Street had been highly sought-after, so Hannah and Seamus's fellow students were rather amazed to find that they had all been invited. Ellen and Visha seemed totally relaxed, gliding about the room in their best frocks, engaging in brief conversations with stars from the Gaiety or esteemed academics. But most of the others were congregated near the French windows, ready to make a dash for it into the garden if anyone too intimidating were to ask them a question. Daniel and Angus were making regular trips to the supper table bringing back plates laden with food to share with their friends.

Several clear notes rang out followed by much shushing. Lily was tapping the side of her Waterford crystal glass with a silver fork.

"Thank you. Thank you, everyone. Shushhh. Thank you. I'd like to say a few words before the party becomes any more lively, and then you can resume enjoying yourselves."

"I hope you all enjoyed the concert as much as I did." A burst of enthusiastic applause and a few cheers. "I am so grateful to tonight's conductor, Mr Felix Brennan, for organising the orchestra and the venue. And, of course, for being the teacher of two such outstanding pupils." More applause.

"Everyone gave their time for free in support of the Red Cross. We have raised more than thirty pounds for their essential work tonight. We must never forget that while we were listening to such divine music brave young men were being killed – on both sides. Yes, British and German soldiers. Seamus, our young viola-player will be at the front in the New Year. He and my talented niece shared the genius of Beethoven and Mozart, and we also heard some Mendelssohn and Schumann. That music should remind us that the Germanic nations are not monsters. They are as civilised as us." There were a few murmurs of agreement mixed in with as many indignant harrumphs.

"But I don't mean to court controversy tonight. It is a night of celebration. My cellar is nearly empty but we should keep drinking while there's anything left in it." Loud cheers. "And it's nearly Christmas. So, I should like to give Hannah, my talented and beautiful niece, her present early." Lily walked over to the corner of the drawing room to a table with a strange shape on it draped in a shawl.

"I have taken some trouble to acquire this gift but I know Hannah will love it and it is a small reward for delighting us all tonight."

Lily whipped away the shawl, as if she were a magician unveiling her latest trick. The room gave a collective gasp when they saw the handsome gramophone player, with a stack of discs by its side. "Hannah, well done. You were magnificent tonight. Your mother – my darling sister, Evaline - would have been so proud. And Happy Christmas."

Hannah stepped forward, thanked and embraced her aunt. She inspected the gramophone and stroked the wooden case. She glanced at the discs; one included the Sinfonia Concertante and two others were of Beethoven quartets, with the rest offering Schubert's Unfinished Symphony, Haydn's Creation, Tchaikovsky's Violin Concerto and a disc of opera excerpts amongst other things. But right at the bottom were two discs of music by people she had never heard of: The Maple Leaf Rag, the Entertainer and some other ragtime dance music.

"Can I play these now, Aunt Lily?"

"I don't see why not. Maybe wait for a little while until some of the older guests have left."

Hannah looked around for John. She wanted to share the excitement of her gift as she knew he too would enjoy being able to listen to the recordings. But she couldn't see him anywhere. In fact, she hadn't seen him since shortly after they had arrived.

"Have you seen John?" Hannah asked Maisie.

"I think he's taken his mother home. I heard your Aunt offer them her car."

"I guess this is not exactly her sort of gathering, is it?" ventured Eamonn. "Too much alcohol and jollity."

Maisie nudged Eamonn. "And I suppose she would have been tired after playing for that big man who sang those very loud songs."

"Ah yes. Tired. That's what she'll be." Eamonn was thinking how tireless Mrs Fitzgerald was when it came to drilling her students in Latin.

Hannah took the bottle from the table behind her friends and filled her own glass. "Oh, I'm sorry. Any more for you two?"

By eight o'clock, any dignitaries had said their goodbyes and the drawing room was left with just the orchestra clan and the students. There was room to move about finally.

Hannah dragged Seamus over to the gramophone and handed him the instructions. "Be a love. Read those. And get this thing going."

It took Seamus mere minutes to master the machine and soon Scott Joplin was pouring out of the shiny black disc.

"Time to dance, everyone!" Hannah started pushing chairs against the wall and everyone lent a hand to clear a space. She hadn't danced since her Dada had let her join in a wedding party in the pub when she was about fifteen. She looked around for Seamus but he was already holding Ellen and helping her to dance as vigorously as her limp allowed. Maisie was with Eamonn, Morag with Daniel and even Visha had accepted the invitation to dance from a dashing French horn player with a splendid beard.

"Right then, Felix. It's time to show these amateurs what real dancing is like." And Hannah grabbed her conductor's hand to introduce him to the delights of syncopation.

******

It was gone midnight when Slattery delivered the last clutch of slightly squiffy friends - not forgetting the bulky gramophone - back to the Maple Academy. The car had never been so dangerously packed with youthful exuberance but Slattery completed the journey with admirable sobriety and steadiness, despite the car being rocked regularly by the lurchings of seven excited teenagers. A triumphant concert, more wine than they had ever before been allowed, dancing to ragtime, the end of term in two days' time and the coming of Christmas was a potent cocktail.

The front door was unlocked thankfully – no-one fancied getting Mrs Fitzgerald out of bed – and they all tiptoed inside with exaggerated shushings loud enough to wake the dead. Once Slattery had deposited the gramophone in the drawing room and said goodnight, Seamus began hugging Ellen, then Maisie, Visha and finally Hannah. Eamonn followed suit and even Daniel tried out an awkward embrace on Visha.

"I love you all so much. You are my very dearest friends and you always will be. I shall never forget you." Seamus looked around at them all. The reminder that they would soon be waving Seamus off to the front on Tuesday sobered the atmosphere instantly. Mrs Fitzgerald's sitting room door opened and John walked out.

"Welcome home. You wouldn't all be drunk now, would you?" He smiled at them all. "Best not do any more chatting or you might wake the dragon. I have been put on duty here to make sure everyone got home safely and that no-one is sick over my mother's silk rugs. Drink some water and get yourselves straight up to bed now."

They filed obediently past John and on up the stairs. John shook Seamus's hand and gave him a congratulatory whack on the shoulder as the soon-to-be soldier squeezed past him. Hannah made sure she was at the back of the queue.

"You were tremendous tonight, Hannah. I really think you should be aiming for a career as a professional player, you know." John took her hand in his and cradled it with the other. Then he raised her hand to his mouth and kissed it. "I particularly enjoyed playing The Harp with you this time. I think we found new depths in it, don't you? But one day, you'll be too famous to even pass the time of day - let alone play a quartet - with me."

"That will never, ever happen. You know that. Goodnight John." And Hannah followed her friends up the stairs as John locked the front door and switched off lights.

The girls took their time undressing, recalling the highlights of the previous eight hours: the velveted grandeur of the Gaiety, the generous applause, the salmon vol au vents, the gift of the gramophone. Ellen grabbed Maisie and twirled her around the bedroom.

"Oh, I wish I could dance properly like all of you. But I do have one thing you don't." Ellen collapsed onto her bed.

"What's that, Ellen?" Maisie sat down next to her friend and put her arm around her waist.

"You, my darling Maisie, have a sweetheart - and maybe so do you too, Hannah McDermott." Ellen gave a drunken wink. "But I am the only one of us with a fiancé."

As Ellen intended, this statement cause a flurry of gasps and squeals, followed by questions of who, how, when.

"Seamus asked me a month ago. He said he didn't think he could bear to be off fighting without someone special waiting for him back home. I admit, it came out of the blue, but we have always been very fond of each other – and it was very easy to become a bit fonder. I wrote to my parents about him and then he wrote to my parents and even went off to visit them last Saturday. I don't think they can believe that their crippled daughter has captured the heart of such a lovely and handsome boy – or man, I should say. We are going to spend part of the Christmas holiday together before I'll have to watch him leave for France. That's going to be so hard." Ellen's eyes filled up. "But other people have to live through this and sit at home and wait for the end of this evil war, so I can too."

Hannah was shocked that this had happened apparently under her nose and that no-one had asked her permission. She had thought Seamus was hers for the asking.

"How lovely, Ellen. I am so pleased for you both." Hannah kissed Ellen's cheek with determined nonchalance mixed with genuine happiness for her friends.

"Well, it's only because your heart is elsewhere that he asked me. You would have been his first choice, no question. But I just got lucky."

An hour later, the effects of the alcohol were creating louder than normal sleeping snorts from Ellen, and even Visha was breathing noisily through her mouth. Hannah was the only one left awake as she tried to piece together what must have happened and at what moment the string tying Seamus to her had snapped.

Why did she care about losing Seamus so much? She loved John. Yes, she was passionately in love with John and Seamus was just a very dear friend.

After another half hour of tortured analysis, Hannah quietly turned the sheets back and put her legs out of bed. It was cold in the bedroom but she left it without her dressing gown and crossed the landing to stand outside John's door. There was a faint light underneath it.

She gently turned the handle and entered the room to see John sitting up in bed reading by the gentle light of his bedside lamp. Hannah walked up to the bed in silence, then reached down and lifted her nightdress over her head in one flourish. John looked at her for a moment before getting out of bed and walking past her to the door. Oh damnation; she was going to be sent her back to her room then.

John turned the key in the lock and walked back to Hannah, where he removed his nightshirt with matching abandon before drawing her to him and kissing her gently.

"You are divine, Hannah. Kissing you is like drinking from a honeyed spring."

Hannah stroked John's shoulder and then his chest, covered in golden fuzz. His nipples were as hard as hers but she was scared to look lower than his waist.

"I want to revive you with my love, John."

They folded themselves round each other again, kissing more and more urgently. Hannah couldn't mistake the hardness of John's erection pressing against her stomach. Then John lifted Hannah gently onto the white sheets.

# Chapter 21 – December 20th 1917

"Hannah, have you done any packing this morning? Or anything at all for that matter?"

Stasia was marching around Hannah's bedroom, opening her wardrobe and the chest of drawers, checking on progress towards the big move into the villa happening tomorrow, as Hannah watched her from her bed.

"Oh, do leave me in peace, Stasia. I'll do it when I'm ready. Or maybe Aggie can do it for me."

"Don't you dare ask Agnes to lift a finger towards what you should have already done. She has more than enough to do, finishing off the kitchen packing, while still cooking and running around after us all."

"Alright. I'll do it after lunch. Just leave me alone now."

Stasia glared at her sister and then turned and walked out of the room, leaving the door ajar. Hannah gave a frustrated growl and was obliged to get up and slam the door after her sister. She looked around at the half-packed crates for a moment, threw herself back onto her bed and picked up her volume of Yeats. But few poems were read. There was too much from the past few days to sift through and attempt to make sense of.

The concert had been so thrilling and she wished she could perform like that every week to an adoring audience. The discomfort of her nervous anticipation was totally obliterated by the surge of joy she had felt as she played and the wonderful bond she had felt with all the performers on the stage with her, and in particular with Seamus and John.

Saying goodbye to Seamus two days later had been much more painful than she had anticipated. Seamus and Ellen had announced their engagement at the final dinner at the Academy on Monday night. Everyone had toasted their future happiness and wished Seamus the best of luck in his new regiment. It was a warm and touching occasion.

But the next morning, after she had watched Seamus walk out of the front door, him turning to give a final wave to the assembled friends, she had run upstairs and sobbed for half an hour into her pillow, which was embarrassing given that Ellen was coping with his departure with admirable stoicism.

Then, here she was, back in boring old Rowanbridge and not even allowed to enjoy the familiar comforts of home because everything was upside down ready for the move out of Main Street and into the Villa. Stasia had resolved that they would be installed in the new house by Christmas time and what Stasia resolved she let no man put asunder, however unreasonable were the efforts required.

Stasia had been personally supervising the carpentry and painting for the last three weeks after the foreman had suggested, with some trepidation, that perhaps it would be better to delay the move until the New Year to give them time to finish off the villa properly.

But what caused the most contemplation was Hannah's final two days with John. She tried to relive every second of the time they had managed to spend together since she had first entered his bed the previous Sunday night. Their first night as lovers had been thrilling but terrifying, despite John being so kind and patient. He had kissed every part of her, seeking her permission before exploring a new curve or fold. She had done little but surrender to him, save seek out his lips and stroke his golden hair when it fell onto her breasts. When he finally entered her, it was uncomfortable and, in truth, she was rather relieved when it ended. Relieved but triumphant.

The following night had been altogether different. Hannah took her cue from John and began to explore his body just as he did hers. She ran her hand along the long muscles of his legs, elegantly toned from gripping his 'cello over the years. Her hand ventured up to his balls, where her tentative touch made John moan. He took her hand

and placed it around his penis and then showed her how to stroke it. They whispered loving words to each other, always conscious that just a few bricks separated them from discovery. John sucked her nipples hard and then scattered kisses down her body, one hand left behind squeezing her breast. Hannah gasped when John's mouth reached between her thighs.

"May I kiss your rosebud?" Hannah nodded and giggled. Is that really what it was called? She knew what it was, of course. God knows she had touched it often enough in the privacy of her bed, but she had never heard anyone refer to it by name. She knew that people did such things during sex – Aggie's activities in the barn had not gone unnoticed - but she had no notion of the tumultuous sensations it could provoke. When intercourse began she was moistly aroused and came to a shuddering climax many times more powerful than when she touched herself.

As the dawn light crept into the room, Hannah leapt out of bed with a start. That night, they had made love three times; she was sore and sticky and satisfied. She fumbled round in the gloom trying to find her nightdress. Before she left, she woke John.

"I have to go now before the others wake up and discover my empty bed."

John sat up and took her hands.

"My darling Hannah. This is all very wrong but I simply cannot stop myself. I don't know what spell you have cast over me but you have brought me back to life. And I am now all yours - body, heart and soul." And they kissed softly, as John stroked her left breast and tweaked the nipple, knowing this would be the last kiss for many weeks.

Hannah had reached the landing, just about to creep back into her bedroom, when behind her she had heard Seamus whisper, "Be careful, Hannah." She turned around in shock, but he smiled at her. "I will," she mouthed and returned the smile, before slipping back into her cold bed.

Just two nights with John. She could recall every sensation, every smell, every taste. She would have to make those memories last the whole month before she would be back at the Maple Academy.

There was a brisk knock on the bedroom door and Aggie walked straight in, breaking Hannah's reveries.

"Come on, Miss Lazybones. Get up and get moving. You need to get this room finished before lunchtime 'cos we've got to get all the hens rounded up and boxed and taken over to their new henhouses before it gets dark. What are you broodin' over anyway?" Aggie sat on the bed. "Is it still that same boy? You should be over him by now and moved on to the next one. Never let them think they've got a hold on you. That's when they start messing you about."

"I told you, he's not a boy." But Aggie's attention had turned to the half-packed crates.

"Look, if you stand on that chair and pass down the stuff on the top of the wardrobe to me it'll be over faster."

With the heaviest of sighs, Hannah crawled off her bed and let herself be organised by Aggie.

******

"It's my last night in this house, Stasia, so there's no way I won't be spending it in the bar. I'm sorry, but you'll have it all your way very soon."

James pushed his chair back from the table where he had just polished off two helpings of apple pie and custard.

"As you wish, Father."

"Stasia doesn't like anyone having a good time, Dada."

"How would you know Hannah, seeing as you spend all the time moping in your bedroom while the rest of us are driving ourselves into the ground getting ready for the move tomorrow."

"Well, you're the only one who wants to go, so that seems fair enough."

"Shush now, Hannah. Your sister has been a tower of strength and I'm sure this is the right decision for all of us."

James struggled to his feet and stretched, before leaving for his final night as the friendliest landlord in the village.

"How about a few jigs tonight, Hannah? It's a special evening. I know you've been gracing the stages of Dublin with your fine playing but I promise I'll never ask you to play in the pub again after tonight."

"Of course, Dada." Hannah jumped up and took his arm. "I'd love to." She threw Stasia a backwards glance and danced off to find her fiddle.

# Chapter 22 – January 1918

Hannah lowered her book and gazed out of the huge drawing room window, down over the snow-dusted rooves of Rowanbridge. The new villa was barely a half mile outside the village but Hannah felt even more cut off from friends and neighbours in this smart, soulless house, still suffused with the smell of new paint.

Everything she loved seemed to have been taken away from her. Her favourite squishy sofa had been left behind in the Main Street house and replaced by an unforgiving new maroon velvet settee with wooden arms and nothing to snuggle into.

Her poor father had been robbed of his ancient armchair and was now fidgeting about trying to find some comfort in the new bolt upright matching fireside chair as he read the racing news.

"I doubt there'll be any racing today over at Gowran Park. Damn shame when I got a good tip-off from Jimmy who has come good twice this week."

Father and daughter could hear Stasia in the dining room next door issuing instructions to Aggie to "take care" every time a piece of the best china was unpacked from the tea chests.

Christmas had been a very unsatisfactory affair with no tree – Stasia didn't want to get needles on the new carpet – and no visitors or trips out to see anyone. Midnight Mass was the nearest Hannah got to a celebration, with happy people gathered together for wine and singing. James had wanted to go over to the Main Street pub on Boxing Day 'just to see how Jimmy is coping' but Stasia had killed that idea instantly.

The only thing on the horizon was the invitation from the Byrnes, their new next-door neighbours, to come over to tea this coming Saturday afternoon. And that was more a bore than a treat as far as Hannah was concerned.

She put down her volume of Hardy's The Return of the Native on the window seat and stood up.

"I have to get out of here, Dada. I know it's a bit chilly out there but I think I'll go for a walk down to the river before lunchtime."

"That's a grand idea, my angel. Get some good clean Rowanbridge air into those lungs."

Wrapped up as warmly as she could manage, Hannah clattered down the cold black-and-white tiled hallway to the rather splendid kitchen, packed with the latest gadgets, that Aggie was now the queen of, and then out of the back door. No hens came to greet her; they were all penned in out of sight behind the stables. Hannah had to go and seek them out these days.

"Hello there my lovelies. And how are you today? Do you like your new home? Your henhouses are all very grand but they are still prisons, eh." She took the lid off the grain bin outside the gate and threw them a few handfuls. "Now then, my best little brown girl, see what you can lay for me."

Hannah walked down towards the river, but, instead of climbing down to the riverside path, she continued on until she reached the churchyard and her mother's grave. The roses they had placed on the grave on Christmas Eve were now drooping and frost-damaged.

"Ah, Mammy, I hate this new house. Can you see from heaven what Stasia has made us do? Leave behind all the most comfy chairs and the big old desk from the study. She wants to stop Dada doing the accounts. And we see no-one walking past that we can say hello to, except the bloody Byrnes." Hannah bent down to brush the snow off the Christmas wreath. "Mammy, I guess you know that I'm in love. Do you like him? He's a beautiful man and so gentle with me. I've been a bit naughty but I know you'll forgive me. Will you ask Jesus to forgive me too? Tell God he shouldn't have made kissing and the other stuff so delicious if he'd wanted us all to stay pure. But I am still practising my violin hard, honestly, and you'd be amazed if you could hear me play that Bach Partita that you used to play. Well, I suppose you can hear me. Are you proud of me, Mammy?"

Hannah heard a crunching noise behind her. She turned to see Father Stephen walking along the gravel path up to the church door which he opened and went through. Hannah blew her mother's grave a kiss and then followed the priest into the church. He was kneeling at the altar, deep in prayer. Hannah waited for him to stand and then she walked over to him.

"Hello, Father Stephen. Happy New Year to you."

"May you have a blessed and holy 1918, Hannah, and let us all pray for peace."

"Erm, yes. Peace, yes, absolutely. I have a very dear friend who has just gone off to fight."

"Remember to pray for him, Hannah, and I will do so also. Would you like to join me in a prayer for him now?"

"Thank you. His name is Seamus."

Father Stephen and Hannah knelt side by side at the altar. The priest bent his head as did Hannah but after only a minute she looked up at the crucifix and blushed fiercely. Thanks to her lovemaking with John, she only now properly understood the significance of the mime she had performed on the convent crucifix that Good Friday nearly two years ago. But if she hadn't pretended to fellate the tortured body of Christ in front of Father Stephen she might still be at the convent, she would never have joined the Maple Academy and would never have met John. Strange how things work out.

Father Stephen rose and placed his hand on Hannah's head.

"May God send his blessings to you, Hannah, and I hope you have a happy year ahead."

They walked out of the church together. Hannah watched as the priest walked next door, opened his front door and disappeared. If only all priests were as kind.

Hannah had lost interest in walking by the river and dawdled her way back home. Before going inside, she walked up the slope to the bottom of the new garden where, responding to Mr Byrne's request, Stasia had commanded a row of yew tree whips be planted up against the wire fence to shield each house from the observation of the other. But the trees were just a couple of feet tall for now so Hannah could easily conduct a thorough inspection of the imposing Georgian farmhouse that had been in the Byrne family for over a hundred years.

"Boo."

Hannah gave an involuntary jump but soon saw that, thankfully, it was just Tricky on the other side of the wire witnessing her nosiness.

"Hello Tricky, and a very Happy New Year to you. Have you been having a lovely Christmas break?"

Tricky shrugged his shoulders.

"We're all coming over for tea on Saturday afternoon. I'm sure you'll be there."

Tricky nodded.

"Where are you going now?"

"Snow. Beast need hay."

Tricky walked back along the borderline, beckoning Hannah to keep up with him. When they both arrived at the lane that led past the new villa and on up to the Byrnes, Tricky helped Hannah to climb over the post and rail fence. There, waiting, was his cart filled with hay bales, with the horse tied to the fence by one of Tricky's elegant knots.

"Come for the ride?"

Hannah needed little encouragement - anything to delay re-entering the wretched villa - and let Tricky help her up onto the cart beside him. Off they went then, round the back lanes and into Mill Lane, until they came to Cromwell's Tower fields.

The cows were already gathered at the gate, expecting their daily ration from Tricky's hand.

"It's amazing, isn't it, how animals learn who their friends are. Our hens are the same. As soon as they see me they know something yummy is coming."

Hannah held the horse's bridle and stroked its nose as Tricky lifted bale after bale over the gate.

"What's the news from Nicholas? Is he still in France? He must be OK or he'd have been sent home I suppose. When are he and Louisa planning to get married?"

"Easter."

"Oh, how lovely. And I'm pleased they aren't waiting until the war is over. Who knows - maybe it'll never be over. We all need to grab whatever happiness we can, don't you think?" But Tricky had climbed over the gate and was now cutting all the string around the bales with his penknife, winding up the string neatly to put in his pockets and seemingly ignoring her, until it was time to take the cart back.

When they reached home, Tricky scrambled off the cart to help Hannah down. "Thanks for the trip, Tricky. I'll see you soon. Look after yourself." And, for some reason she couldn't fathom, Hannah gave Tricky a quick peck on the cheek before waltzing through the villa's kitchen door.

******

Tea at the Byrnes the next Saturday turned out to be an excruciating affair with old Mr Byrne just staring glumly out of his front windows at the monstrous new building that had destroyed his view, while James tried to make conversation with Mrs Byrne, aided by the odd comment from Stasia. Hannah and Tricky said little but kept up a silent conspiratorial dialogue of nods, winks and eye-rolls with each other while they ate their way through the cakes.

Before they left, Tricky disappeared briefly, returning with a tiny ball of fluff in his hands. He gently lowered a tiny kitten onto Hannah's lap.

"Oh, what a darling little thing." Hannah cradled the ginger kitten, rubbing its ears and chin until it vibrated with purrs. "You are so adorable." Hannah picked up the kitten and kissed its nose.

"Take it."

"I'd love to, Tricky – thank you – but…"

Stasia interrupted instantly. "Hannah, you can't possibly take a kitten. You'll be back to Dublin in no time and then we would be left to look after it."

Hannah had been about to say much the same thing but now decided to take issue with her sister's logic.

"But Tricky has been kind enough to offer it to me and it would be so lovely to have a kitten waiting here for me. Something to look forward to when I come home. Daddy, is it OK for me to have this little baby? Aggie will look after it for me along with the other cats." Hannah went over to James and put the kitten on his knee.

"Yes, I suppose so. It can't do any harm, Stasia, now, can it?"

Hannah's last week at home was brightened by having the kitten, ceremoniously named Honey, to fuss over. Knowing that it irritated Stasia made it all the more fun, though, by the end of the week, everyone in the villa had succumbed to its mischievous charm.

The last day of the holiday arrived; Hannah was tense with anticipation.

"Jeezus, Hannah, how many more times will I have to pack, unpack and then repack your clothes this holiday?"

Aggie was emptying Hannah's top drawer into her case ready for the journey back to Dublin the next day while Hannah was sitting cross-legged on her bed, teasing Honey with a feather.

"You could do with some new camis you know, these are looking a bit worn and grubby."

"Oh gosh, yes, I really do need some new underwear. Why didn't I think of it before today? Is it too late now to go into Kilkenny."

"What are you talking about? Why would you buy your undies in the Monster House when you have the pick of Dublin's posh shops? Just make sure your sister gives you enough money to get something nice. I'd love some pretty underwear, me. Mind you, what's the point? Stuck up here behind the village, I haven't seen any handsome young fellas for a month now. No-one calls here apart from the postman - who must be sixty if he's a day - and the grocery delivery boy. And he's too young even for me."

"That's rubbish, Aggie. I've seen you flirting with the builders outside."

"Yes, but there's nowhere private we can go to up here. Not yet anyway. And they'll have finished the paths and garden soon and then we'll be back to the convent life. It was so great down on Main Street with customers coming in every day, not to mention the Guinness delivery men every week. They were the handsomest. Don't let that kitten piss on the bed. She's not trained yet, you know."

Aggie sat at the foot of the bed, folding every item of clothing and then bending to place it in Hannah's suitcase.

"I saw that Louisa Nevin in town yesterday, when I went into Kelleher's for some elastic. She was with her Mammy looking at all the silks and laces, choosing for her wedding dress I suppose. That is going to be quite an affair. Mind you, she'd be better off not spending too much money until nearer the time because Nicholas could easily get blown up before Easter the way the war is going."

Hannah laughed. "You are such an optimist, Aggie."

"I am a realist, Hannah McDermott, and you'd do well to be as practical as me."

Aggie stood and closed the top drawer before moving on to the second. She threw a tangle of stockings on the bed, onto which Honey instantly pounced.

"Bloody hell. Get that cat off the bed or she'll rip them to shreds. Now then, madam, you can stir yourself and get sorting these into pairs. And don't just put any old two together now. Make sure they match properly 'cos they are all slightly different colours."

Aggie picked up a package wrapped in blue sugar paper from the back of the drawer.

"Have you not had your period while you've been home? This packet is as full as when I put it in the drawer a month ago."

Hannah hesitated. She had to think hard. "I finished just before I came home. I'm due again any day now." But as she sat, painstakingly matching stocking to stocking, she was raking through her memory with mounting panic.

"Aggie, you know you said you once got pregnant? What did you do about it?"

Aggie turned to Hannah. "You think you're pregnant?" Aggie scuttled over to the bed and started whispering manically.

"You do, don't you? Oh Jesus Christ, Hannah, what the hell have you been up to? I thought they kept you under lock and key in that posh Academy place. "

"They do ... but they can't stop us from seeing each other."

"So, you've let some boy have his way with you?"

"I keep telling you - it's not a boy, it's a man."

"A man? A teacher? He should be shot. Forcing himself on a young girl. We should get him locked up."

"It wasn't like that. I wanted it to happen. I made it happen."

"Are you crazy? What happened to becoming a famous violinist? Are you honestly trying to get yourself into trouble – or get yourself married off?"

"I don't know. I'm just in love. You know what that feels like."

"I'm not so stupid as to let my feelings ruin my life."

"Look, I'm sure my period will start soon. I'm only a week or so late."

"Let's bloody well hope so. But look here - just lay off these goings-on, OK? It's all very well for me, with no prospects at all, to go around playing fast and loose with the fellas but not a clever young girl like you, from a respectable family with so much to live for. It'd kill your Daddy. It would, sure."

"Dada is made of stronger stuff, Aggie. Stasia would be none too pleased, mind."

"Now look. If your monthly hasn't started in a week, find an excuse to come home. You can make up some story – maybe tell them your Father is ill – and I can sort you out. The old biddy in Thomastown who helped my problem go away is still in business, I think."

"What would I tell Stasia?"

"Oh, for heaven's sake, you can think about that when the time comes. It's not beyond you surely. You always manage to come up with some pretty fancy lies when you want something. She can be suspicious all she likes, as long as we get that baby out."

Hearing the word 'baby' brought a smile to Hannah's mouth. She picked up Honey who was attempting to climb back onto the bed via Aggie's skirt.

"What are you smiling for? This is not funny, you know."

No, not funny, just exciting, thought Hannah, as she tickled the kitten's tummy.

# Chapter 23 – Mid-February 1918

"Hannah? Hannah, are you alright in there?" Maisie was knocking gently on the ground floor lavatory door.

Hannah stared at the white porcelain. She had been retching for some minutes but had produced nothing to show for it. This dry heaving was exhausting and was doing nothing to quell the nausea.

She stood up and resolved to ignore the sickness and go back to her history class. She turned the key and emerged to find a concerned Maisie hovering around the door.

"Do you feel better now?"

"Yes, I'm fine. It must be the kippers we had at breakfast."

But Hannah knew exactly what had been causing her to run to the bathroom for the last few mornings.

"No, I think you must have the 'flu because you felt ill yesterday as well."

"Maybe. Anyway, we'd best get back to Miss Murray."

Hannah and Maisie slipped back into the classroom and took up their exercise books. Miss Murray was at the front getting very agitated about all the religious issues at stake in the Restoration of Charles II.

Hannah was hardly listening but instead playing out the conflicting thoughts in her head. Clearly, she was pregnant. There was no avoiding the fact. She would lie in bed in the mornings and stroke her stomach which felt as flat as normal, scarcely able to credit that there was anything inside it at all that threatened to cause a major drama. But her breasts had started to feel a little different when John touched them.

In the two or so weeks since term had begun she and John had stolen five nights together. Their intimacy had grown and she felt utterly at one with him, particularly as he had started to withdraw before orgasm saying that this would stop her getting pregnant. Feeling his warm stickiness spread over her stomach felt somehow even more daring than it being inside her; John would gently wipe it off with his flannel and then kiss her damp tummy.

Then, when she had crept into his room at midnight two days ago, he had taken out a small package, with a Manchester postmark, from his wardrobe. It contained a rubber condom. John said he had never used such a thing before but they had worked it out together with much repressed giggling.

Hannah would lie back in John's bed after they had made love and study his beautiful profile as he slept with a half-smile on his lips. He was an utterly transformed man from the ghost she had first met a year and a half earlier. He hadn't said the precise words but Hannah was sure that he loved her.

Would it spoil all this if he learnt that she was pregnant?

On the other hand, there was no way she was going to go back to Rowanbridge to be 'dealt with' by Aggie's shadowy Thomastown biddy, mainly because she had no idea what excuse she would give to her father and Stasia about coming home mid-term.

Hannah wondered whether she could trust her Aunt Lily with the news. She was unquestionably a forward-thinking, mature, modern woman who would surely not be too shocked and might even be able to help her secure a safe solution somewhere in Dublin without anyone in Rowanbridge knowing a thing about it. Aunt Lily had been an actress, after all, and Hannah was confident that she would know what to do about an inconvenient pregnancy. She would pay her a visit next Saturday.

Before dinner, most of the students were relaxing in the drawing room, taking advantage of the roaring fire. The bedrooms were a little too chilly at this time of year for much more than leaping into and out of beds and hasty dressing.

Hannah was holding a hank of lurid magenta wool between her raised hands, while Maeve wound it into neat balls ready to be knitted into some strange creation, when Ellen came into the room waving a sheet of paper.

"Hey, everyone. I've had my first letter from Seamus this morning from the front. Well, I'm not sure whether he is at the front because he's not allowed to say. But he's definitely properly started in the army because he's complaining about the itchy uniform."

Eamonn swapped his fireside armchair for the rug so that Ellen could take the seat and read out the letter to her friends gathered around, stopping from time to time to miss out any parts she pronounced too embarrassing, but making them all fully aware that Seamus had packed in many sweet endearments. There was little about any actual fighting but lots about the military routines, the beds, the food and the camaraderie. But his new friends hadn't erased memories of his old ones.

"Here's a bit for you Hannah. 'Tell Hannah that I am using my rifle on my shoulder to practise my posture and keep my fingering flexible, even in this bitter cold. I shall be challenging her to a duet the first time I am home so she'd better not slacken off the lessons thinking I am going to fall behind her. It's war out here but it'll be the war of the bows back in Dublin soon enough.' Oh, I just can't wait for him to be back here."

"Well, you can tell him to watch out, because I can now slaughter any viola-player from a hundred yards with the fiery fierceness of my scales." Hannah was touched that Seamus had chosen to mention her by name, the only one of his former classmates to be so honoured. Lovely, lovely Seamus.

Ellen folded the letter, put it in her pocket and turned to the growing pile of magenta woollen balls by Maeve's side. "What the hell are you going to knit with that, Maeve? I like a nice cheerful colour with the best of you, but that is taking a liberty."

"I know. It is a little bright, isn't it. Mother found it in the local haberdasher's at a knock-down price and sent it on to me." Maeve held up a ball next to her bright orange hair. "Not sure this is going to work for me."

"I know…" Visha had been a little apart from the throng, sitting on the window seat as Ellen had read her letter, but she now came over to join the group. "Why don't you turn it into blankets for the forces? I saw an article in yesterday's newspaper about women's groups knitting squares that can be joined together to keep the soldiers warm - and the sailors of course."

"Why don't we all do it?" Eamonn suggested. "I don't mind learning to knit if someone will show me." He turned to Maisie and smiled.

"That is a grand idea. I've got loads of little bits of wool left over from other projects and I know Mammy will have plenty more. And she can send us as many sets of needles as we need." Maeve was enjoying the rare delight of being the centre of attention.

"Well, it's certainly more useful than frittering away our time doing jigsaws, or playing chess." Angus turned and gave Daniel a self-righteous nod.

"Aww, you lot are great." Ellen wiped away a tear.

"And we'll all be doing something useful for our darling friends, Seamus and Sourja. Keeping them warm, while we keep them in our hearts."

Maisie's gentle words sent everyone off to their beds thinking how very, very lucky they were not to be sleeping outside that January night, freezing under the French stars.

The next Saturday, Hannah got on the tram to see Felix for her weekly lesson. She missed Seamus's company. And the motivation to practice daily had also vanished now there was no end of term concert to aim for.

The swaying tram was not helping Hannah's morning sickness. She had brought an empty old leather music case with her, just in case the unthinkable happened and she had to vomit during the journey.

"And a very good morning to the famous Miss Hannah McDermott." Felix opened his front door with a flourish and a bow. He stood back upright and peered at his pupil. "Gracious, Hannah, are you OK? You look a bit green. Come in, come in. Actually, no. Just stay there for a minute." Hannah waited on the doorstep until Felix returned with a bowl. "Better safe than sorry."

"Don't worry, Mr Brennan. I won't mess up your floor. It's the tram and the fumes. I'm not actually going to be sick. Can I just sit for a moment, please?"

After a glass of water and two of Felix's plain shortbread biscuits, Hannah felt ready to begin the lesson, but it was hardly a rewarding experience for either of them and Hannah was relieved when the lesson ended. She suspected Felix was too.

"Well, I hope you feel better soon. Make sure you crack that second movement by next Saturday." Hannah had asked to study Bach's D Minor Partita that term and was anxious to get onto the famous Chaconne but Felix wouldn't hear of it until all the other movements were note perfect.

"I shall. Thank you, Mr Brennan. Sorry about today and thanks for looking after me."

Instead of making her way back to the tram stop to return to Dalkey, Hannah walked further along the road to her Aunt's waiting car. Slattery was taking forty winks in the driving seat but sprang to life as Hannah opened the back-passenger door.

"Hello, Slattery. Thanks for coming to fetch me. I'm not trying to be grand or anything by sitting in the back, but it's just easier to look after my violin here." Hannah was not being strictly honest and luxuriated in the sensation of being chauffeur-driven through west Dublin as they made their way to Pembroke Street. One day, she too would have a car and her own driver to take her everywhere. She'd had enough of draughty trams and steamy buses.

Lily was delighted to have some company for her Saturday lunchtime. It was a modest meal by her aunt's standards as Lily was going out for a grand dinner later that evening; Hannah was relieved to find she was only expected to eat an omelette.

"How very sweet of you to come and visit me. You should come more often on a Saturday, especially now that you are alone for your lessons. Do tell me all your news. How is the famous 'villa'?"

Hannah related all the facts that Stasia had listed in her weekly letter taking care not to complain too bitterly about moving out of the old house. She knew that her aunt thoroughly approved of them escaping the ties of the Main Street pub.

"I always thought it less than ideal to be bringing up young ladies in the vicinity of rough labourers, drinking, smoking, spitting, and goodness knows what other bad behaviour you've both been witness to."

Hannah smiled. Her aunt was an ardent supporter of the rights of the working class as long as she didn't have to encounter them in the flesh.

"I don't know how your mother tolerated being made to live in that house and even to serve in the bar from time to time, as I remember. Well, I am so pleased that you are all now going to be living somewhere more fitting."

Lily asked all about Mrs Fitzgerald - saying that she anticipated seeing her at the Abbey Theatre in a couple of weeks - and about her fellow students.

"I cannot bear to think of that talented young viola-player wallowing in mud and blood in the trenches. I am shocked that he felt he should volunteer to go off and fight for such a dubious cause."

Hannah was trying to find the right moment to raise the topic she had specifically come to consult with her aunt about, but, every time she was about to begin, some servant or other would come into the dining room to bring in a plate or take away a dish. Eventually they were settled in her aunt's small morning room with a tray of tea and no likelihood of imminent interruption.

"Aunt Lily, I need to ask your advice - about a rather embarrassing subject."

"Ask away, my darling girl. There's nothing you should feel you can't talk about me with me. I know the world. I am unshockable."

"Well then, I think … I'm fairly sure I am having a baby."

Lily's teacup shook precariously, threatening to tip Earl Grey into her lap. She put her cup and saucer down carefully onto the tray and stared hard at Hannah.

"Could you say that again please, Hannah. I thought for a moment that you said you thought you were having a baby." Lily dropped her voice to a whisper for last three words.

"I did."

Lily stared at Hannah in silence. Unshockable? Not so much then, thought Hannah, but the cat was now irretrievably out of the bag.

"Yes, I thought you were the only person I could ask about what I should do. I cannot possibly tell Stasia or Daddy."

"Why do you think you are … carrying a child?" Lily's voice was now more of an urgent hiss.

"Well, I haven't had a period for over two months now."

"Yes, but it could be anything causing that. It happens frequently, particularly to young girls who don't eat properly. I knew some dancers in my days on the stage who never had their courses. You cannot be pregnant, Hannah. I don't know how much you know about the facts of life, but you would have to have had … intimate relations with a man. It must be something else. I shall send you to my doctor for a diagnosis."

"I have been feeling sick in the mornings this last week and my breasts are very tender…"

"You clearly have some infection, Hannah. We will get it cleared up and you'll be right as rain in no time."

"…and, yes, I have made love to a man. Not just any man, but John Fitzgerald."

"My God."

Lily was poleaxed and could not speak for several moments. Then she rose and paced about the small room, before sitting again.

"Did he force himself upon you? This is a very serious charge. He will have to leave the Academy. It will crucify Letitia. As if he hasn't caused her enough pain already."

"Calm down, Aunt Lily. No, he most certainly did not force himself upon me. We are in love. I wanted him to make love to me. I'm just not sure I want to have a baby. It's as simple as that."

"Simple is it? We'll see about that. Now, let me think."

Lily stood again, paced again, sat, and then poured herself some fresh tea.

"Right then. You must see my Dr Grainger. He is an expert in women's matters. He might perform a little procedure called a dilation and curettage which will sort out everything to do with … your hormonal troubles. But we must act quickly. This week."

"Will I still be pregnant after I have seen him?"

"We do not know whether you are pregnant yet. Dr Grainger will ascertain that. Just leave things in his hands. And say nothing to anyone. I shall try to organise an appointment for next Saturday afternoon after your lesson."

Hannah decided to leave further questions for next week and the rest of their tea-drinking was conducted in stilted conversation about the weather and such until Lily announced that it was time for Hannah to get back to Dalkey so that Slattery would be back to her in time for her dinner engagement.

"Goodbye now, Hannah. Stay well this week. And - please - never ruin a Saturday afternoon again like that. When you are recovered we shall need to talk about John Fitzgerald and the right course of action. But keep away from him from now on. Do you hear me?"

Lily had seemingly forgiven Hannah enough to give her a hasty embrace before opening the front door and waving her off into the care of Slattery, waiting to whisk Hannah back to the Maple Academy.

# Chapter 24 – Late February 1918

Hannah was finding it hard to concentrate on Mr Ord-Hume's explanation of the fertility of the Nile delta when her own fertility was of more immediate concern. Geography was now the only subject she took with the genial old gentleman, which was a shame because he reminded her a little of her father, with his tweedy suit, his ruddy cheeks, his white hair and bushy moustache.

Oh, how she wished she could sit on her Dada's knee right now for one of his enveloping hugs. She would be happy to tell her father all about the mess she was in; he would not judge her and would look after her – but it would mean sharing it also with Stasia, and that would be intolerable. Aunt Lily had proved to be less broad-minded than all her grand statements about feminism and rejecting social conventions had suggested.

If Hannah had thought Mr Ord-Hume would be a willing paternal surrogate she might well have pursued him after the end of the lesson and asked for a hug, but instead she stayed in her chair as a few students came and went, ready for the next lesson – English - and listened to Ellen witter on to Maisie about how much she would have liked to live in ancient Egypt.

When the new class was finally settled, in came John, carrying a pile of Measure for Measure scripts, which they had started to study the previous week. John, her teacher and her lover. She felt an acute pang of guilty pleasure to think of their secret times together. How handsome he looked when he was teaching, confident and cheerful. John made his way around the long table where they all sat, giving out copies of Measure for Measure while studiously avoiding Hannah's eyes - or so she felt.

"Please turn to page twelve, the beginning of Act 2 Scene II. Eamonn, you read Angelo, Morag will you read Isabella please, Angus the Provost and Visha, can you please summon up your very best impersonation skills to play the licentious, Lucio?" The Academy girls were well used to playing male roles but Visha looked not at all pleased to be cast as the rakish friend of Isabella's brother, Claudio, now condemned to death by Deputy Angelo for flouting Vienna's laws on immorality, having impregnated his beloved Juliet.

No part for Hannah today then. She turned to page twelve and there found, tucked into the crease, a small piece of folded paper with her name on it in John's hand. She slipped the message up into in her sleeve for later reading.

As her friends ploughed their way through the text, Hannah noted ruefully that Shakespeare's sexual politics seemed a great deal more modern than her Aunt Lily's. He was clearly directing the audience's sympathies more towards the 'fornicatress' Juliet, heavy with Claudio's child, than to Claudio's priggish sister, Isabella. He made Isabella's attachment to her virginity seem not just absurd but downright selfish – almost immoral in its own way.

Hannah also couldn't help concluding how much better a job she would have made reading the part of Isabella than Morag was doing in her thin Glaswegian monotone. Or maybe that was John's ironic touch, to cast Isabella as a bloodless Calvinistic killjoy.

It was just before midnight when Hannah knocked gently on John's door, answering the request in his note to come to his room that night. It said he wanted to talk to her. Hannah loved to talk with John but she also anticipated that something even more delicious would follow.

Hannah opened the door gently to find John at his desk looking at photographs and holding the strand of golden hair.

"Hannah. Thank you for coming to see me." John rose and came towards her but, instead of taking her in his arms and kissing her as he normally did, he indicated that Hannah should sit in one of the leather armchairs. He sat across from her in the other one. Hannah's thoughts raced as John reached over and took her hand.

"Hannah, this is very hard. The last thing I want is to hurt you but I fear that is what I have already been doing." John rose out of his chair and walked over to face the curtained window.

"You are a totally wonderful, talented creature who has brought life to even this dead, dark soul. You are so generous and loving. I have been utterly entranced by you. But I have been wrong to take advantage of that sweet nature. Terribly, terribly wrong. I apologise for everything that has gone on between us. And now it simply must end." He turned back to Hannah and then returned to his chair.

"You must see that this is for the best. It would scandalise my mother if this ever became known, and all the other students, or at least their families, and it would destroy the Academy. But, most importantly, this is not what you should be pouring your energy and thoughts into. You could be a serious professional musician and you should concentrate on achieving that."

"But John, I love you. And you love me."

"Hannah…" John voice faltered and his eyes filled with tears.

"Hannah, you are very young. People of your age can fall in love one day and out of love the next. That's why it's so very wrong of me to have exploited those emotions to… satisfy myself."

"No, John. I can tell the difference between that sort of flighty feeling - a crush if you will - and real love. I love you and you are all that I want." Hannah put all her conviction into that mantra.

"Either way, Hannah, I think our relationship should end. End now. I know it will be hard to be here together for another two terms but then you will leave and forget all about me and begin a dazzling career." John stood as if to dismiss her, as he might do at the end of a lesson.

Hannah made a lightning quick decision. "Well, you need to know something important. I am carrying your baby."

John slowly sat down again, looked at her intensely for several moments and then took up her hand again.

"Are you sure?"

"Yes. I haven't seen a doctor or anything. But I haven't bled since the end of November and I've been feeling sick in the mornings and…"

"Hannah, this is wonderful news. My darling girl." John stood and pulled her up into a fierce embrace. "Don't worry about a thing. I shall look after you in every way I can, in every way you want me to."

"You don't think it's a bloody disaster then?"

John chuckled. "Well, it's not ideal and it'll cause some big waves that might drown us all. But a new life is always a blessing."

"What shall we do then?" Hannah sat on the bed and beckoned for John to join her there.

"Let's just think this through slowly. Of course, I am so sorry that this has happened to you. It's all my fault. I should have known better but a sort of madness took over. You must not blame yourself in any way."

John sat and thought, all the while stroking Hannah's back.

"Well, I knew perfectly well what I was doing. But how come you were going to stop seeing me and end everything before I told you. Don't you love me anymore?"

"Hannah, you mustn't see it that way. I was simply trying to free you from any obligation to our relationship. There's no way you will want to tie yourself to a man so much older than you - once you come to your senses. A man with no prospects at all when you could have a glittering career as a violinist, and maybe even as a soloist."

"Don't be silly, John. I really, truly love you."

They kissed tenderly and John cradled Hannah in his arms.

"Listen. Hear me out. There is no way you need to let this baby ruin your life. With your family's knowledge, you can go out to Connemara and stay with Shawna and Ruari and Aoife until the baby comes. And then they can look after it for us. I know they would be thrilled to have a baby back in the cottage. And I would maintain it and visit just as I did with Máire. Only this baby will be well and live. I just feel it. You can then go back to your home as if you had just finished school in the normal way, and no-one other than your father and sister need know."

"John, my Aunt Lily already knows. I saw her this Saturday and she is going to arrange for me to see her doctor next Saturday, who I think would help me … stop being pregnant, if you know what I mean. If I hadn't wanted to have your baby I would never have told you and just gone along with her plan. But I do want it, and I want you. I want to have your baby more than anything in the world."

A tear, which had been balancing in the corner of John's eye, now fell onto his cheek.

"Oh God, Hannah, I couldn't have borne it if you had destroyed such a precious thing. Thank you for that."

They embraced again and John rocked Hannah gently in his arms. Then he got up from the bed and knelt in front of her, taking her hand.

"Dearest Hannah, I'm not worthy of you in anyway but if you would agree to marry me, you would make me the happiest man alive."

"John, of course, I will. That's what I want more than anything else in this life. To be the next Mrs Fitzgerald."

Hannah flung her arms around John's neck and kissed him as passionately as she knew how.

Later, after John had made love to her in the most gentle and tender way he could, he caressed and kissed her flat stomach.

"Cuisle mo chroidhe."

"What's that?"

"It means 'the pulse or the beat of my heart' in Gaelic. That's what that little bean means to me."

"Now, you won't be making this baby more important than me, will you?"

"How could I do that, you silly sausage? Without you, there is no bean. You are both cuisle mo chroidhe. Of course."

"That's OK then. I'm not in the habit of playing second fiddle to anyone, you know. Not even my own child."

# Chapter 25 – March 1918

Hannah lay back on the huge white pillows and gazed at the chandelier above her. She held up her left hand and admired the gold band on her left ring finger. Now that was more like it. Definitely better than a piece of broken shell.

And this was certainly a better way to enjoy making love to her new husband: in a huge bed, in a remote hotel in the Wicklow Mountains, far away from disapproving looks and snide remarks, where there was no need to whisper their love or to abandon their warm bed before dawn.

Not only that, but she had even managed to get married just before Nicholas bloody Byrne and that creep Louisa Nevin. One in the eye for the Byrnes. Hannah gave her still flat stomach a gentle pat; all thanks to the little bean growing inside her.

Of course, there had been some very unpleasant scenes before she and John had become man and wife at the Dublin General Register Office last Saturday, in the presence of just four very unhappy witnesses. The day after becoming a wife, she had celebrated her eighteenth birthday in this splendid hotel with her brand-new husband by her side.

But the chain of events from John's proposal to this point had been painful. Two days after Hannah had become engaged, Aunt Lily had driven her down to Rowanbridge, thinking her presence would help break the news and encourage James to accept the news calmly. But Hannah could tell that Lily was not at all happy with her and their conversation in the car from Dublin was icy.

And her poor Dada. Of course, he had done his best to make his darling daughter feel less guilty but there was no mistaking the pain and betrayal in his eyes. Never mind. He would get used to it and Hannah was certain that he would grow to like and respect John in time.

Hannah had thought Stasia would explode with fury when she was told, but she said nothing at first and just marched out of the parlour and up to her bedroom. Over supper that night, Stasia had managed to drop a few casual barbs relating to Hannah's depravity, the Academy's inadequacy, Lily's poor choice and the general evil of John Fitzgerald.

"Stasia, when you meet him, you'll realise that he is a saint."

"Well, clearly not saintly enough to resist the devil's temptations."

Hannah wasn't sure whether Stasia was implying that her own sister was demonic. But who cared anyway.

"He is certainly a very decent man," opined Lily, "just evidently rather weak."

Stasia, at first, pronounced that she wouldn't attend the marriage ceremony up in Dublin but subsequently relented, realising that if she stayed in Rowanbridge people would gossip that Hannah's marriage was not a welcome one to the McDermotts. It was more important to create the myth of a fortuitous match that the whole family was delighted about.

After delivering the unwelcome news, Lily and Hannah were planning to return to Dublin first thing next morning; but, before they left, Aggie had sneaked into Hannah's bedroom to wake her with a cup of tea, accompanied by kitten Honey who leapt up onto the bed. The previous evening, Slattery had let the metaphorical cat out of the bag to Aggie over a fag and a pint – and who knows what else - but Aggie's own antennae had already picked up the signals. She gave Hannah a big hug.

"You're a complete eejit, you know. I told you I could sort you out." She stroked Hannah's rumpled hair as Honey curled herself into the counterpane. "But I do wish you every happiness together, my lovely girl."

As awful as it had been to let her own family know, Hannah knew that she had escaped lightly compared to John. She shuddered when she thought about the reception that John's mother had given his news. That this would be his second marriage to an already pregnant woman under twenty did not go unobserved. Mrs Fitzgerald was coldly furious, insisting her son leave the Academy instantly to go and find lodgings elsewhere, dismissing him from his teaching post and forbidding him from even visiting.

Soon after, Ellen delivered to Hannah a tersely written note addressed to 'Miss McDermott' which made no reference to the engagement and certainly not to the pregnancy, but simply asked her to leave the next morning to go and live with Lily in central Dublin 'until further notice' and forbade her from saying anything about 'any matter' to any of the other students.

Hannah found that command impossible and the next morning, as she packed up a small bag, she shared with her three best friends the fact that she and John were now engaged and that Mrs F had gone hopping mad as a result and banished them both. Hannah left out all mention of illicit lovemaking and the resulting pregnancy though.

"Well, you can see her point of view. Which family would entrust one of their daughters to an establishment that allowed a love affair to develop between a teacher and a pupil. And not just that, with the son of the owner. Very improper." Visha shook her head.

"Well, I'm really happy for you both, Hannah." Maisie was her adorable self, "but I hope that doesn't mean we never get to see you or Mr Fitzgerald again."

"Don't you fret, Maisie. For a start, for how long is Mrs F. going to be able to stop seeing her darling boy? I give her three months tops before she caves in. And you won't miss that old floozy Hannah McDermott at all. We're much better company than her and we don't plague you with all that bloody violin noise." But Ellen looked distinctly tearful as she hugged goodbye to her friend.

So, there had been some painful moments and sacrifices to bear en route to her honeymoon bed, but she'd happily suffer them all many times over again to be John Fitzgerald's wife.

Hannah looked over to the washstand as her husband of three days was preparing for bed. That long lean body, the strong legs, the wide shoulders, the hollows on the side of his buttocks, the fuzz of golden hair in his armpits as he soaped and rinsed them before bed; it all belonged to her now. Hannah felt a throb of desire watching John pull back his foreskin to wash himself ready for her. Hannah anticipated the slight taste of vanilla soap that she would soon be enjoying.

John jumped onto the bed, stood behind Hannah and then slid down behind her to cradle her against his chest, nestled between his muscular legs.

"Now then, Mrs Fitzgerald, can I interest you in a little spot of poetry this spring evening?"

John stretched over to reach for one of the volumes of Yeats that had accompanied them on their honeymoon. He opened the book and held it in his left hand leaving the right free to wrap around Hannah's waist. She leant back against his shoulder, with closed eyes.

> *"He Remembers Forgotten Beauty*
> *When my arms wrap you round I press*
> *My heart upon the loveliness*
> *That has long faded from the world..."*

Hannah adored listening to John recite Yeats; she surrendered to his crimson velvet voice and the intermittent soft kisses he dropped onto her neck, under her thick chestnut mane.

John finished the poem and closed the book, placing it carefully on the bed as he folded both arms around his wife and kissed her shoulders.

"My turn now." Hannah picked up the book, ignoring the increasing urgency of John's embrace. "Stop that now and listen up. This was the first Yeats I ever heard; you read it out to us in class. I think I was already in love with you – not sure - but I definitely was by the end of it." Hannah took John's hands from around her waist and placed them, palms down, on the white linen before she started to read The White Birds out loud.

As the poem progressed, its significance began to dawn on her fully for the first time. Phrases like 'a sadness that may not die'; 'Time would surely forget us and Sorrow come near us no more'; 'were we only white birds, my beloved, buoyed out on the foam of the sea' now shouted out their meaning.

Hannah closed the book and placed it gently on the bedside table. John was silent. How could she not have realised before why John had chosen that poem. He must have been thinking about his beloved dead Ailsa back when he read it to the class, and longing to be with her again, walking along the shore at Cleggan. And now she had, crazily, reminded him of the woman he had lost before marrying Hannah.

No matter. That was all before he had fallen in love with her. Hannah was alive - warm flesh and blood - and a dead wife was surely no match for that. Hannah took up John's hands and placed them on her breasts. He began to stroke her freely, plucking her nipples, brushing over her stomach as he kissed her ear and neck. Hannah felt him growing hard against the small of her back. She placed her hands on his taut thighs as he began to finger the sweet wetness between her thighs. She closed her eyes again, anticipating more exquisite lovemaking.

******

After four days of luxury in the Wicklow Mountains, it was time to go home. Home to John's rather grim rented rooms in Dublin to begin their domestic life together. But, when they got off the train at Dublin, rather than leave the station, John led Hannah to another platform.

"What's happening, John?"

"This is a little surprise for you, my darling. A bit more honeymoon for us and a chance for you to understand more about me."

John announced that they were off to Clifden, to stay with the De Bhailises in Cleggan over Easter.

"You must see Connemara, my darling. That's where my soul lives."

"I thought you had given it to me."

"You have my heart, for sure, Hannah Fitzgerald, but I cannot pretend that my soul has not been captured by the waves and the lakes."

"Well, we'll see about that," said Hannah, in mock sternness. "I shall have to set about releasing it so that you can carry your soul around with you, wherever you happen to be, like a normal human being."

The dusk was falling fast when they got off the train at Clifden; the gulls were circling and shrieking their last for the day as Hannah and John walked out of the station.

"I haven't told them about the baby, by the way. Let it be our secret for now."

Hannah understood why John didn't want to flaunt the pregnancy. Too much of a reminder of the circumstances of his marriage to Ailsa and also the pain of losing her and her child.

Ruari was waiting on the road with the pony and trap. John shook the older man's hand and Ruari slapped John on the shoulder. A simple enough gesture but Hannah could see the strong connection between them. She stepped forward.

"Ruari, please meet my new wife, Hannah."

"How do you do, Ruari. I have heard many stories about you all."

Ruari took Hannah's hand and kissed it.

"She's a beauty, John. You're a lucky man. Welcome to Clifden, Mrs Fitzgerald. I hope you will forgive our little cottage. It's not up to your Dublin standards."

"We don't want Dublin standards, Ruari," reassured John. Hannah wasn't so sure about that. "That's exactly why we've come – to taste the real Ireland."

"Please call me Hannah, Ruari. I'm sure I will love your home. I feel as if I know every corner of it already."

"Come along then. Hop up. Shawna and Aoife will be getting worried."

John threw up their bags and helped Hannah onto the trap to sit beside Ruari. Then they were off to Cleggan as the bats started to fly over their heads.

# Chapter 26 – Easter 1918

"Wake up, my love. It's a beautiful day." John placed the cup of tea he had brought up for her on the bedside table and kissed her cheek.

Hannah moaned but dutifully hoisted herself up to sit against the pillows as John opened the thin curtains.

"Did you sleep well? You seemed to drop off the moment your head hit the pillow."

"Well, it was a very long day, wasn't it? Coming all the way from Wicklow out to Connemara."

"It was stupid of me to expect you to travel so far, especially with you carrying the babe. Selfish. Forgive me. But I didn't want us to have to go back to Beresford Street and those squalid rooms for a while yet."

John ran his hand over the white-washed stone wall.

"Not that this cottage is anything grand. But it is clean and fresh and the sea air will do you a power of good."

John came and sat on the bed and gave Hannah's feet a squeeze. "Drink your tea and I'll bring you up some hot water so you can wash and dress. Shawna and Aoife are waiting for you before they have their breakfast. Ruari went out hours ago."

The door closed behind John, leaving Hannah alone to survey the room properly. They had come to bed by the light of a single candle last night and she had been unable to inspect anything properly.

So…this was where John and Ailsa had lived as man and wife, where they had slept together - in this very bed no doubt - where their baby daughter had been born and where both of John's beloved girls had died. There were no outward signs of its past life; no pictures, no ornaments, nothing save the plain wooden bed, a pine chest of drawers, a deep blanket box and a spindle-backed chair. But, to Hannah, the room was filled with the passion and pain of

John's first marriage and she was subdued as she thought about all the torment her new husband had lived through. She hoped no such tragedies would shadow their marriage.

Breakfast took some time; Shawna and Aoife asked Hannah so many questions that she managed to eat little more than one slice of delicious soda bread, spread with thick butter and bramble jam. The two women were as shinily scrubbed as the kitchen table, with their smiling, open, green eyes and long hair pinned to the top of their heads, one as silvery as the herrings on the plate, the other dark as the slate floor. Whenever Aoife looked away, Hannah took the opportunity to take a good look at her. Is this what Ailsa had looked like too? So graceful and naturally beautiful with a modest manner about her.

The two women asked after Hannah's father and sister, and about Rowanbridge and Kilkenny. They had heard all about her playing and expressed regret that she had not brought her violin with her.

"But maybe you'll sing for us." Aoife looked at her eagerly. "We could sing together. I could teach you. Ailsa and I used to sing some songs in two parts. I can find those somewhere."

"No. I'm no singer, I'm afraid."

In fact, Hannah had a perfectly nice singing voice but there was no way she was going to let herself be moulded into a second-hand Ailsa by anyone, and certainly not by a beautiful young woman whom, by his own admission, her new husband had once been 'a little bit in love with'. And Hannah was not impressed at the way Aoife touched John so freely, a hand on his shoulder as she passed behind his chair or brushing his hand when he handed her the butter.

"If it's OK with you both, I'm going to take Hannah out to see some of my favourites places, while the weather is looking kindly on us." John lifted Hannah's hand to his lips. That was more like it.

"Can I wash the breakfast things first?" Hannah stood and started to clear the table but was forcibly robbed of the plates by Shawna. She didn't resist.

Although the sky was mostly cloudless, there was a strong breeze coming off the sea, as Hannah and John walked down to Cleggan's small harbour. Hannah was relieved that she had her winter coat on and had borrowed a shawl from Aoife. John threaded her arm through his as they walked along the fine pier.

"We could take a little ferry boat out to Inishbofin, that island over there. It has lovely sandy beaches and the ruins of Cromwell's Barracks. There is an ancient legend that an old woman driving a white cow emerges from the lake on the island whenever a disaster is about to happen. It's about six or seven miles out."

"Well, we have some of Cromwell's ruins in Rowanbridge, you know, and plenty of cows too. I don't think I fancy a long boat journey today, John. Not in my condition."

"I'm sorry, my love. That was a stupid idea." John slipped his hand under Hannah's coat and stroked the gentle curve of her belly. "I must take special care of you." He took out his hankie, wiped the drip from her cold nose and kissed it.

They continued their stroll around the wind-blasted headland, passing fields of cows and sheep, grazing on the vivid green grass, and several ruined stone cottages until they came into the small village of Claddaghduff.

"You must be tired out now, Hannah. Maybe we've come far enough. Have a seat on this rock for a minute. Remember, it's a couple of miles to get back to Cleggan, though I can take us back the shorter way."

"I'm fine. Is that a little church over there?" Hannah pointed down the lane to a low isolated building looking out towards the strand.

"It is. That's Our Lady Star of the Sea. It's a very grand name but a very modest place. Nothing much to see."

"Come on. I want to see it. Is it where you got married – the first time?"

John nodded silently as they walked the couple of hundred yards to the church.

The moment Hannah pushed open the door, she wanted to kick herself. The last memory John would have of this modest church would not be his wedding but his little daughter's funeral, barely six months gone.

Hannah walked up the central aisle and slid along a pew, but John did not join her. He walked over to a side altar where a few candles were burning and lit two himself. He watched the flames grow stronger, then dropped a couple of coins into the box and walked out.

A couple of minutes later, Hannah joined him in the cool breeze.

"I'm sorry. I didn't think. Did you light the candles for Máire and Ailsa?"

"Yes. I always get them a candle each. It's stupid really. I have no faith - but I do have hope. And a flame is a powerful, hopeful symbol. More pagan than Christian I reckon." John took Hannah into his arms. "I have hope for our baby and for our life together." He kissed her tenderly.

They were walking back to the road, hand in hand, when Hannah stopped and turned to John.

"Take me to their graves, John. I'd like to see where they are."

"Ah, that's not so easy, now. There are no village graves here at the church, apart from the odd priest. They're all over on Omey Island." John pointed west, out to the sea.

"You have to get in a boat to see their graves?"

"No, not usually. You can get to Omey Island walking over the sand at low tide. I could even drive the trap over there. But it's a fair stretch from here. And you need to get your timings right or the tide can creep up on you, leaving you wading your way home. I'll take you on the pony if you like. Not tomorrow though. You'll be expected to go to Mass on Good Friday with the De Bhailises. But on Saturday maybe. If you're still keen."

****** 

Hannah hadn't attended a Good Friday mass since she had left the convent. Ruari was taking a day off from fishing and drove Hannah and Shawna in the trap the two miles or so over to Our Lady Star of the Sea; Aoife and John walked behind them.

John declined to join them in church and waved to them as they walked up the path, But, as she and the three De Bhailises contemplated the stations of the cross, Hannah could guess what he was doing: he was crossing over the sands to Omey Island to visit his lost loves' grave. Why, otherwise, hadn't he stayed in the cottage? Hannah shrugged inwardly. She couldn't begrudge him that. And they would soon leave Connemara and all the memories that had been reawakened here for her husband.

The gulls were flying noisily overhead as they came out of the church a couple of hours later. John was standing over in the road, letting the pony munch some grass from the verge as he held its bridle. No-one asked what he had been doing during the service. They didn't need to.

The Good Friday story of betrayal, torture and sacrifice had never before made much of an impact on Hannah, but today she had found herself very moved by it and had even shed a tear at Peter's denial of Christ before the cock crowed. The party's mood stayed pensive and solemn when they returned to the cottage. Ruari took down the family bible and read to himself as Shawna took up her delicate lacework and John immersed himself in Bleak House, leaving Aoife and Hannah to prepare supper.

The peat fire cast little light, so Hannah went over to sit at the kitchen table to peel the potatoes, where the light from the oil lamps shone brightest, next to Shawna.

"Fancy us letting you do some cooking, Hannah. You must have people to do that for you at home."

"I don't mind at all, Shawna. I can't really cook at all, apart from eggs. I am a world-class cooker of eggs. But there'll be no-one to cook for us when we're back in Dublin, so, unless we plan to starve, the sooner I start learning a few recipes the better."

John looked up and smiled at his young wife and she silently mouthed "I love you" back at him.

After they had all demolished the fish stew and drunk several cups of tea with fruitcake, Aoife began to sing. It was a slow and haunting traditional melody, the words in Irish totally unintelligible to Hannah, but the melody told her it was about love. Aoife's pure voice rose towards the end.

"That was beautiful, Aoife. Thank you." Hannah's thanks were genuine. "I'm very pleased you didn't let me embarrass myself with trying to match your singing. What was the song all about?"

"It's called Ar Éirinn Ní Neosfainn Cé Hí which roughly means For all Ireland, I'd not tell her name. It's about a farmer who sees a young girl on his land. He is captivated not just by her beauty but also by her kindness and generosity. She has golden hair which reaches the ground, and cheeks like roses. He wishes he could tell her his story and that he wants to look after her and place her in his heart, but he will not tell her name to anyone."

"That's lovely. Are all traditional love-songs so sad?"

"I don't think it is sad, necessarily. It's just about his reticence and modesty. I like to think that eventually he will pluck up the courage to tell her and that it will all end happily." Aoife smiled conspiratorially at John.

"I think many Irishmen need a bit of a prod before they share their feelings." John took Hannah's hand and kissed it. "Come on now, we should be off to bed."

As they lay together in bed, John tried to read but the meagre light of two candles defeated him and he closed the book.

"Goodnight, my love."

"You don't need light for what I have in mind, John." Hannah turned to face her still new husband and ran her hands over his chest. "It's still our honeymoon, you know."

He kissed her deeply while running his hands down her back and squeezing her bottom.

"I don't want to disturb anyone in the cottage, and you've become mightily noisy, you know."

"That's no excuse, John Fitzgerald. It's not like we didn't have plenty of practice at the Academy keeping quiet. I remember how to do that. It makes it even more exciting, I think."

******

The next day, John took Hannah off in the pony and trap to explore Clifden, with a short shopping list from Shawna to complete. As they made their way back, a sudden desire to explore more of John's past hit Hannah.

"John will you take me to see that terrible school you told me about. The one at Letterfrack."

John had taught at the industrial school, run by the Christian Brothers, after his marriage to Ailsa.

"Why do you want to see that dreadful place, Hannah? It's just full of wretched, abused boys and wicked Brothers."

"I know that. And I'm sorry if it brings back awful memories for you. But I just feel that it would help me understand you better and what you've been through."

John looked grim but, instead of turning the pony off on the road towards Cleggan, they continued through Moyard and on to Letterfrack.

St Joseph's Industrial School was set back from the road, behind tall wrought-iron gates, and overlooked by the misleadingly named mountain, Diamond Hill, which glowered rather than glittered. The building looked much like any other school, with its tidy symmetrical layout and rendered frontage but Hannah could tell from the ashen look on John's face and the whiteness of his knuckles gripping the reins that it was a place of horror for him.

"Appearances are so deceptive. It looks like any proper school. You can't tell from here, can you, that what goes on behind those neat windows is an utter abomination. How many places must that be true of? You have to work there – or be a pupil there - to know. It needs to be shut down. I should have done more."

"You did what you could, John. Don't blame yourself. I'm sorry I asked to see it."

"The shocking thing is that there are several lay members of staff and they must all know what goes on. Some of them were decent enough people and some were quite kind and did what they could for the boys. But their silence is part of the oppression. I could never understand why Ailsa's faith wasn't rocked by what she saw with me in there. It's not God's doing, John, she'd say. God has given us free will and we can choose to do evil or to do good with our lives."

Hannah cursed that she had caused John to think of Ailsa again.

"Come on. Let's get back. Shawna will be waiting for the pork, and you need to cheer up. We're on our honeymoon, remember."

John put his arm around Hannah's waist and kissed her, then set the pony off trotting back to Cleggan.

# Chapter 27 – April 1918

The last few days of their honeymoon in Connemara had been a pleasurable mixture of the breezy outdoors and the cosy indoors. John had taken Hannah on several walks along the shore - no shortage of shells strewn at their feet – but he hadn't taken her over to Omey Island to visit the graves of Ailsa and Máire and she didn't ask again. Hannah was grateful that she hadn't had to watch John stand mournfully over a previous wife's remains.

On Easter Saturday night, there had been a small ceilidh in Cleggan's solitary bar; Hannah had been amazed to see what a good dancer John was. They had never danced together before. It wasn't unlike playing music together; they shared an unspoken feeling for the rhythms and an understanding of what steps would work best for each song.

Hannah had watched the fiddler in the midst of the small band; a young lad with black hair and mischievous eyes. Not bad at all, she thought. She conceded to herself that he could play the dance tunes better than her but she reckoned he wouldn't even be able to begin to play the Bach Partita. Hannah was hit by a pang of guilt; she hadn't played her violin for over a month and she hadn't even had the courtesy to let Felix Brennan know that she wouldn't be continuing with her lessons with him. There was certainly no money for those.

In fact, there was very little money for anything now that they were back in Dublin and living in Beresford Street. John had work doing private tutoring but there was no chance of securing a job in a school without a reference, and, even though he was working every day, he only brought home enough for this lodging and for their basic food, light and a few coals for the fire. Hannah was learning the hard way how to make a little money stretch a long way, buying the cheapest pieces of meat and waiting until just before closing time at the bakery to buy bread at a knock-down price. She disliked cooking in the best of circumstances, so she found feeding themselves from what Aggie would have thrown away at home a sordid and dispiriting business.

But there were better physical pleasures than eating. Going to bed and making love was an excellent way to stay warm. They were cuddled together there now, a short time after eating sausages and leeks for supper. They both had books open; John was reading intently but Hannah's attention was wandering.

"I love your body. I love how it's all put together - how your arms fit into your shoulders so perfectly and how your back slopes down to your little bum." Hannah pressed her hand firmly over John's body as she outlined it.

"Yours is so beautiful, even though it's changing a little bit every day." John undid the neck of Hannah's nightdress and opened it. "Your breasts are heavier, and your nipples are much darker, just like chocolate." John bent to lick them. He then stroked the modest mound of her stomach. "And the little bean is getting bigger. Maybe even as big as a turnip now I reckon." Hannah laughed at the image. "And he's starting to make himself public. When are you going to tell your friends?"

Even though Hannah was regularly exchanging letters with Ellen and Maisie she hadn't yet told them about her pregnancy.

"I will. Soon. I just don't want them to think that's why you asked me to marry you - even though I suppose it was." John stroked his wife's cheek tenderly.

Ellen had become an indispensable source of news about the Academy and their friends there. John's teaching position had been filled by an elderly spinster whose taste in literature inclined towards the whimsical and magical and whose physical presence, as Ellen bluntly observed, would offer no temptation to girl, boy, man, woman nor beast.

Hannah and John were relieved to hear that both Seamus and Sourja were still writing letters to their friends at the Academy, though their accounts of their war experiences - Seamus's in particular - made harrowing reading. He was not just horrified and terrified but seemed full of black depression at the futility of the whole shambles around him. Ellen tried to sound cheerful as she recounted his messages, but her anxiety for her fiancé was unmistakable.

Maisie relayed all the news about where the students would be off to at the end of the summer ahead. Eamonn had secured a place at Trinity to read for a degree in Economics. Visha hadn't been able to breach those venerable gates, but she had not been daunted by Trinity's refusal to give her a place to study medicine and had instead applied to Edinburgh University, which had accepted her. Daniel would be off to Cambridge to read mathematics after the summer. Maisie's letters were full of praise and awe for her friends' accomplishments, but she didn't say what her own plans were for after she left the Academy.

Neither Ellen nor Maisie ever said much about Mrs Fitzgerald. Hannah assumed that they wanted to avoid upsetting John but, surely, if there had been anything significant to report, they would find a way, so she assumed that her mother-in-law continued in her own indomitable way. If she was missing her son, she was not going to let anyone know, least of all him.

Hannah looked up from the bed at the stained ceiling as noisy footsteps rumbled over her head. Voices raised in anger. Children crying. God, what a dreadful place this was. Reading, as she was, about Emma Woodhouse's ordered and privileged life was not transporting her to a romantic bygone era but making her feel extremely annoyed and hard-done-by. Hannah looked across at her husband, smiling and laughing occasionally, as he read Shaw's Pygmalion while one hand idly twisted a lock of her hair on the pillow.

Hannah lifted his hand from her head to kiss it and with her other hand took the copy of the play and closed it.

"Is it good, then?"

"It's very witty indeed. I'd love to hear you read the part of Eliza Doolittle. She's a bit of a ragamuffin but she manages to get the better of a professor and ends up as a very refined and elegant lady."

"I'm already a very refined and elegant lady." Hannah removed her nightdress.

"Indeed, you are extremely elegant, with or without your clothes on. But maybe not totally refined – thank God." John turned onto his side, scooped up Hannah with one arm and kissed her mouth, neck and breasts as his hand travelled the length of her body until he reached between her thighs. Hannah moaned as he touched her.

"Is it really called a rosebud?" John laughed at Hannah's ignorance.

"No, silly. But I think its proper name is very ugly; it's called a clitoris. Makes it sound very hard and spiky when it's so soft and divine. Though not always soft…"

He kissed her mouth while rubbing her with increasing pressure. Then he stopped. He brought his hand up to his face and gasped. Hannah opened her eyes. John's hand was covered in blood.

John jumped out of bed and brought Hannah a towel. She was rigid with shock. He threw on his clothes.

"Don't worry, my love, but I need to go and get a doctor."

"No. Don't leave me, John."

"I must, Hannah. I'll be back soon," John dashed out of the bedroom and she heard his panicked steps recede down the stairs. Only a few minutes later he burst back into the room. Hannah looked terrified, rocking and moaning, holding the towel between her legs.

"Jack downstairs has gone to get a doctor for us, so that I can stay here with you. Don't worry, my darling, I'm with you. Look, I think you should lie back and I'll raise your hips onto the pillows."

John arranged all the pillows and blankets under Hannah until her legs were higher than her head, then he sat by her holding her hand and making reassuring noises while she wept and groaned. Nearly half an hour had passed before a very grumpy old man puffed his way up the stairs and into the room, followed by their neighbour.

"Good evening to you. Leave her to me now, man."

John went over to the door and took Jack's arm, "Thanks, friend. We'll be fine now. I'll see you tomorrow."

The doctor was at the bedside.

"How do you do. I am Dr O'Driscoll." He turned to shake John's hand and then began to examine Hannah without looking into her eyes.

"There's not much I can do to be frank that you haven't already done. Madam, you need to stay calm."

The doctor gently removed the bloodied towel from between Hannah's thighs.

"The flow is not too strong. All you can do is stay on your back, madam, until the bleeding stops. I've known babies born when their mother has bled a little for all nine months. You might like to put more towels under yourself though, unless you have the money for a new mattress on top of my bill."

For the next two days, John barely left Hannah's side, sending messages to his pupils that he was unable to attend them this week. He washed her gently in the morning and evening, brought her the chamber pot and then removed it, filled with blood-stained urine. He read Emma to her and some Yeats and made her cups of tea and slices of buttered toast. If the most devoted and loving attention could achieve anything, Hannah would have stopped bleeding. But the pile of soiled towels in the bucket kept growing. On the afternoon of the third day, Hannah felt a sharp cramp and then a bloody mess slithered out of her. When

Dr O'Driscoll inspected it an hour later, he declared that it was all over and the baby was lost.

Hannah and John cried together that night, making their pillows as sodden as the towels beneath them.

# Chapter 28 - May 1918

John folded the newspaper and stood up from their rickety breakfast table.

"It's unbearable. Did you read this? The Germans are nearly at Paris. I wouldn't put it past the government to have another shot at Irish conscription, though I hope we'd put up as much resistance as we did last May. And all these men blinded by tear gas at Éstaires – just barbaric. I thought the Americans would have made more of a difference by now."

"I know. I worry so much about Seamus. Ellen must be out of her mind. She's pretty sure he's in France somewhere."

"I just cannot bear to think of him and Sourja, out there facing bullets and bombs when they were just schoolchildren a year or so ago."

"Well, so was I, but you seem to find me quite grown-up now." Hannah grabbed John's passing hand and put it to her lips. "Anyway, how would you solve this situation now, given you don't believe in the war."

"I don't believe in starting wars, but, once it's begun, best to win it as quickly as possible with the fewest English, French and German lives lost - and none from Ireland as far as I can help it. These idiot English generals couldn't win a game of tiddlywinks, it seems."

John gathered some books together into his leather bag and put on his overcoat.

"I'll see you tonight, my darling." And, with a tender kiss on Hannah's cheek, he strode out of the door.

Hannah sat with her half cup of tea and surveyed the cramped room which was now their home. She put her hand on her flat stomach where there should have been a small bump. Tears filled her eyes but she was determined not to cry any more. It was very sad, yes, but she told herself there would be plenty more babies coming along and that the pregnancy had served one purpose by binding John to her.

And, in a funny sort of way, maybe it was more convenient not to be pregnant. There could be no whispering about the date of any premature birth and there really wasn't room for a baby until they had secured a better place to live. One room on the third floor, sharing a lavatory with five other families, wasn't what Hannah had in mind as a suitable marital home. But it was all they could afford for now.

But Hannah was resourceful. She was now eighteen, a fully-grown woman as far as she was concerned. A couple of weeks after the miscarriage, she had taken it upon herself to earn some money, advertising herself as a violin teacher on a card displayed in the window of the corner shop.

Three afternoons a week she walked - or bought a bus ticket if it was raining - to go and teach children in their own front rooms after they got home from school. It was awful. Most of them had no talent nor any interest in playing though there was one rather promising fourteen-year-old lad whom Hannah had decided to enter in the Feis Ceoil next year. His dedication reminded her that she had once been a promising young player practising hard for the great music festival.

But there were some consolations. Three weeks ago, she and John had been invited for Sunday lunch to her Aunt Lily's. Hannah had gorged on roast chicken and John had enjoyed a glass of wine and conversation about the state of politics and art. No mention was made of the lost baby and it was clear that Hannah had been restored to favourite niece status. Hannah was hopeful that from now on, at least once a month, they would be able to go and enjoy a civilised lunch in Pembroke Street.

Stasia had also declined to refer to the miscarriage in her weekly letters although Hannah had given her the sad news straight away. But her Dada had sent her a letter with five pounds in it and the message "Very, very sorry to hear your upsetting sad news. Sending you a big hug and kiss, my beautiful girl. Get yourself a treat. Your loving Dada." She knew her father would have shed as many tears for the lost baby as her, though perhaps not as many as John.

Hannah looked around at the drab room, the threadbare rugs and the curtains so thin they barely kept out any light. Her Dada would not be happy to see her forced to live like this. She found some writing paper and sat at the table thinking how she could best orchestrate the next phase of their life.

*"Dear Dada,*

*I hope you and Stasia are well and enjoying the fine spring weather for the crops. The hens must be laying well by now.*

*I have gotten myself a few violin pupils, which brings in a bit of extra money to supplement what John earns. But it is still very hard, Dada. Everything is so expensive.*

*How is Jimmy getting on managing the pub? I bet Stasia has to watch him like a hawk, which can't be easy with you away over in the villa. Stasia tells me he and Eileen plan to marry in the summer and then they'll move into the old house.*

*But I've been thinking. How would you feel if me and John came to Rowanbridge to live in the old house instead? We could keep an eye on Jimmy then. John could maybe get a job in Kilkenny as a teacher. It'd be easier for him away from Dublin. And you'd have me back home so I could keep Stasia off your back. And, of course, we do hope to have babies soon and then you could be a proper granddad to them. Doesn't look like Stasia'll be the marrying sort, does it?*

*I won't mention it to John until I know you like the idea and then I'll get him on side before you say anything to Stasia. It'd be lovely to be home for the summer.*

*Sending you all my love,*

*Your darling daughter,*

*Hannah*

*PS Give Aggie and Honey a hug from me."*

Hannah sealed the envelope and balanced it on the mantelpiece ready to be popped into a post-box on her way to her afternoon lessons.

\*\*\*\*\*\*

A few weeks later, Hannah was sitting in a café, avoiding the eyes of the waitress who had already asked her twice what she would like to order and was clearly resentful that a prime table was being taken up by a non-ordering customer on a busy Saturday in Grafton Street. Hannah buried her nose back in her book and discreetly slid a few sugar lumps from the bowl on the table into her clean handkerchief.

"Hannah!" Ellen's familiar squeal made the other customers look over momentarily as three girls – no, young ladies – rushed over to the solitary reader.

Hannah returned the warmth of their embraces; even Visha's normally cool and reserved demeanour couldn't hold out against the thrill of seeing their erstwhile roommate, now all married and full of composure. Maisie's hug came last but lasted the longest.

So much to chat about. Hannah hadn't seen her friends since she had walked out of the door of the Academy in February but they had exchanged news regularly. Even Letitia Fitzgerald wasn't so mean as to forbid letter exchanges.

"Show us the ring then," demanded Ellen. "Oh… is that it?

"It's all about what it means, isn't it, Hannah?" Maisie to the rescue.

"I hope the day for fine jewellery will come, but not while John is eking out a living for us as a tutor. He needs a proper job, running the Academy maybe when his mother finally forgives him - and me."

"Good luck with that one. I don't see Letitia Fitzgerald being one to bend easily."

"Maybe when I present her with a grandchild she will relent."

"Are you pregnant already then?" Ellen's cynicism melted quickly at the thought of babbies.

"No, but I'm sure it won't take long."

"That means you're doing it all the time? He-he! Well, it's one way to stay warm. Go on, tell us what it's like. I've spent a fair old time dreaming what it would be like to be in bed with John Fitzgerald after all, before you came and whipped him away from under my nose. I bet it's fantastic and that he's a great kisser."

"Ellen, honestly. You are just too shocking." Visha voiced her disapproval but it didn't stop her listening intently to the juicy snippets Hannah was prepared to share. But the failed pregnancy was kept secret.

As they ate their lunch, the friends exchanged all the new news they had. Sourja's ship had come under fire but had survived so far, though he had witnessed a fellow officer lose a leg which had severely traumatised him.

"I am going to study to become a doctor," Visha told Hannah," It seems the most useful thing I can do with my life - and who knows how long this war will last. I tried for Trinity, but they turned me down. I have no idea why. It's not as if I'm a Catholic, am I? Anyway, I shall go to Edinburgh where many women before me have studied medicine."

"Congratulations, Visha. Maisie had told me. It's a lot more useful than teaching children to play the violin, especially when most of them hate doing it!"

Visha and Ellen only had one more month at the Academy though Maisie revealed that she was staying on for another year, as she wouldn't be eighteen until October.

"What about you, Ellen? asked Hannah. "What are you going to do?"

"I have no idea. My mother keeps saying I should learn to do secretarial work so I can sit down all day, rather than teach. Fat lot of good learning ancient Greek is going to be out in the big, bad world. Mrs F. should have been teaching me how to type instead. But I really don't want to do anything except be married to Seamus. God knows when that day will come. He hardly ever writes to me now and when he does he just talks about how hideous it all is, how he has to go to sleep with the noise of men screaming from their injuries or crying for their mammies. He sometimes even forgets to tell me loves me. He wrote about a man – boy really – who he had befriended who got into such a state of terror that he couldn't fight any longer. He was court martialled and shot, like a dog. So tragic."

"I think we should be hopeful. The Americans seem to be making a real difference as far as I can tell from the reports." Maisie was an avid reader of all the newspaper coverage of the war and was always the voice of hope.

"Let's drink to that." The four clinked their lemonade glasses and teacups.

An hour later, as they each paid their share of the bill, Maisie said she hoped they'd be able to do this again, every month after the summer maybe, for as long as everyone was in Dublin.

"Well, I think you'll have to count me out. We'll be out of Dublin by next month I hope, and back home in Rowanbridge."

"Oh, Jeezus. Now you tell us." Ellen glared at Hannah, her hands indignantly on her hips. "How on earth have you persuaded John to leave Dublin? He'll go mad in the country without some culture and his politics."

"He doesn't know yet. But I know he'll be very happy to go because it will make me happy and he tells me all the time that that's all he wants in life. I'm going to tell him tonight. I've arranged it all with my father. He's telling my sister today too. I know for a fact she'll be a hell of a lot trickier than John about it."

"Well, good luck." Ellen dropped her arms and kissed Hannah on the cheek. "I know you'll get your way in the end but, I bet you, you'll be back within the year. You'll miss Dublin too you know. I thought you were going to be a famous concert violinist."

"Who knows? There's plenty of time for that. I'm not going to stop playing. And I am only eighteen you know."

"Old enough to be married and trying for babies it seems but not old enough to use your amazing talent. It's a crying shame."

"You've changed your tune. You were always the one moaning about the noise of Hannah practising." Visha enjoyed confronting Ellen with her inconsistencies.

"That's completely different. I wouldn't have to listen to that racket anymore, just go along to her swanky concerts as her very, very dearest friend, Mrs Seamus Flaherty."

Amid laughs and hugs they went their separate ways.

After giving the lesson, Hannah walked back home. She stopped at the local grocer at their road end and, with some of today's earnings, she splashed out on a few rashers and some mushrooms so that she could cook John his favourite supper. That would put him in an excellent mood for when she shared her plans for their new life in Rowanbridge.

# Chapter 29 – July 1918

"No, no, Aggie. Please don't try and carry that upstairs. It's full of books and weighs a tonne."

"Ah, go on wid ya', Mr Fitzgerald. I'm used to carrying stuff a lot heavier than this."

"But really, there's no need. I would be much happier doing it myself."

"Well, OK then. It's very kind of you."

"Not at all. And, please, just call me John."

John took the trunk off Aggie with a smile. She blushed and gave an awkward little curtsey. She had never been treated so considerately in her entire life. And what a handsome gentleman he was - with lovely soft hands. Aggie could see why Hannah had fallen for him.

"John, are you down there?"

Hannah was already upstairs deciding which bedroom they should choose for themselves. John lugged the trunk up to the landing as Hannah walked out of the upstairs drawing room with Honey in her arms.

"Come and see. What do you think? We could have Dada's old bedroom – it's the biggest – but I like this one at the back. It was always kept as the guest bedroom so it's hardly been used and everything looks fairly new. And it looks out over the yard and the veg patch and the fields beyond rather than the busy street. And my lovely hens when they come home too."

Although Hannah had been tempted to take over the master bedroom on grounds of status, there were too many painful memories of seeing her mother decline and eventually die in that bed.

"My darling, whatever makes you happy is just perfect with me." Of all the concessions John had made to Hannah – and God knows there had been many – he really didn't give a damn about the choice of bedroom. He was more concerned about living in a small village with no access to theatres or concerts or political meetings. In fact, he wondered whether he'd meet any other people who supported the cause of an independent Ireland. Maybe there'd be plenty in Kilkenny itself, but he suspected that Rowanbridge was a political desert. People seemed much more concerned about the state of the harvest and who was walking out with whom. He just hoped his wife would not revert to an interest in parochial trivia.

John took the cat from Hannah's arms and placed it on the floor, then picked up his wife, threw her onto the big bed and leapt up beside her.

"We shall do just fine in this room," he said, kicking off his shoes.

"And my old room, next door, will be perfect for a nursery."

John kissed Hannah tenderly.

"All in good time, my love. We're in no rush."

"What do you think of the bed." Hannah gave a little bounce. "Is it comfy enough, do you think?"

"Any bed that has my beautiful wife in it will feel like it's made of fairy gossamer. I look forward to making babies in it with you for years to come." John turned, gathered up Hannah in his arms, and began showering her with little kisses. She laughed and pushed him away, then looked seriously into his eyes.

"Too late for the first one though."

"Too late? What does that mean?"

"It's means that we've already made a baby – in that shithole of a bed in Beresford Street! I wanted to wait until we arrived here and started our new life before telling you."

John said nothing, but gazed into Hannah's eyes, a tiny smile on his lips and a tear in the corner of his eye, before bestowing on her a deep and soulful kiss.

"Oops, I beg your pardon, Mr Fitzgerald." Aggie had burst into the bedroom carrying two suitcases.

"Don't you worry, Aggie." John stood up and took the cases from her. "We were just celebrating the good news. Hannah is going to have a baby."

Aggie did a little jig and clapped and ran downstairs to make tea.

"And call me John." He shouted happily at her disappearing back. Five minutes later Aggie called them down; the tea was ready. John jumped off the bed and held out his hand to help Hannah rise.

"Come on, Mrs Fitzgerald. Let's toast the start of our new life with a cup of Aggie's best," and he slipped his shoes back on hastily before following his wife downstairs.

Aggie had set up a tray in the parlour rather than the kitchen.

"Try a piece of my barm brack, Mr Fitzgerald. I soak the fruit in hot tea which keeps the cake nice and moist."

"It's delicious, Aggie. And remember, it's John."

John delighted Aggie by eating two slices and then went off to take all the musical paraphernalia – the treasured gramophone, their instruments and stands – up to the drawing room, forbidding Aggie to carry another stick.

"No, you just sit and chat to Hannah. She's missed you very much, Aggie."

The two women took out the tea things to the kitchen and Hannah lifted Honey out of her Dada's old fireside chair, watching Aggie potter about clearing away the cups and plates as she sat and stroked the ginger cat on her knee.

"What a grand man you have landed there, Hannah McDermott. I hope you deserve him."

"Hannah Fitzgerald, you mean. I know. I'm very lucky. But then so is he. I'm sure Dada and Stasia will soon grow to love him and see him for the angel he is. Is Stasia very mad?"

"Hopping mad, I'd say, judging by the tightness of her lips and how mean she is to your Dada. But you'll be able to judge for yourself tonight."

"Ha-ha. I've got the house. I've got Honey. And I've even got you, my Aggie." Hannah leapt up and seized Aggie's waist and spun her round. "She must be spitting tacks about losing you. But you're mine now. All mine."

"Well, it took me all of two seconds to decide which house I'd prefer to be a slave in. At least with you, I get to have a laugh from time to time. Honey gets her Mammy back. And it's grand to be back in the thick of it on Main Street instead of buried away in that stuffy old 'villa' away from all the life of the village."

"With the men from the pub. Don't pretend. I know you."

"Yeah, I like the fellas well enough, but not that one." Aggie pointed through the kitchen window. "Disgusting. See? Jimmy Boyle pissing in the yard when the privy is just a few feet away. I shall have to get a bucket and wash it down or it'll stink to high heaven. Maybe Mr Fitzgerald can give him a telling off and stop him taking liberties."

******

Just before six o'clock, Hannah and John left the house to walk to the other side of the village to have supper with James and Stasia. This would be the first time they had all been together since the frosty wedding ceremony back in March and it would be the first chance for John to create a good impression. He was extremely anxious.

"Remember. Tell them that you will be looking for a job first thing tomorrow ready for the new school term. And that you know what hard work is and that you want to give me every comfort."

"Well, that's all true. But I'm not going to pretend to be something I'm not. Are you going to tell them about the baby?"

"Not just yet. Let's leave it another month, just to be sure."

It was a shimmering summer evening. Hannah stopped to sniff the roses and the phlox in the front gardens along

Main Street, and several people waved at Hannah from their front windows or doffed their hats as they walked by on the pavement, happy to see one of their own back home in Rowanbridge.

As they passed the Post Office, a church bell rang out.

"That's the Angelus bell. I bet you never noticed it in Dalkey but here people observe it twice a day. That's something that'll be very different for you. Much more religion around everywhere. In fact, come to think of it, all the schools will expect you to be Church of Ireland or a Catholic. There's nowhere in Kilkenny like The Academy where you can believe what you like – or nothing at all."

"Well, I would do almost anything for you, my love, but that's a boundary I'm not prepared to cross, as you well know."

"Oh, I know alright. You and your damned principles."

As they turned left at the crossroads towards the villa, they saw a solitary drinker outside McLoughlin's bar, nursing a pint of Guinness and gazing into the distance.

"Good evening, Tricky. How are you on this fine evening? Can I introduce you to my husband, John Fitzgerald. John, this is Patrick Byrne. The Byrnes are old friends of our family and now are Father's and Stasia's neighbours."

"I'm very pleased to meet you, Patrick. And, some time, you must tell me all the stories about Hannah growing up that she probably doesn't want me to hear." John laughed as he took Tricky's filthy hand and shook it warmly.

Tricky ignored John but winked at Hannah. "Smart one there, Hannah McDermott."

"I'm Hannah Fitzgerald these days, Tricky. But I forgive you - even I forget sometimes. We're off up to my father's now for supper. Would you like to walk up with us?"

Tricky shook his head and indicated the half-glass of stout.

John and Hannah continued their walk towards the river, leaving Tricky with his pint and good-natured promises of meeting up again soon, none of which Tricky responded to. When she was sure Tricky was out of earshot, Hannah gave John the full lowdown on the Byrnes, including the unwelcome proposal that she had received from Tricky's younger brother, Nicholas, a couple of years previously.

"So, I feel bad for Tricky, him being the older son but always made fun of because he's no good at chat and what with his squint and everything. And Nicholas is determined he's going to get his hands on the family inheritance and leave Tricky out of the frame, assuming he comes out of the war alive, of course. He has a wife waiting for him now, all ready to reproduce. Everyone says Tricky is 'slow' – they mean an idiot – but I don't think he's stupid at all. He sees everything but just keeps it to himself. By rights, Tricky should be the one to inherit."

They passed in front of the school and the church. Hannah debated whether to take John in to see her mother's grave but decided that it should wait a while. After all, she hadn't been to see his dead wife's grave so maybe it wasn't fair to expect him to care about her dead relations.

When they reached the front door of the villa, Hannah tidied John's hair and straightened his tie. They both took a deep breath before they knocked.

James came to the door, greeted Hannah joyfully and shook John's hand warmly, but it was undeniably awkward meeting Stasia again. Her face was frozen into a mask of disapproval as they sat down to supper. After the soup, things thawed a little. Hannah and her father kept the conversation going between them, with gossip about various village residents and the state of the businesses; John chose to ignore Stasia's barbed comments about the war effort, Sinn Fein and the independence movement for the sake of domestic peace. They were obviously aimed at him but there would be plenty of time to cross swords with his sister-in-law on political matters once he had been accepted properly into the family.

"So, let's be clear. There's no need for you two to poke your noses into the comings and goings at the pub; Jimmy Boyle is in charge of all that." Stasia had accepted that Hannah had won her way into the house but there was no way she was going to let her into the business.

"Well, wouldn't it be helpful for us to keep an eye on him? I'm going to be at home all day while John's out working. I'm not exactly the sort to take up embroidery."

"I am more than capable of ensuring Jimmy Boyle does his job without your help. Practice your violin. Isn't that what you're supposed to be doing?"

"Yes, but I can't do that all day long. I'd end up with a lop-sided chin."

"Feed the poultry then. Stroke your cat. Help Aggie out with the cooking. You'll find some way to stay busy, I'm sure."

"Do you play backgammon, John?" James had spent a lifetime restoring peace. "I haven't had a game in a while." James shuffled over to the walnut sideboard and took out a green leather case.

"I'd love to give you a game, Mr McDermott, but I'm not very good, mind. I haven't played since I was about twelve, playing with my father. But let's give it a go."

However good or not John was at backgammon, his new father-in-law was definitely going to win tonight.

# Chapter 30 – December 1918

One day they were at war, and then, suddenly - three weeks ago now - they were at peace, or so it said in the newspapers. There was little to show for it in Rowanbridge. It was still hard to get hold of tea and coffee and impossible to get any oranges, as Stasia bemoaned.

But those families with sons fighting in some part of Europe or across the British Empire silently thanked God and wondered what sort of men would be coming home to them.

Two Saturdays ago, Father Stephen had organised an evening service of thanksgiving in the church for the peace, which was followed by an informal knees-up at both McLoughlin's and McDermott's Bar. Apparently, Father Stephen had been seen dancing with Aggie and then singing at the top of his voice at gone midnight walking home along Main Street. Guinness was not in short supply at least.

Normally, Hannah would have been at the centre of any celebration in the village but, the day after peace was declared, she had lost her second baby, and had now taken up permanent residence in her bed. She was refusing to face anyone, not even her father, who called in regularly to check on her recovery but was not allowed upstairs. James had had scarcely two months to rejoice at her pregnancy before it had been cut short. Aggie would sit the old man down in his favourite kitchen armchair, give him a cup of tea, a piece of cake, and an update on the health – physical and mental - of his younger daughter. Then he would sigh heavily, pick up his hat and make his sad way back to the villa, leaving messages of love for his darling girl. John, Aggie and Honey were the only ones allowed to see Hannah's red and puffy face, drained of all tears.

This tragic loss was nothing like the one in March. This time, despite Dr O'Connor doing what he could to delay her premature contractions, she had gone through a real labour and delivered a real child – a perfect baby boy just six months in the womb but stillborn. John spent hours afterwards just sitting and holding her, telling her how much he loved her and that everything would be fine soon, but, in truth, his grief was as strong as hers – maybe stronger even – but held inside as much as he could manage.

Hannah had refused to look at her dead baby but John had held the tiny body through the night; then, as the dawn broke, he wrapped it in a white sheet and took it to bury somewhere on the McDermott land. There was no way he was letting his son be laid to rest in a churchyard.

Stasia was utterly scandalised by this and consulted with Father Stephen about what the proper etiquette should have been, sending her sister a note afterwards about how the baby's soul would never escape Purgatory unless it was given a proper Catholic burial, but Hannah barely read the message and anyway thought that, if there was a God at all, he would not let an innocent baby suffer in Purgatory. Maybe her own Mammy would take care of her dead grandson up in heaven. But why was this happening to her? Did she deserve to suffer?

Aggie brought Hannah eggs, cooked in every possible form, to tempt her to eat, but they remained cold and unloved on the side table for Aggie to collect mid-morning and feed to the cats.

And now it was December. It was gone half past ten; Hannah was still lying in bed, reading, Honey curled up beside her, when Aggie appeared with a bowl of warm water to encourage her to wash and change her nightdress.

"Come on now, you mucky madam. Let's get you freshened up."

Hannah allowed herself to be disrobed, soaped, rinsed and dried, all the while looking gloomily past Aggie out of the window.

"I've been cursed, Aggie,"

"What are you talking about, you eejit. Plenty of women lose babies and go on to have plenty of healthy ones."

"No. She has cursed me. I should never have gone to Cleggan and slept in her bed. Oh God, and even made love in her bed."

"Who are you talking about, you mad woman?"

"John's first wife. She died in that bed and so did their daughter. She is never going to let me have his baby."

"You're raving, my girl. I don't have time for all this nonsense." Aggie gathered up the dirty laundry, the bowl and towel and left Hannah to her melancholy muttering.

An hour later, John appeared with a tray of tea and a letter.

"You have a letter from Dublin, my darling. Could it be from your Aunt Lily? It's not from my mother anyway. Still not a peep from her."

"Let me see. Oh, it's from Ellen." Hannah sat upright and opened the letter eagerly. As John poured her some tea, she read hastily.

"Come on then. What's the news?"

"Well, Ellen is back home living with her parents, but she has seen Seamus a couple of times. He's fine - nothing broken, no scars or scratches even - but she says he's very low. Not the happy Seamus we all know and love. She's asking to bring him here to see us. She thinks if he could see old friends - and maybe play his viola - it would cheer him up a lot."

"Well, that's a good idea. I'd love to see them. Maybe playing would help you too?"

"Ellen asks how the pregnancy is going. Oh, God. She has no idea of course - how could she know? I'll have to write and tell her. If she could see me right now she wouldn't bet on me being able to cheer anyone up." Hannah let out a giant sob.

"Come on now, my love. It's time to look forward – and I mean both of us." John wiped Hannah's eyes with his handkerchief and helped her blow her nose. "The war is over, there's an election soon, Christmas is coming and then there'll be a brand spanking new year when things can only get better."

"Listen to you. You sound like me." Hannah laughed through her tears.

"Yes, well, I'm all spent now, trying to be the positive one. That, as you know, is your job." John held out his hand and dragged Hannah out of bed and into his arms for a fierce embrace.

"Right, wait there." John dashed into the drawing room, cranked up the gramophone and ran back as Scott Joplin started to boom out. "You know I don't do this really, but today we are both going to dance."

Eventually, Aggie made her way upstairs to see what all the noise was about, only to see Hannah and John whirling around the parlour, making all the silver and china on the sideboard rattle precariously.

"Well, thank God for that. I was on the verge of handing in my notice if you hadn't come out of that stinking bedroom soon."

Hannah was persuaded to dress for the first time in weeks and, at midday, she even made her way downstairs where she sat in the old armchair by the kitchen fire, Honey on her knee, as Aggie stood at the sink, washing John's shirts.

"Yes, you just sit there, your Highness, and watch me scrub away. At least I don't have to be up and down those bloody stairs all day for the tragic heroine. Aww now - don't cry again. I know you're sad but you have a lot to be thankful for."

"I know that. And I am determined to stop moping about."

"The first thing you should do is go and pay your poor Daddy a visit. He's been out of his mind not being able to see you and calling in here almost every day. Have a walk round this afternoon."

"I shall. And I shall show Stasia that I am made of sterner stuff."

Hannah pushed Honey off her knee and walked over to the back door, picking up the jar of chicken feed on her way out to the yard.

"Yeah, they've missed you too," shouted Aggie at Hannah's back.

After a decent lunch, Hannah wrapped herself up warmly and set off for the villa. She refused John's offer to accompany her and decided to go around the back way, down Mill Lane and past the Tower, so as to avoid bumping into any nosey – and sympathetic – neighbours. She couldn't bear the thought of anyone being kind to her just yet.

Leaning on the gate by the Tower was Tricky, busy at his habitual pursuit: twisting the gatepost rope into elaborate knots.

"Afternoon, Tricky. Are you waiting to take the cows up for milking?"

Tricky started, turned and mumbled what was probably a yes.

"Sorry about ... baby." He couldn't look at Hannah.

"Thank you, Tricky. It's very hard but we shall recover from this. No news about Nicholas and Louisa starting a family yet then?"

Tricky shrugged as if to say he didn't know or care.

Hannah reached the villa and knocked on the front door. Eventually, Stasia came to the door, a tall man in a tweed overcoat hovering behind her.

"Hannah! Well, what a surprise. Go on in, Father. I just need to see Mr Hughes here out."

While Stasia concluded whatever business she had been conducting with the said Mr Hughes, Hannah tiptoed into the drawing room to find her father taking forty winks in his armchair. She crept up behind him and covered his eyes.

"Guess who."

James was thrilled to see Hannah up and about. He showered her with love and sympathy.

"A little grandson. That would have been so lovely. We could have taught him to run the farms. But it wasn't to be."

"Dada, you can teach a granddaughter to run a farm too. Stasia's making a pretty good fist of it, surely."

"Oh, she certainly is. She's been interviewing this week for an estate manager to take the load off me. You must have seen one of them leaving. Now the men are coming back from the war, we have a chance of finding someone suitable."

Stasia opened the drawing room door sharply, ushering in Bessie carrying tea, and, once the maid had left again, she sat down to pour.

"I'm very sorry you've been through this, Hannah. Having a child is not a God-given right though, you know. Just because you want something you can't always have it. It's not easy."

"I didn't think it was. But we have been very unlucky."

"Well, now you're up and about maybe that husband of yours can get back to looking for a proper job, not just doing odds and ends of teaching."

Hannah gripped the teacup a little more tightly.

"My friend Ellen, from the Academy, wrote to me this morning. Do you remember her? She got engaged to Seamus, my viola-playing partner, before he went off to the war in January. He's home and unwounded but in a very bad state with his nerves, she says. She wants to bring him down to Rowanbridge to see us and cheer him up."

"Huh. Well, you're going to have to buck yourself up if you're going to try and cheer up someone else, and someone who has been through a greater trauma than you, if you'll forgive me saying."

Hannah glared at her sister and dug her fingers into her palms to prevent any tears forming.

"Every man who has been at the front must have seen some horrors. It's a wonder they can sleep at all." James shook his head.

"Well, like Hannah, they have to put it behind them, Father. Life must go on. I've just met a Mr Hughes who fought in France for four full years but I didn't hear a word of complaint or regret from him."

"Some people have no feelings."

"Nonsense. They just know how to keep them to themselves."

"Now you two, please be nice to each other. Everyone's been having a tough time and we need to be kind and considerate. Who knows what sadness anyone is carrying round with them. Now, Stasia, what did you make of this Mr Hughes? Is he up to the job?"

"He was impressive. He was an accountant before the war so he has all the business acumen and discipline we need. He's looking for a more outdoor life now. Says he will never get enough fresh air after living in trenches for four years even if he lives to one hundred. I liked him. Very promising."

On her way home, Hannah was drawn into the churchyard.

"Did you lose any babies, Mammy? I don't want to ask Dada. But, if you did, you'll know how I'm feeling right now. But I am not going to let it get me down any longer, for everyone's sake. If you are in heaven, will you do what you can for my two lost babies, please. Get them out of Purgatory if they're in there. That's where Stasia says they are but she's just trying to make me feel bad because I'm not going to mass or anything. She can be a proper bitch at times. Whoops, sorry. Maybe she really does think that mass and praying and stuff would make a difference. If it does, Mammy, can you let me know somehow please."

# Chapter 31 - Christmas 1918

"**OK**, ready for the next one." John was balancing on wooden steps on the pavement tying bunches of holly and ivy to the ropes that were festooned above every window and door, helped by Aggie holding onto the steps and Hannah in charge of dispensing the greenery.

"You'd think the country couldn't get much greener but this is going to be literally the greenest house in the whole county of Kilkenny."

John was on top of the world; Sinn Féin had trounced the opposition in the recent General Election, and he had played a big part in the local campaigning for Cosgrave, giving out leaflets on the streets of Kilkenny and in Rowanbridge itself when he wasn't doing his teaching. Ireland was at last within sight of ruling itself for the first time for centuries.

"You obviously don't want my sister to talk to us ever again. She's never going to forgive you for putting that big poster for de Valera in our front window. But maybe that's no bad thing, eh Aggie?"

The front door of the pub opened and Jimmy Boyle threw beer slops into the road.

"Jimmy. Please use the drain in the yard. It's really doesn't look very good. And the pavement is getting badly stained with all the Guinness thrown over it." Hannah had no problems telling Jimmy Boyle what she thought of his slovenly behaviour.

"Miss McDermott has never had a problem with it and it's her I answer to. Begging your pardon, ma'am."

Aggie gave him a look to kill but Jimmy stared her out, taking a final pull on his cigarette, which he then dropped onto the pavement. He turned and shut the pub door behind him.

"Insolent bastard."

"Aggie, don't let him bother you. The pub is not our concern, you know." John came down the stepladder.

"But Aggie's right to be bothered, John. We're the ones who have to live next to it. I'm going to tell Stasia that she has to sort him out. But come on in now everyone. I'm freezing."

The main Christmas celebrations passed off as tradition dictated: Midnight Mass with plenty of drunken carol-singing; Christmas Day up at the villa with roast pheasant and pork and Father Stephen making up the fifth place at the dining table; Boxing Day tea with everyone - Aggie and Bessie included - playing charades at the Main Street house after stuffing themselves with sausage rolls and trifle.

Eventually, Hannah and John were back to just their own company, which was a relief to John though Hannah preferred a full house at festive times. But there was another missing presence in their lives as they sat on the hearth rug in the drawing room, in front of a glowing fire, sipping Tullamore Dew,

"I would have been very fat by now you know, if we hadn't lost the baby."

"You're perfect, whatever size you are, my love."

"But I'd be more perfect if I could give you a baby, wouldn't I?"

"Don't be silly. I am the luckiest man alive to have you with me here always. I wish I could give you the child you deserve."

"I do want a baby, John, but it's more important to me that you love me. I love you." Hannah kissed John's cheek.

"And I love you, too, my precious girl. I just hope you'll never regret marrying me."

And they stretched themselves out on the rug, taking advantage of the empty house to reacquaint themselves tentatively with each other's bodies, after three celibate months.

They had just two days alone together before Aggie came back to work, recharged and ready to get the house prepared for their guests. There was a lot of huffing and puffing coming from upstairs as sheets were aired, rugs beaten and windows polished until Aggie was satisfied that the two guest bedrooms were fit for sophisticated Dublin visitors.

It was the same physical entity walking through the front door on the afternoon of the 29th as the one who had shared the triumphant stage with Hannah at the Gaiety a year ago now. But the Seamus Hannah ran to welcome looked as if he had been tossed around in the sea for a year and then washed up on the beach, empty and broken. Ellen followed him in, carrying his viola case.

"My darlings. Come on in. Come here and give me a hug." Hannah's joy at seeing her dearest friends again was mixed with loss and sadness. She squeezed Ellen tightly and turned to embrace Seamus, but he drew back.

"Hannah. I thought I might never see you again." Seamus took Hannah's hand in his cold and shaking one.

"You silly old thing." Hannah gave Seamus one of her best beaming smiles but she was shocked to see the state of her friend.

"I've been telling him for the last month he's gone daft. Maybe now you're here, with Hannah right in front of you, you'll admit I was right." Ellen put her hand gently on her fiancé's arm, belying her cross words.

John came forward to shake both Ellen's and Seamus's hands.

"I can call you John now, I suppose," said Ellen with a cheeky wink, "But don't blame me if I slip up and call you Mr Fitzgerald sir, occasionally."

"You will be forgiven, Ellen, though in return I might just ask you to write me an essay on the metaphysical poets."

Aggie came out of the kitchen to say hello, with a big tray of tea and cake which John carried up to the drawing room. There was so much to talk about. Too much. Certainly, too many very big things: a brutal war, a lost child, a huge political upheaval. But they avoided such topics to start with and ended up just gossiping about their mutual friends from the Academy.

"Eamonn, you might know, got into Trinity to read Economics, and Daniel is in England, at Cambridge reading mathematics. Did Hannah tell you? No surprises there, eh John? Visha has gone off to Edinburgh to do medicine. She's enjoying it but says that Scotland is even colder than Ireland. Isn't it amazing how well they've all done! Mrs F. is proud as a peacock."

"I wish I could have made her that proud and happy." John smiled ruefully.

"Oops, sorry. Have you not seen your Mother still, John?"

"No. Not since March. I write to her at least once a fortnight but I get nothing back."

Hannah took John's hand. "I think it's disgraceful." She felt free to share her frustration with her closest friends in a way that she couldn't with her sister and father. "Maybe if he'd been off fighting in the war, risking his life, she'd treasure her son a bit better."

John patted the back of Hannah's hand. "All in good time, my love. Don't fret. It takes a lot for my mother to change her mind once she has taken a decision. But I'm sure it will happen. Maybe if we had a child she would come round…" John regretted what he had said the instant it left his mouth and he attempted to cover up his faux pas.

"Seamus, how do you feel about a spot of playing before supper? Hannah has been practising the Mozart duos for you whenever she has a spare moment. Not that she's competitive or anything. And I would love to hear you two play together again. You make such a magnificent partnership."

"Ellen has made me bring my viola but I've hardly touched it since coming home. It feels like another age – another planet - when Hannah and I – and you – were performing together. If we'd known the slaughter that was going on in our name as we played I doubt any of us could have done it."

"But that's all over, Seamus." Ellen stood up and brought over his instrument case. "Time to look on the bright side."

"Over? Ha! Not for the maimed, the blinded, the crippled. Not for the bereaved. Not inside my head." Seamus snatched the case from Ellen and flung it down beside his chair. "I'm tired. I can't play tonight anyway. I feel such an idiot for falling for all that jingoistic rubbish. Why on earth did I think I should go off and fight a war that Ireland has no business being in, for God's sake? I'm with you now, John. We need our independence."

"Yes, the sooner Ireland can decide its own course of action the better. I shall keep doing what I can until we get our freedom, even though there is not much political activity round here, not even in Kilkenny. But we got our Sinn Fein man elected this month in Kilkenny. It's a start. Maybe you can get involved in the movement when you feel well again." John smiled at the younger man.

Hannah rose from the sofa and went to sit on the arm of Seamus's armchair. She put her arm around his shoulder.

"Have a good night's sleep, Seamus, and then see how you feel tomorrow. No rush. No-one's making you play. Only if you fancy it. Now, come on down to supper. Aggie will have boiled the cabbage to a pulp if we don't go soon." Hannah took Seamus's violently shaking hand. Ellen shook her head sadly at John.

After supper, they sat in the drawing room again, drinking tea and idly chatting about the election and Seamus's plans to become a solicitor when he was well again.

"We can't get married until I get a job and law training could take me three or four years, even if all goes to plan. I've told Ellen that she shouldn't feel bound by the engagement. I'm sure there's many a Dublin man would love to whisk her away."

"Don't be stupid. Who on earth is going to want a funny old cripple like me? I was lucky to ensnare you, Seamus Flaherty, and you're not getting away that easily. I shall just wait for you." Ellen slipped her arm through her fiancé's and kissed his cheek.

"Well, it's definitely the right idea to pursue a proper profession, Seamus. It's not easy finding work." John stood and went over to the gramophone. "Look at me. No school will consider me without a reference. Can't blame them, I suppose. I've managed to get a decent number of personal students and I teach music to a few more, but it's tough, isn't it my love?"

"We're fine. We manage. Better to eat spuds with the one you love than caviar with anyone else. And we live here for free, so we're lucky." Hannah had chosen not to tell John that her father slipped her a pound note every week, so that she could pay Aggie and other bills.

John beamed at Hannah. "Maybe we can't play tonight. But we can listen. This will bring back some wonderful memories."

John put the recording of The Harp Quartet onto the gramophone, wound it up and then went to sit next to his wife. Yes, so many memories thought Hannah. Who would have predicted she'd now be married to the 'cellist she had fallen in love with as they played this glorious music.

As the second movement began, Seamus leant over and lifted off the needle. "Sorry, I can't listen to it with all that noise downstairs." Drunken singing was coming up from the pub, intruding on the Beethoven.

"Never mind. The competition is a bit loud, isn't it. We have to forgive them. It is Christmas, after all." John took the disc off the gramophone and carefully put it back in its sleeve.

"Do you get that noise all the time?" asked Ellen.

"It's not as bad as that normally. Jimmy lets the punters do what they want. Just one of the things you have to get used to, living cheek by jowl with a pub. I've lived with it all my life. I quite like it, though I doubt John is quite so relaxed. In fact, why don't we go down and join in? I was hardly ever allowed to go into the pub but I'm now a grown married woman." Hannah sprang up and grabbed Ellen's hands.

Seamus shook his head. "Not me. You all go though."

"I'm not sure we'd be welcome, you know, my love," said John.

"Just me and Hannah then? Ah well. Another time maybe. Hannah, how about we have a sing-song up here instead then, and drown them out?"

"Why not, if you want." Hannah looked over at John and he nodded tolerantly.

"Go on then. Let's see if we're a match for them downstairs." John went over to the piano. "Come on, Ellen. Have a look through this pile of songs. I can play for you all."

"How about you, Seamus?" Hannah held out her hand. "You have a fine voice. I remember you singing to me on my seventeenth birthday. Do you recall?"

"Do I recall? I practised that bloody song for weeks in my room. The last time I did any singing I was in a trench with two dead bodies behind me and frozen wet feet. I'll leave it to you girls, thanks."

"Let me see, let me see." Ellen was raking through the sheet music methodically; as one pile of songs shrank a new one of discarded titles grew beside it. Of the four, Ellen was the most expert in popular music. "This one. Please play this, John. Not very Christmassy maybe, but it's one of my favourites." Ellen passed the copy of 'You Made Me Love You' to John.

John started playing and Ellen and Hannah stood by the piano arm in arm, singing along, as Seamus sat and watched people he loved enjoying themselves, a smile slowly growing on his face.

*"You made me love you*
*I didn't want to do it*
*I didn't want to do it*

*You made me want you*
*And all the time you knew it*
*I guess you always knew it…"*

When they finished, Ellen threw herself into Seamus's lap and gave him a long kiss on the lips which was at least partially returned.

"Yep. You, Seamus Flaherty, definitely have the 'brand of kisses that I'd die for'."

\*\*\*\*\*\*

The next morning was bright and sunny and the chatter over breakfast stayed light and frivolous. Everyone - Seamus included - did their best to create a happy carefree atmosphere. And it seemed to be working. Seamus was relaxed and ate heartily, much to Aggie's delight.

"Now then, Mr Flaherty, can I tempt you with another egg? Or maybe some soda bread with my famous rhubarb jam?"

"Infamous jam, you mean Aggie. The jam that even the pigs won't touch."

Aggie made a mock swipe at Hannah's head as she ducked and grabbed the maid fondly around the waist and squeezed hard.

"Well, I think I feel up to getting my viola out. Let's see what horrific noises come out of it. It's been such an age since I played."

"You have to break the ice at some point. And it'll make a change for me to have done more practice than you for once."

"Maybe Ellen will let me take her for a walk around the village while you two play." John looked enquiringly at the young woman.

"I would love that, John. Thanks. Though you know it'll take me an age to get all the way round, don't you, me with my stupid limp? There was a time when I would have given anything to be walking out with John Fitzgerald, you know." Ellen winked at John. "Isn't that so, Hannah?"

"Too late, too late. He's all mine now. Missed your chance, you cheeky besom."

Up in the drawing room, Hannah heard the front door close behind Ellen and John. She opened her violin case and took out the instrument; both players tuned up. Hannah opened her rosin box to wax her bow. There, still, was the broken shell that Seamus had given her on Dalkey beach. She shut the lid quickly.

"What shall we play then?"

"It has to be the Mozart duos, Hannah. Playing those with you were the happiest times of my life."

"Only so far, Seamus. There's lots of happiness ahead for you, big man. You just have to let it happen."

They started to play and fell back into the rhythm of the Mozart as if the last year had never happened and they had never been apart.

"Gosh, that is such wonderful music. What shall we play next?" Hannah put down her violin and started to shuffle through the music in her bag. She felt Seamus's hands on her shoulders. He turned her round to face him.

"Just listen to me for a minute please, Hannah. Let me say what's in my mind – in my heart. I must say this but I shall never say it again." Seamus took both of her hands in his and gently stroked the neat knuckles with his massive thumbs.

"I fell in love with you at the Academy. Head over heels. You know that. I know you know. But I didn't know how to say anything to you. So, I just sat back and watched you slip under John Fitzgerald's spell. It nearly killed me. That's why I had to get away, even though it was to the trenches."

"Seamus, I…"

"No, just hear me out." He put a finger gently onto her lips. "I do love Ellen, but only as a friend. There's no way I can marry her; it would be cruel. I don't love her as I should a wife; I love only you, my dearest, darling Hannah. And maybe it's not too late. I'm alive. I'm not married. You are married of course but you… you don't yet have children."

Seamus pulled Hannah into his arms when he heard her faint, anguished sob and bent her head to his chest.

"I'm so sorry, Hannah. I didn't say that to cause you pain. What I meant was that you could be free - if you want to be. You have no ties apart from your marriage. We will have our own children. Come and live with me. I will always love you and I want to look after you…forever."

Hannah was trembling as she drew away from Seamus.

"You are my very dearest friend, Seamus. I know you would look after me. You would provide for me. I trust you with my life. And yes, I knew that you were in love with me at the Academy. That was lovely. I liked knowing that you were in love with me. I even thought, from time to time, that maybe I was a bit in love with you in return. I could have helped you talk to me about it, I suppose. I'm sorry. But I didn't because I fell in love with John. And I love him more every day. We've had our trials, it's true, but we will overcome them. I will never love anyone but him. I am tied to him for all time."

\*\*\*\*\*\*

The next day was New Year's Eve. After Hannah and John waved goodbye to their friends, they spent the day alone together up in the drawing room, reading new books, sipping whiskey and listening to the recording of Tristan and Isolde, which John had bought his wife as a first Christmas present.

They were sitting on the sofa in front of the fire, Hannah with her legs over John's knees, him gently rubbing her toes. Hannah studied John's finely wrought face – his deep-set eyes and his sensuous mouth - framed by his golden hair, absorbed utterly in a recent volume of Yeats' essays. There was no question that he loved her deeply but was she worthy of him? She had never thought herself unworthy of anything before.

"I don't think Seamus and Ellen will be getting married after all, you know."

John put down his book. "No. That's because he's in love with you, poor chap."

"Yes. I haven't encouraged him though, John. You do know that, don't you?"

"You don't need to do anything for men to fall in love with you, Hannah. We are poor moths drawn to your flame." John kissed her hand softly.

Yes, she thought, this is the man I will love forever. She lifted her legs from John's knee and leapt up.

"Right, enough canoodling. I shall make you some scrambled eggs for your supper and then we can go to bed where you can make passionate love to me on the stroke of midnight."

"Ha! Why shouldn't we start 1919 as we mean to go on."

# Chapter 32 - April 1919

Nicholas Byrne was riding down the lane from the big house as Hannah was marching up it, heading towards him with a determined jaw. She was here to see her father about the news that Aggie had just brought back from her morning errands.

"Good morning, Hannah. And what a grand morning it is. Just look at those flowers."

Hannah looked up at Nicholas, perched high on his dappled grey mare. There was still a slight awkwardness between them, despite nearly three years passing since Hannah had rejected him.

"Morning, Nicholas. You can see why Wordsworth was impressed by a great big crowd of daffodils, though, to be honest, they aren't my favourite spring flower. Rather too yellow for my taste."

Nicholas dismounted. "My mother put some white tulips on my father's grave on Sunday. They looked very fine." Old Mr Byrne had been dead a couple of months now, killed off by the 'flu epidemic along with four others in the village, including a seven-year-old and a newly married girl.

"How is your mother coping?"

"Not well at all. It's a terrible sadness she has. But then, he was nearly seventy, which is a good age I suppose. Not like losing a child, like yourself."

"I can't stay chatting, Nicholas. I must go in. I have some urgent matters to discuss with my father. Please give my regards to your mother and Louisa – and Tricky of course. Though I seem to see him most days. Did you know he's given up going to McLoughlin's bar and now comes to our pub, even though it's a longer walk down?"

"Well, he has all the time in the world to fill. Please pass my best wishes to your father. And I hear that congratulations are in order for your sister. Louisa and I are very happy that Stasia has found happiness at last."

Nicholas tipped his hat to Hannah, remounted and rode off.

Mr Hughes was coming out of Stasia's office carrying several ledgers as Hannah walked into the hall. He looked terrified at the sight of her.

"Good morning, Mrs Fitzgerald. Your sister is in there. Shall I let her know you're here? I know she'd like to talk to you."

"No, don't bother, Mr Hughes. I'm sure she's very busy and I need to see my father - urgently." Hannah glared at the man until he retreated and walked back down the hall.

James was poring over the racing pages in the morning paper, marking off certain runners in that afternoon's meet at Gowran Park that Jimmy Boyle had given him tips for, but he immediately put it aside as Hannah walked in.

"Right then. Give your old Dada a kiss and then sit down. I'm pleased you're here because there's some big news..."

"I know already. Aggie told me. How come she got to know before me? And I've just had Nicholas Byrne, of all people, ask me to pass on his congratulations to Stasia."

"I have no idea how Aggie knew. Servants. They do gossip so. Maybe Bessie told her and the Byrnes' cook at the market this morning. But I only found out yesterday myself. I had no idea what was happening under my very nose."

No-one had seen Stasia's engagement to Edmund Hughes coming, but it was now a fact. Stasia had led Edmund into the drawing room the previous evening and announced it triumphantly to her father, who was shocked and delighted in equal measure.

"Obviously, I'm happy for Stasia and I shall go and congratulate her in a little while. I've just seen Mr Hughes too. He didn't exactly look like a man in the grip of a great romance. More like a dog beaten into submission."

"That's a terrible cruel thing to say, Hannah. You are very naughty and I hope you won't say anything like that to your sister. I'm sure they love each other very much. It has been a fairly rapid affair but why should they wait if they know what they want to do, especially as Edmund is a good ten years older than Stasia and he's just been through a hideous war. Not everyone is going to find a grand passion as you and John did."

"I'm sure he's a decent enough man, and maybe the best Stasia could do. He's just very boring."

"Nothing wrong with being boring. He's a hard worker and trustworthy - no silly ideas about politics and suchlike."

"You mean… like John? Anyway, the reason I wanted to see you immediately, and before anything else gets decided, is to talk about our inheritance."

"Good heavens, Hannah. I have no intention of dying for at least another twenty years."

"That's as maybe. And of course I don't want you to die, silly. I would be heartbroken. But I don't want Stasia and me to be in the mess that Tricky and Nicholas find themselves in. The father dies without a will and then there's a big row between the children."

"There's no row between the Byrne boys."

"Yes, but that's only because Tricky has just let Nicholas take everything, even though, by law, he should inherit it all and, by any sense of fairness, he should at least inherit something. That might be what they've agreed but I wouldn't be quite so … compliant."

James laughed loudly.

"Don't laugh. I'm serious. I think it would be only fair to sort things out between Stasia and me now. Divide up your assets and things between the two of us."

"You mean make over the farm, the pub, shop and all the land to the two of you?"

"Why not? You're not planning on any having any other children are you?"

"Ha! No. But I did read King Lear once…"

The door opened and Stasia walked in with Mr Hughes a step behind her.

"Good morning, Hannah. I'm pleased you're here."

Hannah went over to kiss her sister.

"Many congratulations, Stasia. I am very pleased for you. For you both." Hannah shook Mr Hughes's hand.

"Thank you, Hannah." Stasia took her sister's arm and they sat down together on the unforgiving sofa.

"You'll recognise my ring of course."

Hannah saw that Stasia was wearing their mother's engagement ring.

"Edmund offered me his grandmother's old sapphire ring but I like mother's diamond one better." Stasia stretched out her left hand to show off the familiar ring to Hannah. "Edmund, come and sit down over there. We are very lucky to have found each other. Edmund will be an enormous help to me running the farm and the businesses as Father gets older. But we don't intend to marry immediately. We shall probably wait a year or so. There's a lot to arrange, isn't there Edmund."

So, Stasia had taken Mammy's ring without a moment's hesitation. Hannah was surer than ever that she needed to persuade her father to make a fair settlement between them, and sooner rather than later.

"Where are you living at the moment, Mr Hughes?"

"He's living over in Paulstown, but I think there's no reason why he shouldn't have a room here in the house until we marry. It will be so much more convenient for everyone. And quite proper."

"Oh, I don't doubt that for a moment. Anyway, welcome to the family, Mr Hughes."

"Please call me Edmund, Mrs Fitzgerald. Or, maybe, I should say Hannah?"

"God, yes. No need for any formal nonsense. Don't stand on any sort of ceremony with me. We're going to be brother and sister after all." Hannah flashed him one of her most winning smiles.

James stood up and went to the sideboard. "We shall all be one very happy family together and maybe we can have a little toast to your future happiness." James rummaged around and pulled out a bottle of whiskey.

"What are you thinking, Father! It's still morning."

"Go on, Dada. I'll join you in a toast. I think I remember Stasia toasting our happiness at our wedding so I'd like to return the favour."

"Well, thank you for those kind wishes but we'll leave you and Father to enjoy your drink. Edmund and I need to get on with the monthly accounts and making up the wages."

"Stasia, before you go, your sister thinks that your marriage is a good occasion to consider the future of the businesses. I'm not going to be around forever and I want to be sure you are both well looked after."

Stasia took in a deep breath. "Hannah has no need to fear for the future of the businesses. I have them all under control."

"That's just what I'm worried about, Stasia. While Dada is still around I know he will look after me. But I think it would be fairer for us each to have our own patch and stop any squabbling."

"That's you all over, isn't it Hannah? You always want what you can't have. You think you and your teacher husband are capable of keeping a business going, do you? You have little chance of that, and he has absolutely none."

"You underestimate me, Stasia, as you have always done. I assume it's OK for me to have Mammy's emerald ring now, as you have had the first pick."

"Now, now, my lovely girls. Let's not spoil this happy occasion when we should be doing nothing but celebrate."

"It was Hannah's decision to raise the subject, Father, not mine. Come along Edmund."

# Chapter 33 – January 1920

The Kilkenny notary blotted the two documents, one a copy of the other, and shook the hands of James McDermott and John Fitzgerald, as Hannah looked on from behind the desk.

"There you go." James shook John's hand and then slapped him on the back. "Congratulations, John. You are now the owner of one house, one pub, one shop and a few fields, all of which I have loved all my life, so you'd better take as much care of them as you do my daughter." Hannah jumped up and threw her arms around them both.

"And of course, to make things fair and equal, I shall be signing away the villa, the farms and all the land to Edmund and Stasia as soon as they have married in May. So then I shall be a proper penniless tramp and I'll be begging for scraps at your door. I hope you'll take me in."

"Always, Dada. You know you will always be welcome to live with us in Main Street."

In fact, the notary had insisted they make James's living arrangements legally binding; clauses had been written in dictating that James had the right to live for six months of the year in each of his daughter's homes.

"I shall be around whenever you need me for any advice. In fact, I shall be mightily hurt if you don't ask me for help."

"I'm not so arrogant as to think we won't need our hands holding, sir."

"Right then. Let's go and celebrate with some steak and kidney pudding and a pint or two at Flanagan's."

Over their hearty lunch, Hannah revealed to her father that she was pregnant again, with the baby due in June. James squeezed Hannah's hand joyfully and discreetly wiped a tear from his eye.

"I was thinking that your dress was a little tight and that you must have overdone the Christmas pudding. Well, that means that you need to take things very easy. John, don't let her go charging around trying to be the boss. Let Jimmy keep doing what he's been doing in the pub. He knows all the ropes. There's not a lot to do in the fields for a couple of months. Just get yourself familiar with the shop. One thing at a time. And I shall be there to do whatever Hannah would have been doing. Just until the babe is born. Of course, eventually a child will be able to help out."

"You would never let us help out much, Dada."

"That's because your mother wanted you to be proper ladies. I'd have had you and Stasia washing glasses just as soon as you could reach the bar."

"Talking of Stasia, she's asked me to be her maid of honour but there's no way I shall be dressing my bump in peach coloured satin. I don't want to tell her that yet - just in case we lose this pregnancy too - so keep it a secret for a month or so. OK? Edmund has plenty of young nieces who will be thrilled to be bridesmaids, I'm sure, and will do the job just fine."

"Anyway, congratulations all round," and James clinked his glass of stout against theirs.

******

"And we're getting low on treacle, ground almonds and tapioca too."

Hannah was sitting in the shop – her and John's shop - doing her third weekly stock check with Eileen, so that she could put in their regular order to the wholesalers. She was enjoying having control of the small village shop that she had known all her life. Not exactly a toy but it felt something that she would soon easily manage, leaving the pub and the fields for John to worry about, though, with her father now installed back in his old bedroom at the Main Street house, she felt that nothing could go too wrong.

"Fine. Right. I'll be off. You're doing a grand job here, Eileen. It's great to have someone we can trust in the place."

Very different from the situation with Eileen's fiancé, Jimmy Boyle, in the pub, thought Hannah.

"Thank you, Mrs Fitzgerald. See you tomorrow."

Instead of going back home, Hannah walked the other way along Main Street, towards Loughlin's Bar. She fancied sticking her head inside the door, just to get a feel for the place that was competing with them for the village's drinkers. It was locked but she found a section of unfrosted windowpane that she could just peek through if she stood on tiptoes. Wooden floor, low beams, benches and stools; nothing to write home about and nothing that McDermott's didn't have. In the corner was a piano. Now that was an extra touch she envied.

"Good day to you, Hannah. Checking out your rivals?"

Hannah spun around to find Mrs Magee, her old governess, watching her as she did her spying.

"Ah, how are you Mrs Magee? I haven't seen you for a while."

"Well, you don't come to Mass, do you, Hannah. That's where I see most people. But maybe I'll be seeing you more often now you have the shop. I pop in most days for something. That Eileen is a gem, isn't she? Though I hear that you'll soon be busy with a little one of your own. I'm so happy for you. I wish you and your husband the best of luck this time. Stasia whispered your news to me. I hope you don't mind me saying. Your sister is so very pleased for you. And you must be pleased for her too, bagging that handsome Mr Hughes. There was only one wedding in the village last year, so it'll be lovely to see Stasia married off finally."

"She wasn't exactly a lonely spinster, Mrs Magee." Hannah smiled. "She's only a couple of years older than me."

"That's as maybe, but there are definitely fewer fish in the sea since we lost so many good men in the war. Not enough to go round. Tricky Byrne might even get lucky one of these days." The old woman nudged Hannah and laughed conspiratorially. "I'll leave you be, Hannah. There's a bitter wind today and I have a weak chest as you know. Good morning to you."

Hannah made her way slowly towards the river. Bloody gossips. Was there no way to keep a secret in this damn village. Well, she should have expected her pregnancy to become common knowledge as soon as she had told her sister, and it wouldn't be that long before it would become impossible to hide. Was Stasia really 'so very pleased' for her as Mrs Magee asserted? Hannah doubted it. Stasia had greeted Hannah's announcement as coolly as ever.

As Hannah walked on, she saw Father Stephen come out of his front door and walk straight into the church. Time for Friday confessions.

She crossed the road, opened the gate to the churchyard and made her way to her mother's grave. The chrysanthemums that her father and Stasia had put on the grave last Sunday were holding up well against the icy wind. Hannah knelt and picked off the soggy, dead leaves that were nestled around them.

"Well, Mammy. Here I am again, with a baby inside me. Put in a good word for me, if you can, please. If you bump into John's first wife, Ailsa, up there can you just tell her to back off and lift her curse. Surely we've suffered enough and should be allowed to have a child of our own."

Hannah stroked the top edge of the tombstone and turned to go back home, but, without thinking, she walked into the church instead. It was quite dim with low, watery winter light making its way through the tall windows; two candles were lit on the altar and there was a glow coming from the rack of devotional candles in front of the statue of the Blessed Virgin in the side aisle. Hannah was grateful for the gloom. She didn't want anyone she knew to see her. She sat on the pew at the back, watching a straggle of villagers shuffle in the main door, make their way up to the confessional booths, and finally whisper their penances as they fingered their rosaries before shuffling out again. The lingering smell of burnt incense was familiar.

"Are you OK there, Mrs Fitzgerald?"

Hannah opened her eyes with a start. Had she been asleep? Father Stephen was sitting beside her looking concerned.

"Oh dear. Oh yes, I'm fine, Father. I just came in to get out of the cold for a minute. I'm sorry. I was somewhere else entirely."

"It's good to see you in the church. It's been a while."

"Yes, well... I have given up on religion these days and my husband is an atheist."

"Yes, I heard that. But you're not, I hope."

"I'm not sure. I was losing patience with the Catholic Church even before I went off to Dublin, and the war only made things worse."

"Yes, I remember your ... difficulties with Mother Veronica." The priest smiled. Hannah hoped he couldn't see her blushing face.

"Oh God. You remember that was me. I hope you've forgiven me."

"Of course. I was a naive young chap and you were just teasing. At least, I think that's what was going on. We shall never speak about it again, if you like."

The two sat in silence for a while.

"Well, I don't think I'm going to get any more customers today... unless... you'd like to come to confession of course..."

"No thank you, Father. Although my confession would keep you entertained in there for a good half hour at least." They both laughed.

"I see you visiting your mother's grave quite often. Do you pray to her?"

"Heavens, no. I just go to chat, to get things off my mind. It makes me feel peaceful somehow."

"That's all that prayer is, you know - talking to God."

"I don't want to talk to God, only my Mammy."

"Fair enough. Your sister has told me that you are expecting a child again. Congratulations."

Hannah rolled her eyes.

"I'm sorry. Was I not supposed to know? It's wonderful news."

"I don't mind you knowing, Father. It won't be long before I'll be as big as a house anyway. It is good news - it means I get out of being Stasia's maid of honour for one thing – but I am anxious, after all the trouble we have had in the past."

"Yes, I imagine you must be. Would you like to say a prayer now, to ask God for a healthy baby and a safe birth?" Hannah shifted on the pew and stared at the priest.

"Now, you see, that's exactly what I hate about religion. Are you telling me that an all-powerful God would let a baby die if its mother didn't pray to him? No, thank you." She stood and smoothed down her coat. "I must get back."

"I hope you don't mind if I say a prayer for you and the baby, then."

"Please yourself, Father. Good-bye."

Hannah walked towards the door.

"Hannah!" She turned back at Father Stephen's call. "You must feel free to come in here whenever you want. I promise not to ask you to pray ever again. But if you want to talk to me - or if you just want to get out of the cold - you will always be very welcome."

# Chapter 34 – May 22nd 1920

"Hannah, come on down, my love. We'll be late if we don't go right now. Your Aunt Lily is waiting in the car to take us to the church so you don't have to walk." John was dressed in his best suit, shouting up the stairs, as Aggie, dressed in her best coat and hat, tried to fix the carnation into his lapel button. "If we end up being late for your sister's wedding, I am emigrating, okay."

Stasia and Edmund's wedding was just one of the exciting changes that 1920 was bringing.

Very soon after the papers had been signed back in January, James's fancy had taken him right back to the Main Street house where he had resumed residence in his old bedroom and the big armchair in the kitchen so he could gossip away with Aggie and discuss the hot tips that she had gleaned from her gentlemen friends for the next day's racing. It left Stasia living in the same house as Edmund with only Bessie there as chaperone, but there wasn't a single person in Rowanbridge who thought for a moment that Stasia's virtue would be compromised in any way.

This arrangement was working well for John too because James was always on hand for advice when any new issue had arisen to do with managing the businesses. Keeping beer well, tipping draymen, cashing up, ordering enough – but not too much – stock; all presented their challenges. But John was a fast learner and none of them had caused him bother for long; none except Jimmy Boyle.

Jimmy had worked for the McDermotts for nearly seven years now. He respected James McDermott, but these Fitzgeralds had swanned in from Dublin, first taking the house he had hoped to live in and now taking over the pub he had been running largely without supervision and in the way he liked to do it.

Hannah didn't care whether Jimmy Boyle was happy or not and she rarely had to speak to him directly, conveying her wishes via John or her father. John sensed resentment in every word Jimmy said, and a large part of him sympathised with the man. It was true: they had taken away his prospects and his status.

As the grey winter months turned into a pastel spring, Hannah found it impossible not to get wrapped up in the preparations for Stasia's wedding to Edmund Hughes: helping Stasia choose the silk for the bridal gown, deciding on hymns and flowers for the church, ordering the catering for the wedding breakfast. Hannah was rather surprised – shocked even - when Stasia had sought her sister's views on these, and the other more intimate 'matters of the bedroom', as Stasia referred to sex. This made her happy too. So, Stasia was a nervous twenty-two-year-old virgin bride, just like anyone else.

"Is there anything I should do to … prepare myself for our wedding night, Hannah?"

"Not really. I think you'll find it all comes quite naturally to you when you're in love."

"I know that I won't be the first woman Edmund has been to bed with – he is thirty-two after all – so maybe I should just put myself in his hands."

"Just make sure he goes nice and slow. Plenty of kissing and stroking and stuff. Don't even think about intercourse until you're good and ready. You know. Well-lubricated down there."

"Good God, you make me sound like a rusted-up wheel, Hannah."

Hannah couldn't wait to see her Dada walk Stasia down the aisle, all trussed up in his fine morning dress, with the cravat she had tied for him that morning before Slattery had come to take him over to the villa ready to accompany his daughter to the church.

Lily had arrived three days ago at the villa and taken up residence there to perform all the duties of the mother of the bride in her dead sister's place. True, it wouldn't be the starring role, but Lily was making the best of the celebrity cameo, with a lavish new scarlet-and-black outfit, complete with a black-sable stole and a wide-brimmed scarlet straw hat, bedecked with black ostrich feathers.

Hannah had very little interest in her outfit for the wedding. Her swollen belly was hard to dress attractively but Hannah would have been happy to be twice as big. This baby was here to stay and in another three weeks or so she would be able to hold it.

Ever since she had told John back in January that she thought she was about three months pregnant, he had treated her like the most precious, fragile creature; shielding her and padding her against any bumps, banning her from the pub, making her stay in bed as much as possible but all the while telling her not to get her hopes up. But when she had passed the eight months mark he let his joy be seen, driving out all anxiety for them both. Nothing was now going to take this baby away from them.

"With any luck, our baby will have an independent Ireland before it reaches its first birthday," he would tell Hannah as he stroked her bump. Hannah didn't give a damn herself but she was delighted that the progress towards Home Rule was yet another thing adding to John's happiness.

Hannah sat at her dressing table to fix on her wedding hat. She felt clumsy and ugly all the time, with swollen ankles and a painful pile - which she felt very indignant about - but she was always shocked when she saw herself in a mirror. The bump was quite neat and she still looked like a good-looking young woman, if you looked no lower than her breasts. Hannah ran her hands over her bulge and bowed her head. "Not long to wait now, baby," she whispered to her invisible child.

But, before babies, there was a wedding to celebrate.

"Hannah! Come along, my love. It's nearly twenty to eleven. Stasia will be there before us if you're not quick."

As Hannah rose from the dressing stool and turned to pick up her gloves, a sharp stabbing pain made her gasp.

"Coming!"

Hannah walked to the top of the stairs but another jab stopped her stepping further, and she felt a flood of warm wetness running down her legs.

"John. Aggie. Help! What's happening?"

\*\*\*\*\*\*

John had been boiling water for what seemed like days now. Some of it was needed for the delivery scene sure, but much more was destined for the endless pots of tea he had had to make with Aggie on duty up in the bedroom.

The first person to arrive post-wedding, at about three o'clock, had been James. He said he was just popping in to see how things were going, now that he had made his speech, and he would go back to the wedding celebrations soon. It was now eight o'clock in the evening and James was still sitting downstairs in the kitchen, trying not to let Hannah's screams from upstairs upset him too much.

Mrs Magee had knocked on the door at tea-time asking after Hannah and she had stayed 'for just one cup' and then, soon after, Nicholas Byrne had brought Louisa round to offer her help and he had been sent off in his fancy new car to fetch Dr O'Connor back. They were all still down in the parlour, drinking tea. Tricky had called in too but had sloped off when his brother answered the front door.

It was just gone eight o'clock when James opened the front door to Lily Murphy, Father Stephen in tow. Lily swept upstairs, still wearing her extravagant red hat, dragging the priest up with her. There was a definite hint of the cardinal about her. James followed the two of them up the stairs slowly, steeling himself to withstand his darling daughter's howls at closer range.

When they walked into the drawing room, John bridled inwardly at the sight of the priest. Why was he here? Was he expecting to give the last rites to mother or baby?

"Get me a glass of something, James. I can't tolerate that noise without some alcohol. How long has she been howling like this, John?"

"I'm not exactly sure, Lily. Soon after lunchtime? What is the time now anyway?"

James poured out four glasses of whiskey. The priest and Lily accepted theirs and Lily sat down as far from the bedroom door as the drawing room furniture would allow, but John waved the glass away.

"What's been happening at the wedding since I left, Lily?" asked James. "I felt bad about leaving Stasia but I'd done my bit and all I could think about was Hannah. I had to be here."

"Well, it's all winding down now. I'm sure Stasia will forgive you in the circumstances." James and John exchanged a look.

Father Stephen stood, shuffling awkwardly from one leg to the other, sipping the whiskey and looking very uncomfortable.

"Mr Fitzgerald, I know you and your wife are not regular members of our congregation but I hope you don't mind me looking in. Stasia – I should say Mrs Hughes now – and Mrs Murphy here thought there might be need of me."

Father Stephen threw back the drink and knocked on the bedroom door. Aggie shouted an irritable "Come in" and the priest opened the door. Hannah was standing by the bed, held up by Dr O'Connor on one side and Aggie on the other. He ventured no further in, staying on the threshold of the room, saying a Hail Mary as he took a small bottle of holy water from his jacket which he then poured into his hand and sprinkled – no, flung – in the direction of the group of three. Hannah's moans continued.

Aggie took a towel and wiped the sanctified drops from Hannah's face, muttering under her breath that holy water was going to do a fat lot of good, as the priest made the sign of the cross, bade them all good evening and made a relieved exit down the stairs and out into Main Street.

Hannah had wanted Aggie by her side as soon as contractions had started in earnest. Hannah had been holding Aggie's workworn hand for the last four hours, giving panicky squeezes at accelerating intervals, accompanied by some yelping that she was terrifying herself with. At first, she thought a dog must have sneaked into the bedroom and been trodden on by Dr O'Connor but apparently the noise was coming from her own mouth.

At about nine o'clock, there was a knock at the front door. Louisa Byrne opened it to the newly married Mr and Mrs Hughes, all togged out in their going away outfits, though they were merely going to a Kilkenny hotel for a couple of nights.

"Of course, Hannah couldn't let the day be mine alone could she," Stasia commented as she walked past Louisa and on up the stairs, depositing Edmund in the drawing room with John, James and Lily, before walking purposefully into the stifling bedroom.

Stasia looked at the exhausted figure of Hannah kneeling on the bed, draped on Aggie's shoulders, bedraggled and dripping with sweat, with her nightdress twisted up around her waist as Dr Connor listened to the baby's heartbeat.

"Let's hope all this is worth it, Hannah. I just came to say 'Good luck'. I shall be praying for you and the baby tonight. And I've brought you my bouquet and a piece of cake for you. Maybe not for now, eh? Edmund and I are just off to the Grand. I won't kiss you but I shall be expecting good news in the morning. Goodbye now and may God bless you."

Stasia placed the flowers and the paper-wrapped pack of cake on the dressing table and left. Hannah grunted a thank-you which turned into a roar as it left her mouth.

By eleven o'clock, only John and James were left sitting up in the drawing room; John pacing and James nodding. Everyone else had gone off to their beds. On the sideboard, ham and tomato sandwiches, made by Louisa much earlier, were curling up next to some exhausted pork pie slices.

Suddenly the screaming stopped. James woke up and the two men looked at each other. No baby's cry. They had no words they dared say. It was another quarter of an hour before the bedroom door opened and Aggie staggered out, making a beeline for the plate of tired food.

"Oh God, that's so good," sighed Aggie as she stuffed her mouth and fell onto the sofa. John looked at her, speechless.

"It's all fine. Go on in. Off you go. All over now."

John walked into the bedroom to see Hannah lying back with closed eyes, holding a tiny bundle. John couldn't even see its face but his heart leapt.

"Congratulations, Mr Fitzgerald." There were several bowls of bloodied water on the table and the floor and Dr O'Connor was now putting on his coat and packing up his bag.

"Your wife did a grand job but she is now very, very tired and she'll need to stay in bed for a week or so. Just a few stitches. I'll be back in the morning but don't hesitate to fetch me if there's any more serious bleeding."

"What about the baby? Is it fine?"

"Oh yes. No worries there." Dr O'Connor picked up the bundle from its sleeping mother's arms and handed it to John. "Say hello to your daughter, Mr Fitzgerald." He shook John's hand and left.

John gently folded back the blanket shrouding the baby and looked into his daughter's face for the first time. The tiny snuffly nose, the perfect pink pout and the screwed-up eyes were topped by a few wet shreds of golden hair. John crept out of the room to show James his new granddaughter.

"Here's your granddad, ma cushla." John gently placed the baby into James's arms. Both men had tears running down their cheeks.

"Ah, the precious angel. She's perfect." James planted a soft kiss on the baby's forehead, his bushy moustache making her wriggle, and then carried her into the bedroom to congratulate his daughter, only to find her fast asleep.

"Hannah must be exhausted. That was a hell of a day's work. Give her my love when she wakes and tell her I'll see her in the morning. I'll be off to my bed but I expect I'll get woken a few times. It's a while since this old house has sheltered a new baby." James tenderly passed the baby back to John and made for his bedroom.

"I'll be off too Mr Fitzgerald if that's OK." Aggie was standing at the drawing room door with a tray loaded with plates and cups. "But I'll be back good and early tomorrow. Lots of washing to start on. Sleep well – if you can."

"Thanks for everything, Aggie."

John sat in the armchair and stared at his new daughter. He was drunk with love and relief. He took the baby's tiny fist and put his little finger into it. She grabbed it fiercely.

"It's just you and me then, for now, cuisle mo chroidhe."

He rocked the swaddled baby and sang to her so softly that only the new-born's ears could have picked it up.

*"Seoithín, seo hó, mo stór é, mo leanbh*
*Mo sheod gan cealg, mo chuid gan tsaoil mhór*
*Seothín seo ho, nach mór é an taitneamh*
*Mo stóirín na leaba, na chodladh gan brón.*

*A leanbh mo chléibh go n-eirí do chodhladh leat*
*Séan is sonas gach oíche do chóir*
*Tá mise le do thaobh ag guídhe ort na mbeannacht*
*Seothín a leanbh is codail go foill."*

John was back in the wind-swept cottage next to the sea, cradling his first-born who had always smiled at that lullaby. John kissed the head of his new sleeping babe and carried her back to the bedroom. He kicked off his shoes and gingerly sat on the bed next to Hannah, placing the baby between the two of them, then leaned over and kissed his wife gently on the lips, trying not to wake her, but Hannah's eyes sprang open.

"Are you pleased with me now?"

"Pleased? My heart is bursting with joy, you clever sausage. Just look at this miracle that you have produced. She is perfect and I love you both to the ends of the earth. I'm a very lucky man and I shall spend the rest of my life trying to deserve you both and trying to protect you from anything that might hurt you."

"Well, it hurt like hell. I'll probably never let you touch me again. But I have beaten the curse."

"Beaten the curse?"

"Ailsa's curse. She has never wanted us to have a child together. But now I have given you back a daughter."

"I think you must have a fever, my love. I don't understand what you're saying."

"I know what I'm talking about. You'll see. But you don't need to mourn Máire anymore. Our daughter can take her place."

"It doesn't work like that, my sweet."

"Anyway, she's all yours."

"What shall we call her?"

"I told you; she's all yours, so you get to choose – just as long as you don't call her Letitia after your bloody mother."

The baby began to cry. John picked her up.

"She's hungry, I think."

"Oh God. I shall have to get used to being a milk-cow I suppose."

Hannah opened her nightdress and John helped her put the baby to her breast.

"You have more experience than me at this malarkey, I suppose."

"You'll get used to it, my darling. I think it's the most wonderful sight in the world."

John rested on his elbow, watching the baby suckle noisily as Hannah lay back on the pillow with closed eyes.

"I could spend all day just watching the pair of you. My precious girls."

Hannah didn't reply; she had dropped back asleep. Soon after, the nipple popped out of the baby's mouth; she had fallen asleep too with a blissfully full tummy.

John lifted the baby from Hannah's breast and cradled her tenderly, as he lifted the sheet to cover Hannah.

"You are such a clever girl. We're going to have loads of fun together; there's so much I want to show you. Beautiful places to visit, beautiful music to listen to and play. And you will get to see a proud and free Ireland in your lifetime - I know it. You deserve that. Welcome to the world, my beautiful Countess Cathleen."

BV - #0005 - 210420 - C0 - 216/140/14 - PB - 9781913425173